TENNIS SHOES ADVENTURE SERIES

GADIANTONS AND THE SILVER SWORD

TENNIS SHOES ADVENTURE SERIES

Tennis Shoes Among the Nephites

Gadiantons and the Silver Sword

The Feathered Serpent, Part One

The Feathered Serpent, Part Two

The Sacred Quest
(formerly *Tennis Shoes and the Seven Churches)*

The Lost Scrolls

The Golden Crown

OTHER COVENANT BOOKS BY
CHRIS HEIMERDINGER

Daniel and Nephi

Eddie Fantastic

COVENANT TALK TAPES BY CHRIS HEIMERDINGER

Chris Heimerdinger's Adventures with the Book of Mormon

The Name That Matters Most

TENNIS SHOES
ADVENTURE SERIES

GADIANTONS AND THE SILVER SWORD

a novel

CHRIS HEIMERDINGER

Covenant Communications, Inc.

Cover illustration by Joe Flores

Cover design copyrighted 2000 by Covenant Communications, Inc.

Published by Covenant Communications, Inc.
American Fork, Utah

Printed in the United States of America
First Printing: February 1991

07 06 05 04 03 02 01 00   11 10 9 8 7 6 5 4 3 2 1

ISBN 1-57734-612-2

For Jim Brogan,
who inspired it.

And for Jorge Riveros and Edgar Corral,
who shared in it.

Acknowledgments

I feel compelled to recognize the efforts and encouragements of several persons without whom this work would not have been pursued with as much vigor and dedication. I thank Daniel Schlyter, whose critique of the first draft saved me immense embarrassment; Joseph Allen and Cecilia Bartz (my mother), whose Spanish translations were offered freely and cheerfully; Blair Leishman, for helping me with the proper Spanish pronunciation for the cassette reading; Lee Simons, whose bubbling enthusiasm toward my first book gave me the confidence I needed to write another; and finally, my wife, Beth, my first and foremost critic, and the one whose comments make me the most angry—though I've discovered it's the criticisms that make you the most angry which are usually the most correct.

PROLOGUE

I remember the fog, twisting just below the summit like icy white fingers around a helpless victim's throat. The hill was very high, almost too high to be called a hill, and it was blanketed by an Eden-kissed jungle, rife with every life-sound that God ever saw fit to give a single patch of earth. But the summit itself appeared barren, only a tiny cluster of trees, cushioned in a nest of billowing grasses, and silhouetted against an angering sky. In the center of it all was the blackened trunk of a lightning-scarred tree, the fire having long since consumed its branches. This trunk marked the very pinnacle of the hill, nature's totem, jutting skyward to remind us in which direction we might find heaven.

Blinking my eyes, I saw a man standing there as well, a product of the mist. His head was hoary, his features olive and aquiline, and his garments were from an ancient age. He stretched out his arm and earnestly beckoned me toward him, as if nothing else mattered, as if communion with me was his last vestige of hope. So I began walking, but he never drew nearer. In spite of my determination and the hastening of my pace, I couldn't seem to reach him.

This was my dream, the only dream of the night, Saturday, August 8th, three weeks before I returned to BYU to face my junior year.

The same night as the accident.

CHAPTER 1

You know what frustrates me about girls? They're like a pound cake in a hot oven. If you don't let 'em cook for just the right amount of time—if you open the oven too soon by letting 'em know you *like* them or some terrible thing like that—then you've got yourself a tortilla instead of a cake. My problem is, I ain't much of a cook.

This girl had been hittin' on me for weeks. Every morning, as I'd pass by her window on the way to my nine o'clock class, she'd be patiently perched behind a bowl of Honey Nut Cheerios, seemingly waiting for me to pop into view. Then she would wink—a perfect, methodical wink, like she was in a play in the de Jong Concert Hall and had to communicate the gesture to the balcony's back row. I would smile the "kool smile" and send her a coy, two-fingered wave, walking by with my pectorals pumped higher than normal. Oh, how I looked forward to this game every morning as I left my apartment.

This girl rivaled the most beautiful girls I'd ever seen. There was something about long hair, black as ebony, and stormy eyes with a shine like a distant lighthouse that had always melted my heart. I lay awake a night or two imagining how I might influence fate and meet this girl. At last, fate was good to me one Friday, just after my American Heritage class.

I was passing through the Wilkinson Center en route to my car parked behind the law building when—lo and behold!—there she was, seated on a bench beside the courtesy phones. After dousing myself in an unction of charm, I moved in for the kill.

"Well, hi!" I called over to her.

She looked up with a blank, confused expression, as if she'd never seen me before.

Awkwardly, I identified myself. "I live in the other ward at King's Court Arms."

No response. "I, uh, pass by your window in the mornings."

"Oh, you do?"

She didn't fool me. This chick knew darn well who I was. A little red "trouble" light went off inside me, but every God-given instinct I possessed about life and women was clouded by those eyes. I introduced myself as the notorious Jim Hawkins.

Her name was Renae Fenimore, and after only a few minutes I asked that all-imposing question. After she'd batted her eyes a few times, I learned that she was free that night.

I might have overdone things a little: New wardrobe at Jeans West, a splash of my roommate's *Polo,* flowers from Gary's Floral, dinner at Magelby's, sundaes at Carousel, and a starry night drive that took us to Utah Lake and around the Provo Temple.

For all that, you might think I was expecting a good-night kiss. But *au contraire!* After all, being a returned missionary, and being the second counselor in my elders quorum presidency, and being just an all-around upstanding kind of guy . . .

Okay, so I was a little disappointed when she didn't grace me with a good-night kiss. Instead, she slipped inside her apartment without so much as a handshake. I'd have gone to sleep that night sulking if I hadn't heard her sultry voice beckon me back. Renae leaned out the door, her hair dancing in the soft October breeze, and blew me a kiss. The kiss hit me hard. In fact, I think it knocked me unconscious, because I don't remember driving back to my apartment.

After that I might have gotten a bit impetuous. By the second date I was already imagining which temple we'd be married in. She must have seen the "Moroni spire" in my eyes, because her attitude got real chilly. On our third date, she sat me down in a booth at the Cougareat and flogged me with a speech about moving too fast and feeling overwhelmed and dating other people and . . .

She went on, but I was too busy sweeping pieces of my heart off the floor to listen.

Afterwards, I punched myself in the mirror. I *knew* better! I'd only played this dating game for *six years!* (Well, four if you subtract my years in the mission field—but *still!*) Anybody knows you don't phone a girl every night after making her acquaintance. They think you've got no taste, like you could fall in love with *anybody*. Can I help it if I recognized a good thing when I saw it?

As the weeks slipped by, I'd pretty much resigned myself to the fact that if Renae and I had signed a marriage contract in the pre-existence, the angels had torn it in half. I was just getting ready to cut loose my heart and let it brave the elements again when I learned that my roommate, Andrew, had asked Renae to Homecoming—*and Renae had had the nerve to accept!*

Andrew! Of all people! Andrew Southwick was the most obnoxious BYU roommate I ever had—what I narrow-mindedly called a California money Mormon who lets you smell his family's wealth in everything he wears, says, does, or drives. All the apartment's amenities were his: the VCR, TV, microwave, stereo. Of course, we could use his stuff anytime we wanted—as long as there wasn't something *he* wanted to watch, listen to, or cook. In such cases, he'd toss anyone else's sandwich out of the microwave—with only thirty seconds left!—and replace it with his own.

Our apartment had four single bedrooms and two bathrooms. Two people shared one bathroom and two shared the other. I was the unfortunate sap who got the quarters connected with Andrew. He'd carefully timed the available hot water. If I wasn't out of the shower in precisely seven minutes and twenty seconds, I'd hear the thump, thump of his fist echoing on the bathroom door. On occasion I'd endure some scorching showers to try disrupting Andrew's timing system and give him a nice chill.

In one respect, Andrew reminded me of an old childhood friend of mine named Garth Plimpton. Both Garth and Andrew were voracious readers. They'd practically committed to memory every Church commentary ever printed—although their conclusions about such material seemed exactly the opposite.

The only time I found Andrew even remotely entertaining was when our apartment engaged in intellectual conversations about the gospel—an event which occurred almost nightly. Andrew always played the part of "devil's advocate"—a role in which he seemed quite at home. When I first returned from my mission, I'd have sworn I knew everything about the gospel. But Andrew trumpeted controversies even the most flagrant anti-Mormons hadn't heard of. He was an expert at getting me and my other roommate, Benny, so twisted in our words that we'd have to throw up our hands and parrot, "All I know is, the Church is true." Which, of course, only sated Andrew's ego all the more.

I used to wish Garth was around at these moments. Certainly he'd consumed many of the same books and pondered all the same issues, seeking answers from a thoroughly different spirit. Mr. California needed a serious slice of humble pie, but Garth Plimpton was far across the country, a busy undergrad in archeology at Harvard.

Now my next roommate, Lars Packard, was a different egg altogether. He and I never "bucked heads," so to speak, but I'd still put him in the category of the "weirdest" roommate I ever had. Lars was a UFO nut. All over his room were posters of flying saucers, almond-eyed aliens, and Easter Island, along with newspaper clippings of documented sightings, Area 51, and Roswell, New Mexico. If it had to do with close encounters between humans and little green men, Lars was the resident expert. He belonged to UFO clubs all over the country. During gospel discussions in our apartment, he'd often chime in with a view more off-the-wall than all of ours put together. Lars was always trying to tie extraterrestrial phenomena and Mormonism together. The guy was bizarre, but at least he was docile. Most of his time was spent secluded in his room, reading or playing with his computer. He'd never served a mission—at least, not yet. And if he went to church, it wasn't with our student ward at BYU. Since his family lived in Sandy, Utah, he generally zipped home every weekend.

My obituary would have read, "Jim Hawkins died of insanity his junior year at BYU" if it hadn't been for Benny. Benny Burns and I had become friends the previous winter semester as sophomores living in the on-campus housing establishment of Heritage Halls. As the semester ended, we committed ourselves to the task of finding an apartment with single bedrooms. Thus, when we discovered King's Court Arms, we'd nailed two birds with one stone—a single room, and at least one roommate we felt we could get along with.

Benny had only one character flaw. He was *too much* like me. I suffered from the same ailment that Joseph Smith claimed he had during those obscure days before he translated the Book of Mormon. In short, levity. Although I was sure I had a much worse case of the same disease. That is, the tendency to take nothing in life seriously—not even the Church.

Unfortunately, Benny had the same problem. During the first few months of my junior year, being around Benny, my attitude became more and more cynical, my sense of humor more and more "off-color," and my convictions more and more lax.

In spite of all this, would you believe they called me to the elders quorum presidency? I was the worst second counselor in latter-day history. Though it was my duty to set the example, I probably went home teaching once all semester—and that was only because I heard she was cute. Part of the problem was assigning Benny to be my companion. He spent all his extra hours cultivating a year-old romance with a brunette named Allison, so we let the months slip by and justified the whole thing by saying students don't really want to be home taught anyway.

Every better habit I'd thought had frozen solid in my psyche during my two-year mission in Oregon appeared to be crumbling away. In Oregon, the Spirit had seemed as bold and readable as a *New York Times* headline. Coming home, I was so frustrated with the lack of fire in my ward that I considered putting them all on report with the First Presidency.

Only a short year later, I was finding it a real struggle to get through a single chapter of scripture. I was lucky if I prayed once every other night—or maybe it was once every third night. Three hours sitting in church was like an eternity of watching paint dry. Sometimes I'd just take the sacrament and go home.

I knew my attitude was wrong. I knew it was *really* wrong, but I couldn't seem to muster the energy to turn things around. I guess I thought I needed to get married. That would be the perfect excuse to end my gospel vacation.

Thanksgiving was looming on the horizon—only four days away. A big reunion was scheduled in my home town of Cody, Wyoming. My oldest brother, Mitch, and his family were flying out from Virginia. My second oldest brother, Steven, and his family were driving over from the nearby town of Lovell. And the newlyweds!—my third oldest brother, Judd, and his new wife, Krystal, would be driving down from Billings, Montana. My Uncle Spence and Aunt Louise would be there. Even my little sister, Jenny, the BYU sophomore, was adding to the crowd by bringing home a new boyfriend. Including my parents, our house would face a hungry mob of sixteen people!

The timing seemed perfect. I desperately needed to breathe the ol' homestead air and reorient my bearings. That's why I was so taken aback, so dumbfounded, when I called home and got such an unexpected reaction.

My mother picked up the receiver.

"Hey! How's my favorite mom?"

"Jamie?" Mom confirmed. She was the only person on earth allowed to address me by my true given name.

I continued, "Just calling to let you know we'll be leaving here about ten o'clock Wednesday morning, so don't expect us till around six. Unless, of course, I drive the whole way, in which case, we should be there for lunch—"

"*Jamie,*" my mother repeated, cutting me off. Her voice was unusually tense. "Maybe you shouldn't come home right now."

My jaw dropped in consternation.

"Excuse me?" I said, hoping my mother had developed a sense of humor similar to mine, and was thus giving me a taste of my own medicine.

"I don't think it would be safe. There are people looking for you. Were you 'into something' last summer?"

Mom was truly shaken up.

"What are you talking about?" I questioned.

"Like drugs or . . . I know you wouldn't be involved in anything like that—but maybe you made some people angry?"

I couldn't believe I was hearing this.

"Mom, you're sounding crazy. I don't have the foggiest—"

My dad came on the line. "Jim?"

"Dad, what's going on?"

"We were hoping *you* could tell *us*. Some men came to the house. The first one on Friday, and three others less than an hour ago. They were looking for you."

"What for?"

"Jim, please. Don't hold out on us. Your mother is very frightened."

"Dad, I *promise*, I have absolutely no idea."

"The one on Friday acted friendly enough in the beginning. He asked where you were. We told him you were off at school, and that you'd be home for Thanksgiving. He asked when Thanksgiving was—which we found odd enough—but when we asked for his name so we could pass on any messages, the man walked off, refusing to answer!"

"Did he say what he wanted?"

"No, he never did. Jim, *think*. For your mother's sake—who are these people?"

I stammered, "I couldn't-couldn't even begin to guess, Dad."

"The men tonight wanted to know the same thing—where you were and when you'd be home. This time, your mother wouldn't tell them. The one who knocked—an older man—asked us another question as well. It was very unusual. He asked if you owned a sword."

"A *what?!*"

"A metal sword," Dad repeated. "Then he gave us a warning. It almost sounded like a threat. He said if the first man returned, we should *kill* him. Not send him away. Not have him arrested. He said 'kill,' and he meant it. That's what's got us so upset."

"Dad, this is *insane!*"

"We've called the police. The first man has been back in the neighborhood. We saw him standing under the streetlight in front of the Molhollends' yard when we came home last night. He was watching the house."

"This is *nuts,*" I proclaimed. "What am I supposed to do?"

"Don't misunderstand us, son. We want you to come home. We've been looking forward to it. But I'm not sure it would be safe. If only you could give us some idea—"

"Dad, I *need* to come home."

There was silence on the line. It seemed like forever.

My father finally spoke. "I'm not going to tell you not to come home, Jim. I just wish we could get to the bottom of this beforehand."

"It seems to me the only way we can do that is if I come home. What did they look like? Can you describe them to me?"

"Indian," my dad answered. "They all looked sort of Indian. Not quite like the ones around here, but—the first one was even dressed like one."

CHAPTER 2

I thought I'd felt every emotion there was in the course of my first twenty-two years, but paranoia was new to me. I wasn't quite sure how to deal with it.

I convinced my dad that I had no explanation for the mysterious visitors. Nevertheless, I racked my brain to think of who they could be. What might have happened the previous summer to inspire anyone to seek me out? For the most part, my summer had been dreadfully dull—six days a week digging irrigation ditches up the north fork of the Shoshoni River. There wasn't much opportunity for making peculiar acquaintances.

But one thing Dad had mentioned *did* strike a chord. It was the business about the sword.

One Saturday in August, I'd worked a particularly long day in the trenches and was unable to break away until shortly before dark. As I was driving back into town, I came upon the aftermath of a terrible accident.

There's a stretch of highway west of Cody called "Colter's Hell"—so named for a deep chasm of the Shoshoni River Canyon running parallel to the road. On that night the name became appropriate for a new reason. Some guy had been wandering in the middle of the highway at twilight, perhaps a little tipsy from an evening's merriment at the nearby Bronze Boot Nightclub. He was struck by an oncoming car, killing him instantly. But then the car skidded out of control, smashing through the guardrail.

When I arrived only seconds after the impact, I found the '85 Buick Skyhawk teetering on the cliff's edge. It was a seventy-five foot drop into the swift-moving river. The driver of the Buick—a middle-aged lady in a blonde wig that sat askew off the right side of her head—was still inside, frozen with fear. She knew the slightest movement could topple her vehicle. Still, she had no choice—she had to try. My efforts to talk her out were futile—and every few seconds I could hear the rocks grinding under the chassis as the car continued to slide. I realized that if I didn't act immediately, I'd spend the rest of my life wondering if my hesitation had cost this lady her life.

Tossing open the door, I got a firm grip on her wrist. She was not underweight, so I have to credit a little help from both heaven and my adrenal glands. As the Buick dropped away, flipping end-over-end and smashing onto the river rocks below, we were both lying safely in the stickery weeds near the edge of the road.

Within minutes two patrol cars had arrived, and soon after that, an ambulance. Other motorists had gathered, so I never got close enough to see the body of the pedestrian who had been killed. But I remembered overhearing the police say that the victim had no identification. Nobody seemed to know who he was or where he'd come from. Someone had also mentioned that he'd been oddly dressed.

Before I continued home, I wandered over to the edge one last time and gazed down at the hulk of overturned automobile. There was barely enough daylight left to see the river swirling around its tires. I shuddered at how close we had come to disaster. Maybe I'd been delayed at work that day for good reason. It didn't occur to me at the time that Providence may have had more motives than one.

As I raised my eyes slightly, I saw something flicker on a cliff shelf just below the section of guardrail where the pedestrian's body had landed. I found myself curiously drawn toward it, and climbed down carefully to see what it was. Upon reaching the shelf, I wrapped my fist around the hilt of a shiny silver sword. It was quite heavy, with polished stones inlaid into the base of the hilt. The blade was razor-sharp on both edges, stretching all the way from my hip to my ankle, and topped with an angular tip. The surface appeared to be only a silver plating; there were tiny places where the surface had been chipped away, and a rusty, copper-looking metal was visible underneath.

My initial feelings as I hefted the sword were strangely diametric. At first I was unmistakably repulsed, as if touching something dead. Then all at once I felt exhilarated, as if I drew a kind of energy from this object. As I stood there, I envisioned myself as a dauntless knight in King Arthur's court, looking across "Colter's Hell" for dragons and damsels.

The voice of Officer Finlay broke my spell. Todd Finlay was a thin man with sandy blonde hair, a drooping face, and gold-rimmed glasses. Unfortunately, he wasn't one of the more respected members of the Cody police force. Locals had put him in a category much more akin to Barney Fife than Joe Friday.

With his thumbs hooked in the loops of his belt, Finlay watched me climb back up the cliff, dragging the sword. Intrigued, he asked to see it. After holding it aloft in both hands, he touched his index finger to the edge. The metal sliced into his flesh, seemingly like butter, and a drop of blood trickled down the blade. Cursing, Finlay dropped the sword and wrapped his bleeding digit in a handkerchief.

The driver of the Buick said the sword wasn't hers. Whether it had been knocked out of the pedestrian's arms on impact, or whether it had been on that ledge all along, we had no way of knowing. Officer Finlay said he'd have to put it on file at the police station. If still unclaimed after ninety days, I could have it back. Those ninety days had expired the first week in November. Dad's story about mysterious visitors had reminded me of my intention to see if it was still there when I got home for Thanksgiving.

It was hard to focus on school those last two days before vacation. There was an exam in my Doctrine and Covenants class on Tuesday, and I greatly feared I would bomb it. Benny planted me down at the kitchen table Monday evening to review the test questions.

"Which section discusses eternal marriage? Quick! No time to think!" he cried.

"One hundred and thirty," I answered.

Benny made a sound like a penalty buzzer. "Wrong! One hundred and thirty-*two*."

Heaving a sigh, I mourned, "I'm gonna need a miracle tomorrow."

"Don't sweat it," offered Andrew, slicing tomatoes for a BLT. "No career recruiter is gonna care what your religion grades were."

"They will if it takes my GPA below 3.0," I responded.

"I'm tempted to say," Andrew continued, pulling his bacon strips out of the microwave and carefully unraveling them from the grease-soaked paper towel, "the required religion credits at this institution are a sore waste of time. I'm glad I got them out of the way as a sophomore."

"I think the whole point," said Benny, "was to take one religion class every semester so we could—"

"Keep a balanced curriculum. Yes, I know. I suppose that's good for the proletariat, but truth be known, I could teach circles around most of the religion professors *I've* had at BYU."

I wanted to believe that Andrew's arrogance was the result of deeply sown insecurities, but I'd never picked up such hints. He seemed thoroughly convinced of his intellectual superiority, and he made no apologies for it.

"Maybe in details," I defended, "but not in doctrine."

Now I'd done it. Study time was over. Them was fightin' words, and Andrew wasn't about to let them slide.

"I don't understand your distinction," he challenged. "Details *are* doctrine."

"With you it's facts without Spirit," I said wearily.

I'd tried to sound righteously indignant. But the fact was, I was in no spiritual condition to judge *anyone*. Besides that, until I'd forgotten about Andrew's shanghai of Renae for Homecoming, I couldn't claim to be neutral about anything he said or did.

"Well, I'm not an apologist, if that's what you mean," said Andrew. "I don't expend vast amounts of energy, like most Latter-day Saints, justifying contradictions in LDS history and doctrine."

"What contradictions?" Benny countered. "You're not gonna find any contradictions in the scriptures." Then, as if remembering Joseph Smith's proclamation that the Bible was true only so far as it was translated correctly, he added, "at least not in the Book of Mormon or the Doctrine and Covenants."

Andrew casually spread a layer of mayonnaise on his toast. "Don't be so sure. The D&C section you just mentioned contains one of the most glaring contradictions in all of Mormonism."

"What do you mean?" Benny asked warily.

"Section 132," Andrew reminded him. "That's where Joseph Smith declared polygamy to be a principle of God, despite the fiery sermon denouncing such practices in the second chapter of Jacob."

"Now hold on," said Benny, grabbing his "three-in-one" like a Colt 45. He turned to the book of Jacob.

Andrew began devouring his sandwich as confidently as he felt he was devouring our egos. "Let me save you some time," he offered between chomps. "Read Jacob 2:24."

Benny read, "'*Behold, David and Solomon truly had many wives and concubines, which thing was abominable before me saith the Lord.*'"

"Now read D&C 132:38."

Benny read, "'*David also received many wives and concubines, and also Solomon and Moses my servants, as also many others of my servants, from the beginning of creation until this time; and in nothing did they sin save in those things which they received not of me.*'"

Andrew swallowed another bite and sat back in his chair, swabbing a spot of mayonnaise off the corner of his mouth with a napkin. "So in one scripture it's all 'abominable,' and in the next it's divinely sanctioned—except in those things which they 'received not of the Lord.' Even *concubines* were approved!" He mocked our supposed western drawls. "Now, if'n you don't think that there's a contradiction, I suggest you take a course in basic logic."

"You're pulling it out of context," Benny accused.

Andrew shrugged. "So read it *in* context. You'll come to the same conclusion. In fact, verse 39 of section 132 solidifies the problem even further. There are several other errors I could point out, but I've got homework." Andrew started for his bedroom.

Benny interrupted him for one last question. "If you're so sure of all these errors, how come you're still a member of the Church? Do you have a testimony?"

Andrew grinned. "Of course. I'm at BYU, aren't I?"

He disappeared into his room and closed the door, leaving Benny and me to wallow in the spirit of contention left behind.

"Well?" asked Benny.

"Well, what?" I responded.

"What's the solution?"

"I don't know."

"Is he right? Is it a contradiction?"

I shrugged. Benny seemed genuinely upset. I recalled a General Authority once saying that an anti-Christ was anyone who tried to destroy another person's testimony. Andrew, despite taking the sacrament every Sunday, seemed guilty of that objective on more than one occasion. Still, I couldn't put the blame on Andrew. We'd asked for it as surely as if we'd ordered a hamburger.

"Benny," I consoled, "you can bet that Andrew Southwick is not the first one to ever discover such things. I'm sure the answer is written down somewhere."

Benny nodded slowly, staring off into space.

"Hey," I told him, "the Church is still true."

He crinkled his face and huffed, insulted that I might think his testimony could be so easily shaken. "I know that!" He got up to grab his coat. "I gotta meet Allison."

As was typical these days, when Benny got upset, he retreated to the arms of his girlfriend.

Lars, the UFO freak, had been on the couch with his nose buried in an engineering textbook during the whole conversation. Now that there was a lull, he looked up to ask me if I'd like to attend a Wednesday night meeting of the newest UFO sensation in Utah. This club was the "best," or so he said, and was even based in Salt Lake City.

"They're called the Bernardians," he explained. "They believe in advanced alien life on the second planet of Bernard's Star—eight light years from Earth. If I bring someone else, I don't have to pay dues."

"I'll be on the road to Cody," I apologized.

"I'll go with you, Lars," offered Benny, zipping his coat.

"That is, if you drop me off at the Salt Lake airport afterwards. My flight leaves at 11:10."

"Deal," agreed Lars. "I think you'll like it. Don't let what Andrew says get you down. Remember, ours is the only religion on earth that clearly teaches that there's life on other planets. If you need your testimony reconfirmed, one of those meetings is the best way I know to do it."

I rolled my eyes. If it took a UFO club to confirm a testimony of truth, humanity had sunk to a sorry state indeed.

* * *

On Wednesday morning I dragged my duffel bag down to the parking lot of King's Court Arms. For all I knew, a Mafia assassin was waiting in the backseat of my Mazda 626—or rather, my sister Jenny's Mazda 626. To my relief, there was no shoot-out. I was beginning to think there was a perfectly rational explanation for what had happened in Cody, and that my parents had overreacted.

Since Jenny lived in campus housing, she'd allowed me to use her car for most of the semester. Periodically she would gripe that I ought to buy my own set of wheels, but to be honest, I think Jen suffered from a weird sort of driving phobia. Even when we were in the car together, she always insisted that I take the helm. During the time that I was gone on my mission, Jenny'd had a close scrape with two oncoming semi-trucks on a two-lane road. Ever since, she seemed more content to be a passenger.

I filled up the tank at the Quick Stop, bought some tortilla chips and other assorted grub to make us all as ill as possible before arriving, then headed up to Heritage Halls to retrieve my sister and her new boyfriend.

I think Jenny and I were about as close as a brother and sister could ever get. I'm not saying there weren't times we didn't want to pull each other's hair out—without such moments it wouldn't have been a true brother/sister relationship. But there was a unique bond between us. I couldn't quite explain it, but it tended to make me overprotective. Ever since Jen had blossomed into a Cover-Girl caliber blonde in high school, there was a lot to be overprotective about.

Jenny would have intimidated most guys into oblivion if not for her special talent: she was an expert flirt—the kind about whom legends are told. She knew how to get the shy types to make the first move; how to get the "God's gift" types to think she was the only girl on earth; and how to get the "no-time-for-social-life" types to flunk all their classes. Her problem was, she was *so* good at flirting that she'd never acquired an instinct for *selectivity*. That's why she respected my opinion so much.

I felt certain that my future brother-in-law should be . . . well, like me!—handsome, amiable, and street-smart. However, I required that he rise *above* me in spiritual areas—in fact, he had to be the most turbo-stalwart priesthood holder ever to grace the gospel. Not a wishy-washy, "question-everything" wimp like myself.

Her latest catch was named Parley—a name which I suppose was not his sin, but his parents'. The guy was built like a tank, towering about 6'4"—and that was without the cowboy boots. My 5'3" sister would have needed an elevator for a good-night kiss.

Parley must have been briefed about the importance of my opinion. Thus, he thought it best that I be cowed into complacency. When I arrived, he approached me with three gargantuan strides, causing me to wonder if he'd be able to stop before I was trampled into the pavement. But stop he did, and at just the right distance to be sure our "look up to" and "look down upon" relationship was firmly established from the beginning. Crushing my fingers in a viselike grip, he exhaled the words, "How ya doin'? Jenny's told me a lot abou'cha."

"And you believed her?" I said.

The joke was lost on him somewhere in the stratosphere. He raised an eyebrow in confusion.

My sister giggled and slapped my arm. "Oh, come on. There's only great things to tell."

Just then the joke hit Parley. He pretended a belated laugh, which sounded worse than if he hadn't laughed at all.

Only eight hours to go, I thought.

Jennifer opted to take the front seat. Parley looked gravely disappointed. I think he'd been hoping to cuddle with her in back for the entire trip while I acted as chauffeur.

"So how long have you two been dating?" I asked along the interstate between Park City and Evanston, Wyoming.

"A little less than a month," Jenny answered. "Par and I met on the fifth floor of the library."

"And the rest is history," added Parley, reaching his hands around the seat to give Jenny a shoulder massage.

"Things must be going well," I concluded, "if she's already inviting you back to the homestead for Thanksgiving dinner."

"Oh, that was Par's idea," Jen corrected.

"Oh, yeah?"

"Yep," Parley confirmed. "You got an awfully special sister here, Jim. I had to see what kind of parents would raise such a girl."

The fog was lifting off this scenario. My sister had woven her web a little tighter than she might have been hoping, and now this poor lug was under the impression that he couldn't live without her. When we stopped for fuel in Rock Springs, Jenny followed me inside to the cashier so she could ask what I thought of him.

"Well, he's the *biggest* one I think you've ever caught."

"But do you *like* him?"

"What do *you* think of him?" I hedged.

"He's sweet. Not as sweet as Bryan, but sweet."

"Bryan? I must have missed that boyfriend. So what's the story with this one? Are you in love with him?"

"Do you think I should be?"

I paused in writing out the check to the cashier. I don't think he minded. He seemed to be enjoying the conversation. "Jenny, if you're not sure of your feelings, don't you think you might be misleading the guy by inviting him home to meet your parents?"

"He said he had no place to go for Thanksgiving. I couldn't feel good about leaving him in Provo. Besides, with all the strange people coming up to the house, I figured you could use a bodyguard, right?"

"Jenny, you can't play with guys' heads like this!"

The male cashier looked at Jenny and nodded in agreement.

"I'm not!" she defended. "I mean . . . I don't know *what* I want. Parley seems to have all the right characteristics. He's loyal. He's responsible. He's 'teddy-bear' cute! He's also got a job lined up in sports medicine after he graduates. I need my *family* to help me decide who I should fall in love with."

"Why can't you trust your own feelings?"

"For the same reason I need to rent videos at Albertson's instead of Blockbuster."

"Huh?"

"There's too much to choose from at Blockbuster. They all look so good that I have no objectivity. Sometimes I spend as much time *deciding* on a video as it would have taken to *watch* it. Then I choose something lousy. I need an Albertson's social life. I can't handle Blockbuster."

The cashier looked as perplexed by the analogy as I was. If only Jenny knew how grateful some of us would have been for even as many options as Albertson's.

Four hours later, I could see the peaks of Cedar and Rattlesnake Mountains rising in the distance. And not a moment too soon before Parley told another Polack joke. The climate was at least ten degrees colder up here than it was in Provo. The ground was free of snow, which was a bit unusual for this time of year. Nevertheless, Beck Lake had a thin sheet of ice kissing its surface. As we rounded the turn that brought us into Cody's city limits, I couldn't help but feel that my hometown was awfully quiet for six p.m. There were only a few cars on the road and only a handful of customers in the parking lot at K-Mart.

I might have thought it was *High Noon.* The train had pulled into town and I was on it. In anticipation of a showdown, the townsfolk were clearing the streets.

Don't be ridiculous, I thought. I saw no villains in black hats waiting at the corner beside the McDonald's as we turned off the main strip. Again I decided it was all some big misunderstanding.

But if that were true, why was I biting my fingernails while turning the steering wheel? It was my hometown, and yet I felt strangely unwelcome, as if there was a voice in the icy wind urging me to turn around.

CHAPTER 3

I felt a rush of relief as I pulled into our old familiar driveway. This was home base; nobody could tag me "it." I parked behind my dad's Ford Taurus and beside my brother Steven's Toyota Celica. I looked both ways down the street. There was an old lady making her way along the sidewalk in front of the Watkins' house, enjoying an evening stroll. Otherwise, the neighborhood was still. Whoever my parents thought was prowling about must have taken a few days off to spend Thanksgiving with relatives.

My mother greeted us all with her usual warmth, even offering Parley a hug, saying, "Since you're here for Thanksgiving, you might as well consider yourself one of the family."

Everyone had arrived except Mitch and Judd and their respective clans. My Uncle Spencer waved to us enthusiastically from the couch, sandwiched between two throw pillows, watching the opening kickoff of one of the various football games. My older brother Steven was beside him chewing chunks of ice from a tall glass, as was his trademark. My two-year-old nephew, Cory, was busy pulling pots and pans out of the cupboard. When he saw Jenny and me, he dashed over for a hug from his favorite uncle and aunt.

I got my fair share of "How are ya?"s and "How's school?"s. But it wasn't long before Dad brought up the subject on everyone's mind.

"Have you figured out who these people are yet?"

"No, Dad," I replied.

"That man—the first one who came to the door—was waiting on the corner in front of Molhollends' driveway when I came home from work," Dad reported.

Dad got home from his job as superintendent of Cody Public Schools at five p.m. That meant someone had been there only an hour before we'd pulled up.

Dad added, "The police are starting to think I've lost a few nuts and bolts. I've asked them to drive by the house six times in the last four days. Each time they come, the man is gone. I don't want you going out of the house this weekend, Jim."

"Dad, I can't live that way," I protested. "If they want to talk, I'll talk. I've got nothing to hide."

Parley stepped over to us at that moment and promised, "I'll stay with him every minute, Mr. H. If anybody tries anything, they'll have to deal with me."

"Thanks, I can take care of myself," I said.

Parley sniggered at that concept and walked away. Nevertheless, Dad was somewhat comforted by Parley's proposal, so I agreed to let Jenny's boyfriend tag along whenever I left the house. That opportunity first presented itself shortly after eight o'clock. Tonight was pie-making night for Mom and Aunt Louise. In bygone years, Mom had waited until Thanksgiving Day to bake such confections, but the convenience of warm pie via the microwave had shattered such traditions. The house was smothering in the aromas of cherry, blueberry, pumpkin, pecan, and lemon meringue. The anticipation was too torturous for a household infested with five ravenous males. It was mutually agreed between Dad, Steven, Parley, Uncle Spencer, and myself that the blueberry pie would not live to see Thanksgiving Day. But the grief we felt upon discovering no vanilla ice cream to accompany it was too tragic for words. Immediately I volunteered my services for the arduous task of going to Steck's IGA in quest of ice cream and several other crucial items that Mom had forgotten to add to her last shopping list. Dad objected at first, offering to go himself, but I knew the game on television was one he'd anxiously awaited, so I sat him back down in his La-Z-Boy and whistled for Parley.

As I stepped out onto our front porch, I felt the sting of a shrill wind out of the canyon, making the chill factor far worse than the temperature. The streetlights were blazing and the stars were veiled by a thin sheet of cumulus. As I exhaled, my vision was blurred by my own vapors. But when the vapors cleared, I could see a figure standing under the light post across the street. Parley saw him as well and leapt from the porch, taking several threatening strides across the lawn.

"Hey!" he yelled, awakening anybody who might be asleep in this neighborhood or the adjacent neighborhood. "You got somethin' to say? Come here and say it!"

But the man had already scampered around the high wood fence on the northern edge of the Molhollends' lawn and disappeared.

Parley looked as though he might take off to catch the man. I jumped after him to grab his arm. "Parley," I cried, "If you scare him away for good, I might *never* know what's going on!"

"Just lettin' him know we can't be intimidated," said Parley.

When we arrived at the IGA, there were only four or five cars in the dimly lit parking lot, which seemed unusual for the night before a major holiday. There was a video store situated in the store's entranceway. As the sliding glass door closed out the cold behind us, Parley sent me off to find the groceries while he selected a couple of movies.

"You like Arnold Schwarzeneggar?" he asked.

"Make a stack, and I'll tell you which ones my mother might allow past the front door." With that, I continued into the main part of the store.

Presently, there was only one cashier working. She had a line three persons deep and a conveyor belt loaded down with Butterball turkeys. Otherwise, the store was remarkably quiet. I yanked out a shopping cart and proceeded to make my way toward the dairy section along the back wall to fill my mother's request for eggs and eggnog.

As I stood beside the egg rack, deciding between large or extra large, I happened to glance toward the frozen foods aisle and saw a man standing there, watching me through a Western Family macaroni display—failing miserably if he was trying to appear discreet. The man was old and wizened as if he suffered from a kind of cancer, or as if some creature that made a habit of sucking life from the human soul had latched onto his face. He was dressed almost comically—like a duck hunter—in a bright red vest, khaki pants, hiking boots, and a visor cap that read *Wyoming, Love It or Leave It.* My heart rose into my throat. His features were Indian. I couldn't have said what *kind* of Indian—the Navaho and Crow that I'd seen in our Fourth of July parades seemed to have a different look. Maybe he wasn't Indian at all, but that was the best comparison I could make in my limited experience.

I nodded cordially and shifted my attention back to shopping, playing casual, hoping he'd wonder if he had the wrong guy. He remained the exact same distance away as I strolled past all the aisles in the store to reach the ice cream. In each aisle, another man was waiting, watching. Most of them were similarly dressed, although the slogans varied on each visor cap.

Had they followed me inside? I didn't remember seeing any other cars pull into the parking lot as we were walking toward the entrance. Surely Parley had noticed them. Where was my faithful guard dog now that I needed him?

I reached the frozen foods aisle and tossed a half-gallon of ice cream into the cart. I doubt it was the brand I wanted, or even the flavor. I didn't care, as long as I lived long enough to taste it. There were other things Mom had wanted, but I ignored my list and headed for the cashier. I was grateful to see that nobody else was in line.

The cashier cheerfully proceeded to ring up my items. I said nothing to her, which I'm sure she thought was rude. Instead, I kept track of each man's position at all times. There were five of them. As I pulled out my wallet and handed the lady a ten-dollar bill, they closed in, stepping over the chains of unattended checkout counters. I took my change and waited for the cashier to hook the plastic bag over the metal holder and slip my eggs, eggnog, and ice cream inside. She seemed oblivious to any peril, thinking perhaps these men were friends of mine. She forced a smile despite my rudeness, handed me my groceries, and told me to have a happy Thanksgiving.

I made a beeline for the door. The five men immediately pursued. I hurried to the video store where I had left Parley. My only hope was that he would see my dilemma and come to my rescue, mouth a-foaming. But Parley was gone! The only person in the video store was a teenage girl at the counter, glued to the TV on the wall, while it played *The Little Mermaid.* I prayed with all my heart that Parley was in the car. I turned back to verify that I was still being followed. The older, decrepit man was leading the way. He seemed amused by my determination to escape, and when he smiled I could see wide gaps between many of his teeth.

As the outer door slid open, I launched into the darkened parking lot and made a mad dash for my car. The men bounded after me. I yelled Parley's name and dropped my groceries onto the asphalt. It was a three-way tie to the door of the Mazda. As I tried to open it and climb inside, four powerful arms slammed it shut again. The five men stood around me like panthers.

I spun around and faced the wizened wraith with the gaps between his teeth. "What do you want?!"

He just stood there, as if basking in the satisfaction of finally having me in his grasp.

"Hello, Jimawkins." He ran my name together as if it was one word. "It's been a long time."

I was panting and shaking, but I managed to reply, "Long time since what? Why are you chasing me?"

Another man came forward. This one was younger, though his presence was no less ominous. The corners of his eyes were long and sharp, making them dagger-thin without squinting. Somewhat annoyed at the older man, he acted as if he was reassuming a position of leadership.

"We've come to protect you," said the second man. "To warn you. That way, when the time comes, you may be willing to do us a similar favor."

"Who are you?" I demanded.

The older character removed his cap, revealing a rosy scalp and a thin gray patch of hair. At first I thought this gesture was an awkward attempt to be polite, but then he made a wry grin, stuck out his chin, and asked, "Don't you recognize me?"

"Of course not," I answered. "I've never seen any of you before in my life."

But even as I was proclaiming my ignorance, something about this wizened wraith seemed mystically familiar. Who was he? A character from a horror movie? A phantom from a childhood nightmare? Whatever the connection was between us, I was certain it wasn't good.

The old man pretended to be hurt. "Has it been so long? Soooo, your memory has been excised!" he mused. "Very interesting."

"There's nothing interesting about it," I insisted. "You've simply got the wrong guy."

A third man let out a guffaw. The slogan on his cap read, *I'd rather be fishing*. I seriously doubted that. This man's neck was nearly as big around as his head. The dagger-eyed man put a stop to his cackling by slapping a palm on the man's breast.

Then the dagger-eyed man stated, "We only wish to ask you one question. If you answer it, we will present you with information that will save your life. If you do not answer . . . we will not help you."

"I have nothing to say," I insisted. "I'm afraid you're going to be disappointed."

He plowed ahead with his question. "You saw a man killed three moons ago. You were there when they took his body away, were you not?"

I thought for a moment. "The accident at Colter's Hell? Yes, I was there. I have no idea where they took the man's body. The police can tell you—"

The older man interrupted, "We are not interested in his body. We are interested to know if he was carrying a weapon. Perhaps . . . a sword?"

"Yeah," I admitted. "He had a sword."

"Ah! Yes!" the old man responded excitedly. "Very good. Can you tell us where we might find it?"

"I gave it to the police."

His grin faded. "The police? And where might we find the police?"

"Where? You keep crowding me like this, holding me against my will, they'll likely find *you.*"

A fourth man motioned to the older man that finding the police was not a problem. This man, and the last one standing beside him, looked to be typical white Caucasians. I half wondered if they were locals. The other men definitely appeared to hail from another part of the country, or the world.

The dagger-eyed man motioned his men to back away. "Forgive us. We mean you no danger. We are only soldiers in the cause of . . . *righteousness.*"

The others snickered at his word choice.

He continued, "You've helped us immensely. Now I'll give you a warning."

He reached inside his inner vest pocket and pulled out a handgun—a powerful .357 Magnum. I stiffened in mortal dread. But the weapon was not aimed between my eyes. The man with the dagger-thin eyes held it by the barrel and placed it in my hand.

"There is a man who wishes to kill you," he said succinctly. "He will do so without the least hesitation—unless you act swiftly and kill him first. This instrument should be quite adequate for the job."

I glanced down the barrel, as big as a cannon. "Why?" I asked. "Why would he . . . want to kill me?"

"That would be a foolish question to ask him," he replied. "He will not take the time to answer."

The man with dagger-thin eyes waved his companions to follow him into the alleyway. They followed him swiftly into the darkness—all but the wizened old wraith, who lingered behind to study me a moment longer.

Pointing at my right hand, he commented, "That's a nice ring."

He was referring to my ring with the shiny blue stone that I'd worn for . . . I don't remember how many years.

"I knew a craftsman in my city who made such rings. He was a very talented man."

The wrinkled, sinister man gazed one last time into my eyes, curved his lips into a final grin, then slunk off into the night behind his comrades, leaving me alone beside the door of the Mazda, still holding the loaded pistol in my palm. After the last of them had faded out of sight, I opened my car door and dropped the weapon onto the backseat, as if it was something poisonous.

I began to fear for Parley. Where had he gone? Had they lured him back outside and overpowered him? Had they knocked him unconscious—or worse—and dragged his body into the alley? But there hadn't been enough time!

Suddenly Parley came rushing out of the store. "There you are! I've been lookin' all over for ya! You had me goin' nuts!" He paused to pick up my sack of groceries on the pavement. Egg yolks came oozing out from a hole in the bottom of the plastic. Parley looked back at me with a confused gape on his mug and asked the obvious, "Is everything okay?"

As it turned out, Parley had decided to take a quick trip to the rest room about the time I was accosted. Had he been a *real* guard dog, I might have shot the worthless mutt. I didn't want to tell him what had happened. I still wasn't sure myself. I told him that something had spooked me and I overreacted. I had to collect my thoughts and slow my heartbeat. The best way, I decided, was to go back into the store and replace Mom's fractured eggs.

We skipped the video, an idea which somewhat rankled Parley. But I didn't particularly want to wait around while he decided between *Predator* or *Terminator II.* On the way home he noticed the .357 Magnum lying on the backseat and picked it up.

"How long's *this* been here?" he wondered, rolling the weapon over and over in his hands.

"I, uh, keep it under the seat for extra protection," I said.

"Nice." Parley looked down the barrel. "Almost too much gun for one man."

As we arrived home, I sighed in relief to see that no one was standing under the light post. I pulled into the driveway and parked in the usual spot behind Dad's Taurus. I wanted to take back the pistol from Parley and keep it at my side, but carrying a loaded firearm into the house would only freak out my family worse than they already were. I opened the car door and proceeded toward the porch when a voice whispered from the other side of my brother's Celica.

"Jimawkins?" The voice slurred my name into one word, just like the wizened character at IGA.

I nearly leaped out of my socks. I'd been warned of an assassin. I'd been warned that he would strike mercilessly, with lightning speed. In the next blazing instant, the pistol discharged. Parley, also startled by the voice, had responded like a shell-shocked marine and fired a haphazard bullet through the window of my brother's car. As I ducked down to shield my face, I glimpsed a shadow dart out from behind the Celica and move around the Mazda to make a rear attack on Parley. Before I could call out a warning, Parley squawked in pain and the pistol fired again.

My dad had reached the front door. As I cautiously arose and gazed across the hood of my car, Parley was face down in the flower bed, lying in the remains of my mother's summer chrysanthemums. Standing over him, now wielding the Magnum, was the same mysterious man we'd seen earlier under the light post, his features still half-shrouded by shadow. Upon seeing me stand, he threw his hands over his head.

"Please—!" he cried. He stepped forward, laid the pistol on the hood of the Mazda, then raised his arms again. "I mean no harm to you or your family!"

His face was now better illuminated by the porch light. He was young. Early twenties. Perhaps my age. He wore an old coat with greasy stains and huge rips in the lining. I couldn't help but wonder if he'd obtained it from somebody's garbage. Underneath the coat were the clothes my father had described—a kind of pullover tunic that exposed his legs to the cold, and sandals with leather straps crisscrossing up the calf. His jaw was square, his hair was black and thick, and his skin was unusually tan for November. All in all, his features were very similar to the men I'd already encountered tonight, though his countenance seemed less . . . desperate?

Nevertheless, I snatched up the pistol and pretended to command the grit of a gunslinger, though my hands were shaking like Jell-O.

"Don't move!" I cried. It seemed an appropriate injunction, even if the object of my command was already as still as an oak. I looked over at Parley, still unmoving. "What have you done to him?"

Just then Parley stirred and groaned. He started rising drunkenly to his feet. As his dizziness subsided, his eyes filled with fury. He'd been humiliated by this stranger, despite his being at least five inches and fifty pounds his inferior. All Parley remembered later was a powerful hand seizing him from behind and pinching off some unfamiliar nerve point. Now the cowboy's fists were in full gear, but my family quickly surrounded us. Dad and my brother, Steven, held Parley at bay while the drone of a police siren drew nearer.

"Why have you been terrorizing my family?" I demanded.

"I've been waiting for you," the man explained. "I've come to seek your help. For the sake of my people and yours, please, listen to me."

"What do you want from me?! I've never met you—or your friends at the store!"

"Trust me," he said, "if you've met others like me, they are not my friends—or yours."

I lowered my voice and uttered one final question as the police car screeched to a halt in the gutter in front of my house. My voice was imploring, begging for something I could understand, something I could believe. "*Who are you?*"

"My name is Muleki," he answered. "You knew my father, Captain Teancum."

CHAPTER 4

Every time I closed my eyes to sleep, I kept seeing his face—the man who called himself Muleki—pleading with me silently while the police clamped him in handcuffs and stuffed him in the backseat of the patrol car. Even as they pulled away, Muleki wouldn't take his eyes off mine.

I did fall asleep eventually, but never deeper than dream-state—and my dreams were all messed up, like the dreams I usually have when I'm running a fever. The plots didn't make sense; people didn't talk right; events were out of sequence—yet my brain was unwilling to acknowledge that there was a problem.

Worst of all, that hill kept appearing—the one with the tiny cluster of trees, and the man in the mist, still beckoning me onward, still driving me crazy.

At a quarter past one, I bolted up, disgruntled and utterly exhausted. Propping my shoulders against the headboard, I buried my face in the sweat of my palms and heaved a dreary sigh. Then I said a prayer, brief and ungrateful, pleading that I be granted the sleep I deserved. My thoughts drifted off before I'd properly closed the prayer, and I found myself drawn in by the blue stone ring on my right hand. The room was pitch-black except for a single beam of illumination coming through a sliver in the curtains from the light post across the street. As I sat up in my bed, the beam fell directly across the ring.

I stared at the shiny blue stone. It seemed funny that I had persistently worn it all these years. The last time I took it off was shortly after my mission. Normally I'd worn it on my pinky, but fooling around one day, I got it stuck on my ring finger. A nurse told me not to worry unless I felt it was cutting off the circulation, so I made up a corny game. Like Arthur's sword-in-the-stone, I decided the girl who could remove that ring would be the girl I would marry.

"*Menochin,*" I said out loud.

Now why did I say that? The name popped into my head like the "ting" of a bell. Then suddenly I began to see other things, like memories from a former life, startling enough to make a Mormon consider the possibility of reincarnation! I saw an ancient city with a towering wall, a bustling marketplace and lazy green river. I saw a mighty warrior, invincible in the fury of battle. And finally, I saw a little four-year-old boy leaping into the arms of this mighty warrior and calling him "Father" while the warrior called him "Muleki."

Muleki.

I'd have sworn I was dreaming if I hadn't hit my skull against the headboard and glanced at the clock to verify the hour. I staggered into the kitchen and guzzled a cup of ice-cold water from a pitcher in the refrigerator. Then I wandered into the living room and slouched in my dad's easy chair. There in the darkness, I resolved to learn every mystery that this man who had been hauled off by the police might possess. If my mother would have it, there'd be another place setting tomorrow for Thanksgiving dinner.

* * *

"The holiday spirit come over you, eh?" commented the officer on duty at the Cody Jail.

I'd informed him that I was completely willing to drop the charges of trespassing and harassment and allow the prisoner, who'd maintained the singular name of Muleki, to go free. When the prisoner was brought out to me, still wearing the moth-eaten coat and ancient-style tunic, it was apparent that he hadn't enjoyed much sleep the night before either.

"He said some bizarre things during the night," the officer reported. "I was gonna turn him over to someone at the state hospital in Lander tomorrow. I'm still not sure that wouldn't be the best course of action."

"I'll take care of him," I promised, and Muleki was placed in my custody.

"Thank you for coming, Jimawkins," Muleki said.

"Jim. Just call me Jim. And here—" I peeled off his greasy jacket and dropped it in the waste can beside the door. "You won't need it. My car is heated."

We exited through the station doorway. He followed me out to the parking lot, folding one arm over the other to keep warm. The courthouse clock above us sounded the half-hour gong. Muleki jumped into a defensive stance and stared up at the clock's green-glass face.

"Hop in," I instructed.

Muleki looked down at the Mazda's door handle, hesitating.

"It's all right," I said. "I didn't lock it. Just pull up."

I felt silly explaining it to him. He wasn't a two-year-old. Yet only after I'd demonstrated by opening the door on my side was he was willing to give it a try. The task a success, he slid carefully onto the seat and placed his feet firmly in the center of the floor mat.

I left the gearshift in park while I started the engine and got the heat flowing to cure Muleki's goose bumps. Then I turned to glare at my bewildering passenger. He continued sitting there in a posture of perfect discipline, his arms at his side.

"I can't believe I bailed you out," I said. "I'm goin' on nothing but instinct right now, partner, so don't let me down. I had a long, lonely night, and I saw a lot of weird things. I'm countin' on you to explain them to me."

Muleki hardly reacted. He just listened. Suddenly I wasn't sure where to begin.

"Have you had breakfast?" I asked.

"They gave me a meal in the prison. Eggs—I don't know from what kind of bird—and bread. A yellow juice, very sweet, and strips of meat. I did not eat the meat. I feared the animal it came from was unclean."

"You mean bacon? I'm sure there wasn't anything wrong with—" Then it hit me what he meant. "Are you a Jew?"

"My kinship is Jershonite, from the lineage of Mulek," he responded, "though my blood is no longer pure."

I took that as meaning yes. "So you've eaten, then?"

"Not really. You came before I could finish. I've eaten very little since coming to this land. My food ran out several days ago."

"Are you a foreigner?"

"I'm a citizen of Zarahemla," he replied.

"*Please! No more of that!*" I threw my hands over my face. My hopes of averting a migraine so early in the day were waning. Lowering my hands, I said, "Let's start from the beginning. Tell me again who you are."

"I am Muleki, son of Teancum. Captain of the Guard in the Palace of Helaman, Chief Judge of Zarahemla."

I continued staring at him open-mouthed. I seriously considered handing him back over to the police, admitting that the state hospital thing wasn't such a bad idea. He must have perceived my utter disbelief, because all at once his face blossomed with understanding.

"Ah, then it's true what I first suspected. You *don't* remember. Helaman said this would be possible."

"You guessed it, buddy!" I exploded. "I don't remember anything! And it's driving me *nuts!* Do I have amnesia when it comes to trying to remember a year of my life or what?"

"You were not with us that long."

I vigorously shook my jowls and blew all the air out of my lungs. Then I closed my eyes and inhaled, long and slow. Opening them again, I stared straight ahead at the emptiness of space and admitted, "Sometimes I see faces. I hear voices at night. I'm not sure what's real anymore. I don't even know why I've come here today, except that there's something nagging inside me—telling me that *you* know the answers. I'm begging you to help me. Please, if you have any answers . . . please, just tell me what you know."

"There were two of you," Muleki began. "I saw you when I was a little boy. You were with my father. Both of you looked so pale, like so many of the other people in this land. The one who was with you had many spots on his skin, and his hair was like amber."

"Garth?" I wondered. "Was Garth there, too?"

"They say his full name was Garplimpton," Muleki confirmed.

My body stiffened. This couldn't be happening. Oh, how I'd hoped this guy really was a nut case. How I'd wished I could have gone forward with my life as it was before. But that was impossible now. Every whit of logic within me screamed that his words were ludicrous, yet something else whispered that they were perfectly true.

We went to the Irma Grill, since it was the only restaurant open on Thanksgiving Day. I ordered him a full-course breakfast of eggs, toast, hash browns, and a stack of pancakes. When the meal came, he dug in with both hands. As several patrons seated nearby winced at the sight of yolk and syrup dripping down his palms, I prevailed upon him to use a spoon. He downed that breakfast as if it were his last meal. I considered telling him to slow down—there'd be a lot more eating before the day was over. But I wondered if any amount of food would have intimidated that appetite.

I listened intently as Muleki told me about a cavern at the base of a volcano in a land called Melek. He also told me about a secret passage atop Cody's own Cedar Mountain that served as a bridge between his time and mine. But having one question answered only brought up dozens more. Unlike I had hoped, my frustration wasn't subsiding.

"How old was I?" I demanded.

"You were much younger. About thirteen."

"How long did I stay in this . . . time warp?"

"Only two moons, but in that short period of time you saved my father's life and helped defeat Amalickiah, the Lamanite king."

"If you're a Nephite, how come we understand each other?" I challenged. "Shouldn't we be speaking different languages?"

"I don't know," replied Muleki. "I've spoken to only a few people since coming, yet I understand every word they say. It's a powerful gift. It seems that anyone who makes the journey possesses it."

I needed a fast drive on a long stretch of road with the cold wind blowing in my face. His words were like peroxide, offering a potential cure, but inducing greater pain. As he spoke, memories slowly filled in the darkened gaps of my mind. The images remained quite blurry—but I could see them. Why had they been taken from me in the first place? Why had I been so tortured? Was it so wrong to remember such an adventure?

"There was a girl," I recalled "She had black hair and brown eyes. I'm almost certain she gave me this ring. Her name was Menochin."

"Yes!" Muleki exclaimed, grateful that my memory was returning. "She is my cousin."

Shyly I inquired, "Is she still around? I mean . . . "

"Of course. She is a great woman. She is the wife of Judge Helaman, son of Prophet Helaman."

"You mean she's *married? Already?*"

"She has been for fifteen years. She has seven children. Two boys—Nephi and Lehi—and five girls."

My shoulders slumped. I sat there in consternation. I couldn't believe it! My heart was telling me that Menochin had been my first love. How could she betray me like this? I didn't even get a Dear John! Then it occurred to me—if I'd met Muleki when he was four years old, that would make Menochin . . . *over thirty by now!*

As if reading my thoughts, Muleki explained, "The bridge between our worlds is not entirely stable. You've not aged as much as I have. When I return, I hope it's to the same day I left, but I knew there was a possibility it would not be."

"Why *have* you come?" It was time to ask.

Muleki placed his spoon beside his plate. "Like my father, I am a soldier," he explained. "I have come to prevent a great evil from being unleashed upon your land. And I have come to insure that this evil cannot return to mine—at least not in the wrong hands. I am searching for a sword—silver-plated—with precious stones in its hilt."

"That sword again!" I blurted. "What is it with you people? You come all the way to another dimension of time and space just to retrieve a measly sword? The men last night asked me for the same thing."

Fear swept over Muleki's face. "Did you give it to them?"

"No. I didn't have it to give."

"But you have seen it?"

"Yeah, a man was carrying it with him along the highway west of town. A lady ran over him with her Buick."

"I know this man," Muleki declared. "His name was Rerenak. He was one of the most foolish people ever born."

"No doubt," I agreed. "What kind of idiot would wander in the middle of the highway at dusk?"

"One who was unfamiliar with the workings of this world," answered Muleki. "One who was a member of the secret band of Gadianton."

My heart skipped a beat. "You mean a Gadianton *robber?*"

"He was not an important member. Yet he was very ambitious. He stole from his band the most precious article they possessed and thought to use it in this world as a means of gaining great power. Only, he forgot the oath that he swore when he was initiated—that his life belonged to the Evil One if ever he betrayed his clan. There was nowhere he could hide. Thus, he died for his crime."

"Let me get this straight," I said. "He died because he took *a sword*? This thing must be pretty valuable."

"Only to those whose works are done in darkness. The Sword of Coriantumr was forged by Akish from the ore of Ephraim Hill when the Jaredite peoples covered the face of the land. It was passed down through the generations of wicked kings."

"What could be so terrible about a sword?" I asked.

"You already know much more than is necessary," said Muleki. "It isn't wise for me to tell you more."

"How did you know I had seen it?"

"We found the woman who killed Rerenak."

"*We?*" I felt myself swallow. "Are you a Gadianton?"

"I am not," Muleki said. "But I've been in false league with them for nearly a year now—though I've never taken any oaths. I've learned many of their dark ways. This enabled me to save Helaman's life and to end the wicked days of Kishkumen."

My head was spinning. "You killed Kishkumen? *The* Kishkumen? The same one as in the Book of Mormon?"

"I wouldn't know. I've never read this book." Muleki went on, "When Gadianton fled Zarahemla, I followed his band into the wilderness. My mission was to find Coriantumr's sword and take possession of it. It was a quest for which I was willing to give my life. When Rerenak stole it from Gadianton's tent, I volunteered to be part of the company that would retrieve it. They allowed me to come because I knew a way to reach the volcano in Melek that would not pass through populated regions."

"And the men I saw last night—?"

"They were the other members of our company."

"But they wanted me to kill you," I reported. "They claimed you would kill *me* if I failed to strike first."

"I'm not surprised. They would prefer others to do their dirty work."

"One of them acted as if he knew *me,* but I can't seem to place him. He was an older guy—really withered-looking."

"That would be Mehrukenah," said Muleki. "Since Kishkumen's death, Mehrukenah is Gadianton's personal assassin—the most powerful member of the band besides Gadianton himself. Though he is older and seems quite feeble, don't be fooled. A viper would never bite him for fear his poison would be worse than its own. If you betrayed Mehrukenah during those days when you knew him, beware. It is said that he has no enemies from his younger days. None of them are still alive."

I tried again to reach inside my memory, but I just couldn't place him. I continued, "Another one had really shifty eyes, with sharp corners."

"That man is Shurr. He is Gadianton's brother, and though he is guilty of many savage crimes, I consider him weak and reckless. Gadianton made Shurr the leader of the company only because of Shurr's loyalty. He is to be the sword-bearer, and only he may touch it when it is found. Gadianton fears what Mehrukenah may do if he gets hold of it first."

"The last one is Boaz," Muleki concluded. "He is also a member of Gadianton's inner circle. These men are as dangerous as any men who have ever walked the earth. Never try to defeat them with craft or wit. They would chew you to pieces. The only way to crush them is with the righteousness of God."

Wouldn't you know it? Just the thing I felt I was running a bit shy of.

"But I saw five men," I stated.

"The others were recruited the first few days after we arrived. One is named Clarke. The other is Bridenbough. They were already well indoctrinated in the ways of the band. Apparently your world is not free from Gadianton's stain. I don't know much about them, except that it was with their help that we found the woman who killed Rerenak. She was the one who told us you had the sword. I knew it was not by chance that you found it first. My Uncle Moriancum spoke often of your courage. I broke away from the others and tried to warn you, but, regrettably, I was five days too early. I'm sorry your family has suffered. I'm even more sorry that you have been troubled. If I can have the sword, I will depart immediately and your life will be no more disrupted by this business."

"But I gave it to the police," I confessed.

"The police?"

"When I was bailing you out, I asked the desk officer where it was. He told me that because of the holiday, nobody would be in to dig up something like that until tomorrow."

"Then I will leave as soon as I can, tomorrow," promised Muleki.

"What are you gonna do with the sword after you return?"

"I will destroy it," he proclaimed.

"How? Melt it down? Break it in half?"

"No," said Muleki, smiling painfully at my naiveté. "There is no fire that could melt it and no stone that could break it."

This was getting a bit melodramatic. "Then how do you intend to destroy it?"

"By laying it to rest in Ether's coffer."

"Ether's *what?*"

"It's a stone box in the earth."

"Where's it located?"

"At the highest summit point of the Hill Ramah in the land of Desolation."

"What's putting it in a box supposed to accomplish?"

"Please don't force me to tell you any more," Muleki begged. "If I thought it could help you—if I thought it could save your life—believe me, I would tell you."

Muleki might have read the cynicism on my face and decided not to cast any more pearls before swine. It just didn't make sense to see such stress stirred up over an inanimate object.

Staring at Muleki across the table, I felt sorry for him. The beleaguered Nephite seemed to be terribly lonely. For the last year he'd endured the company of the most evil men of his day, pretending to be one with them. Such an existence could take the wind right out of the human soul. I'd always been taught to avoid anything involving the occult like the plague. It was said that the scars caused by such tampering might never heal. The discipline it must have taken Muleki to come away from this experience with his salvation intact was no less than superhuman. Even so, I saw a certain misery in his eyes—the misery of a soldier who'd survived a hundred wars only to be tortured the rest of his days by the haunting memories.

When I asked Muleki what his plans were after his mission was accomplished, he shrugged his shoulders and finished his meal. Perhaps he didn't feel himself worthy to raise a family and lead a normal life anymore.

In spite of my skepticism, I decided I would help Muleki in his quest. I'd do anything I could to help him obtain the sword and return safely to his people through the caverns of Frost Cave on Cedar Mountain. But a question burned in my mind as we drove home to join in the Thanksgiving festivities: what had Muleki meant when he expressed his fear that the sword might be unleashed on the people of my day? Just what did he suppose would result from such an occurrence? It seemed almost sad; even though the Nephites possessed the true gospel, they still couldn't escape the primeval grip of superstition.

Good thing modern Saints weren't so gullible.

CHAPTER 5

I informed Muleki that I'd explained the situation to my parents before driving down to the police station to get him. I told them it had occurred to me during the night that the strange prowler who'd been stalking their neighborhood over the last week was none other than Muleki Jones—one of the more colorful converts I'd had the privilege of baptizing on my mission in Oregon.

"I laid it on pretty thick," I admitted to Muleki. "They think you were raised by Oregon hillbillies, and that those other fellas are brothers and uncles that aren't too happy about your conversion to the gospel. I don't much enjoy fabricating to my parents, but it accomplished what I'd hoped. Their hearts melted, and they insisted I bring you home for Thanksgiving dinner."

I could smell the turkey roasting even as we climbed out of the car. Mitch and Judd and their families had arrived. A square of cardboard fastened by strips of duct tape had been positioned over the bullet hole in the window of Steven's Celica. As we walked through the front door, the Nephite was greeted by a host of forgiving arms. My mom hugged him breathless and apologized profusely. Dad scolded him for not explaining who he was from the very beginning, and my Uncle Spencer put an arm around his shoulder and proceeded to tell him all about one summer he'd spent on the Oregon coast, not too concerned when I told him Muleki was not from that particular part of Oregon. I think the Nephite was quite touched by the reception. It had probably been some time since he'd enjoyed the company of friendly faces.

Muleki was fairly close to my size, so the first thing I did was have him climb into a pair of jeans and throw on my Cougar sweatshirt. Socks were a new concept for the Nephite, one he accepted with visible reluctance, but he found my old tennis shoes quite comfortable.

I thought Steven would spoil the atmosphere of compassion we'd created when he approached Muleki with an estimate of a hundred and forty dollars to replace his window. Muleki found a pouch that he'd stuffed into his pocket and pulled out a nugget of pure gold.

"Will this correct the damage?" he asked sincerely.

My brother stuttered, feeling ashamed for bringing up such subjects on Thanksgiving. He tried to return the nugget, but Muleki was insistent. Steve salved his conscience by promising to return the change.

Of course, I didn't expect Parley to own up to any blame, even though he'd been the trigger-happy cowboy who'd caused the problem in the first place. In fact, Parley was the only one in the household who didn't approach the Nephite with remorse. I think his pride still smarted from being knocked unconscious in front of everybody.

But a worse blow to his ego was yet to come. It was inflicted when I introduced Muleki to my sister, Jennifer. The Nephite's tender grasp of Jenny's hand befitted a suitor of royalty. For the briefest moment, when her eyes met his, the Queen of the Flirts went immodestly flush.

The rest of the day, and all through Thanksgiving dinner as we stuffed our faces with the finest spread of my mother's celebrated career, and despite the screaming kids and the blasting volume of the football games, it was difficult to overlook the mesmerized silence that took hold of my sister. Jenny utilized some of her more sophisticated predator skills, even going to the trouble of placing name tags by each table setting. Of course, her plate was just to the right of Muleki's. Parley, unfortunately, ended up with a torturous position on the opposite side, where he could watch them in living color.

Parley masticated his food particularly well that meal, and I can't say as I blame him for fuming. Muleki didn't encourage Jenny at all. In fact, he was entirely oblivious to her advances—or at least he pretended to be. About the time Jenny was plopping whipped cream on Muleki's third piece of pie, the cowboy finally grabbed my sister by the arm and insisted that the two of them go for a walk.

I thought I was the only one aware of what was going on until my Uncle Spence leaned over to me and uttered, "Looks like a certain little girl's about to get her comeuppance."

I was sure it was going to be the other way around. I could just imagine how my sister was burying this guy in ten feet of snow job, explaining how her actions were strictly the result of feeling sorry for the stranger, and how foolish Parley was acting, and how he shouldn't carry on so when there was nothing to be jealous about. Sure enough, when they came back through the front door, hand in hand, Parley's temper had suitably quelled—though it threatened further inflammation only thirty seconds later when she dropped his hand before the Nephite could see it.

There were a couple of times during the day when I thought Muleki would blow his cover and make it apparent that he was some kind of alien. He watched the hands on the grandfather clock for a full half hour, waiting for the cuckoo bird to make its second appearance. He leaned behind the television, straining to understand where the moving people were coming from. It was obvious he was having a little too much fun with the ice maker on the refrigerator, and that he was frightened by the doorbell when Sister Watkins came by to borrow a bread pan. But when he began unrolling the toilet paper and inquiring for what purpose it was intended, I think everybody raised an eyebrow. Even a hillbilly couldn't be *that* backward, could he?

The evening floated on: the children were put to bed, the adults suffered through a game of Uno, then finally the party started to break up. My parents' home became a hotel. Mom and Dad had threatened many times over the years, as they watched their children move away, that they would sell the big house and move into a condo. I couldn't believe they'd ever go through with it. Reunions like this were too important to them—and to the rest of us as well.

I slept in my old room again. One of the mattresses was hoisted off the frame and laid on the floor for Muleki. My sister, of course, had to peek through the door after we'd turned out the light to wish Muleki good night. Then the Nephite and I settled in comfortably for a long winter's sleep.

"Jim?" Muleki said just before I drifted off.

"Mmmm?" I responded.

"It was a wonderful day. Better than I've had in a very long time—like the feasts we used to host in the Jershonite neighborhood when I was a boy, before my father died. I will always be grateful to you and to your family."

His words again reminded me of the terrible loneliness he must have borne in recent months. Perhaps the same loneliness that had gripped his heart for years, ever since that day, as a small boy, when he was told his father had been killed by the servants of the Lamanite king. Hearing the report that his father had died a hero likely would not have softened the choking lump in a little boy's throat. Contemplating his pain caused a tear to soak into my pillow.

"Go to sleep," I said. "Tomorrow could also be an eventful day."

* * *

At three minutes to nine a.m., Muleki and I stood before the claims clerk at the Cody Municipal Police Department. I was anxious to retrieve the sword and escort Muleki back to the entrance of Frost Cave. If the lady sensed our agitation, she deliberately ignored it. Not until the digital clock displayed nine exactly was she willing to address us.

"Can I help you?" she finally asked.

"I've come to reclaim a lost article," I replied. "I was told I could have it back if it was still unspoken for at the end of ninety days."

"Do you have a claim number?"

"A what?"

"Do you have a claim number?" She repeated the intonation exactly, like a recording. When the confusion didn't leave my face, she went on to explain, "You should have been given a claim number when it was filed. It would be hard for me to find your article if you don't have a claim number."

"I was never given one," I said. "I handed it over to the police at the scene of an accident last August."

The clerk sighed. "What is the article, sir?"

"A sword, about yea long, with jewels in the hilt."

"We don't have anything like that."

Muleki's brow furrowed.

"Are you sure?" I demanded.

The clerk was growing impatient. "I walk back there every day. I'd surely remember something that unusual. Who was the officer you gave the sword to?"

I thought a moment. "Finlay. Todd Finlay."

"Well, there's your problem," responded the clerk. "Todd Finlay was suspended around the middle of August. He skipped town shortly thereafter. His wife and daughter haven't seen or heard from him since. If he's ever arrested, there's a good case to convict him for abandonment—as well as other things."

"Why was he suspended?"

I'm sure it wasn't entirely proper for her to answer my questions. Nevertheless, the lady seemed to take on a different air. Perhaps her true disposition as the station gossip was starting to emerge.

She explained, "The paperwork says insubordination, but I heard it through a reliable source that Todd Finlay was a drug dealer. Some say he even sold the stuff while he was on duty. If you want to find your sword, you'd better find Todd Finlay, 'cause as far as I know, he never registered it."

We left the police station under a cloud of depression.

"I knew it couldn't be this easy," Muleki sighed.

"Why would Todd Finlay have stolen such a thing?" I wondered.

"If a disposition for evil was already entrenched in his soul," Muleki revealed, "the sword would inspire the rest."

We found Finlay's address in the phone book and drove down Alger Avenue in search of the corresponding numbers. On the final block before the street came to a dead end, we found a tiny frame house with a peeling white fence and dead leaves smothering the lawn. As we tried to unbolt the clasp on the front gate, a miniature mongrel dashed out from under a bush and alerted the occupants. A small hand pulled back the curtain on the front room window and the frame of a haggard-looking, middle-aged woman stepped onto the porch, pinching a cigarette between her fingers.

"What do you want?" she questioned, her tone threatening.

"We just wanted to talk to you for a minute," I replied. "It concerns your husband."

She sucked a long drag of tobacco and stood there on the porch a moment longer, considering our request. Finally she responded, "I don't have a husband anymore."

"Please, Mrs. Finlay," I pleaded. "I promise we won't take very long."

The dog was running in circles, its barking growing more frenzied and insane.

"Vera, get your dog!" the lady yelled.

A little girl of about seven trotted out the door and across the porch. Her clothes were plain, her bright yellow hair unkempt, and she wore no shoes despite the cold ground. I supposed her fear of what might happen if she didn't jump to her mother's command outweighed the need for warm feet.

As she lifted the dog into her arms, she sent us an awkward smile and explained, "He really doesn't bite." She passed by her glaring mother and retreated back into the house.

The woman took another step toward us. "What do you have to say?" she demanded, crossing her arms, almost burning her elbow with the cigarette's dangling ash.

Muleki replied, "We wondered if you could tell us where Todd Finlay might be."

Mrs. Finlay choked out a laugh. "I thought that's what you were here to tell *me!*—or maybe to tell me he was dead. I haven't seen him since August 21st, and to be honest, I don't care if I ever see him again."

"Can you tell us where his kinship is settled?" asked Muleki.

"Pardon me?"

I clarified, "Do you know where any of his family members might live?"

"The only relative I know of lives just across the street from the Methodist church. That'd be his mother. But I talk to her every week or so. She doesn't know any more than I do."

"If there's anything you can tell us," Muleki urged, "we'd be very grateful. We fear he may be involved in something very dangerous. Something he doesn't understand."

"Well, that doesn't surprise me. Todd was always a little off center. He told me the only reason he became a cop was so's he could carry a loaded gun. If Todd's into something weird, I'd just call that par for the course."

"Before he left," asked Muleki, "did you see him with a sword—long and silver?"

Mrs. Finlay opened into a chorus of swear words. Somewhere in the midst of all the profanities, she admitted that she did indeed recall such a sword. "Todd would've slept with that thing if I'd of let 'im. After he got suspended, he spent more time with that hunk of metal—polishing it, talking to it—than he ever did with Vera or me. I think the only thing he took with him the morning he left was his '68 Mustang and that (blankety-blank) sword. Oh, and fifteen hundred in savings. That was everything we had. Only time I've heard from him since was at the end of October. I got a letter with twelve hundred dollars in money orders. I knew that was Todd's way of saying good-bye forever."

"The envelope," I interrupted, "—did it have a return address?"

"Nope. It was postmarked Salt Lake City, Utah, though."

"Utah? Did he know anybody in Utah?"

"Nobody I know of, and I doubt he'd have stayed in any one place for very long."

"Did the money orders have the name of any particular bank on them?" I wondered.

She took another long drag on her cigarette to give herself a moment to think. "There were four checks. Each one for three hundred dollars. They were from a grocery store—Smith's. That was it."

"Did you save the envelope, or maybe a stub off a money order?

"Sure didn't." Mrs. Finlay prepared to go back inside. "I gotta get back to things, boys. To be perfectly honest, Vera and

I'd prefer not to think about him anymore. We never talk about him."

"I'm sorry if we've upset you," Muleki apologized.

"If you find him, don't bother to tell me," she said. Reaching the doorway, she turned again and added, "But if you happen to find that sword, I wouldn't mind you bringing *that* by. Nothing would give me greater pleasure than to bust it up in a million pieces."

We drove home without saying much to each other. Muleki looked up to watch a plane leave a white streak of exhaust across the sky. I think the awesome task of finding that sword was starting to dawn on him. He'd come from a much simpler world. A world where a man could never travel farther than the distance he could walk in a day—not a world where a jet could cart a person to the other side of the globe in a few hours. I know *I* was certainly discouraged. But my worst problem, I hated to admit, was that my heart wasn't entirely committed to this tenuous cause.

"So what's the plan now?" I asked him.

"*My* plan, at least, is to go to this place, Salt Lake City."

"And what a coincidence," I responded, only partially aware of all the implications of my words. "Such a place only happens to be about forty miles from where I go to school."

CHAPTER 6

We first heard the news from the pet department manager at the Pamida discount store on Saturday afternoon. While Muleki was in the dressing room, trying on some additional clothes he could take to Utah, I wandered over to look at the colorful varieties of saltwater fish in the hexagonal tank next to the "Employees Only" corridor. The pet department manager was just inside, talking with another employee about how gutsy it was to stage a robbery at a police station.

"What was that?" I interrupted.

They looked at me as if I was intruding. I repeated, "What did you say happened?"

"The police department—some men held it up this morning."

"What time?"

"Don't know. Early."

Ten seconds later I was pounding on Muleki's dressing room door, announcing that it was time to leave. As we climbed back into the Mazda, I switched on the radio, already tuned to the local station, *KODI*. After listening for several minutes, a recap of the story was broadcast.

The reporter said that five men, heavily armed with handguns and rifles and dressed in hunting attire, had stormed the Cody Municipal Police Department this morning at four thirty-five a.m.

"*. . . They were seeking what personnel on the scene described as a kind of ancient battle sword with silver plating, which may have been filed as lost or missing evidence earlier in the year. When they were unable to obtain the requested article, shooting broke out, injuring one officer and at least one of the gunmen. The five men, escaping the scene in a white Chevy Impala, are still at large, and are said to be extremely dangerous.*"

The newsman went on to describe the condition of the injured police officer, now recovering in a Billings, Montana, hospital—a bullet in the right shoulder—and also to report that roadblocks had been set up on all highways surrounding the town, as well as at several different checkpoints throughout Wyoming and Montana. The words "terrorism" and "baffling" were used frequently throughout the report.

I knew that an incident this unique would surely reach the major wire services, but our local station offered a tidbit of information that the Associated Press or United Press International might have ignored. They said the clothing and weapons used by the gunmen may have been stolen merchandise from an after-hours robbery that took place inside a small sporting goods store on the West Cody Strip the previous week.

"They'll be looking for *us* now," Muleki warned. "They'll think you lied to them and that you still have the sword. Or at least that you know where it is."

It occurred to me that the modern recruits Shurr and Mehrukenah had attracted to their cause gave them some daunting advantages. Without them, how would they have learned to use a gun, or escaped in a getaway car? I'd seen Muleki's gold nugget; it wouldn't take too many of those to earn someone's loyalty. If the Gadiantons could solicit *two* recruits, they could certainly solicit others. Watching out for someone with "Indian-like" features would no longer help us.

Just as I began to shake my head and wonder how I'd gotten

into this mess, another concern crossed my mind. "The police will be looking for us, too," I remarked. "That gossipy clerk is certain to connect the fact that we were both requesting the same unusual article."

As we neared my parents' home, I was afraid it might be surrounded by cops. Fortunately, no flashing red lights ignited the neighborhood. I was grateful that I hadn't given my name to the claims clerk. Nevertheless, the more immediate concern was the Gadiantons themselves. If they were stuck in town, unable to bypass roadblocks, they'd undoubtedly strike out at us at the first opportunity. I knew the only way to protect my family was to leave town right away—tonight!

My parents were disappointed by the news. They'd been hoping everyone could get together for Sunday services in our home ward. I told them that Muleki had a family emergency. The only bus going to Oregon on Sunday left Provo, Utah, at seven a.m. the next morning.

Jenny actually seemed relieved to be heading back early. Or maybe she was just happy to be going anywhere Muleki was going. The only one truly annoyed by our early departure was Parley. He must have realized his influence on my sister was waning. Our sudden schedule change dashed his hopes of taking her on a long country drive that evening to rekindle the flames.

We exchanged our last hugs and kisses with relatives about six-thirty p.m. If we didn't stop for anything but gas, I expected to reach Provo's city limits by about two-thirty the following morning. Parley grumbled about how cramped it would be in our tiny car with four people instead of three. Muleki selected the backseat, trying to keep as low-profile as possible. I'm sure if he'd felt it would keep the peace, he'd have gladly agreed to ride in the trunk with the luggage.

It soon became clear that he'd chosen the worst seat possible. Jennifer was quick to spot the opening. With a speed faster than

Einstein had ever considered, she slipped into the backseat beside Muleki. Parley gave her a lethal glare, then reluctantly plopped into the passenger seat in front, restraining a temper which may have left burn marks on the cushions.

As we passed Beck Lake and turned onto the Meeteetse Highway, the night had already reached its darkest pitch, which in this sparsely populated basin was about as dark as nighttime ever got. We were stopped by highway patrolmen about five miles out of town. They blinded us with flashlights for a few seconds, then slapped the hood and sent us on our way. Obviously, the five gunmen had not been captured. We kept the radio on, hoping to hear an encouraging update, but we lost our reception of all Cody stations just beyond Thermopolis as we entered the Wind River Canyon.

I felt certain the Gadiantons wouldn't be able to follow us to Utah. By now, they'd undoubtedly learned that they needed to be on the trail of Todd Finlay, not us. With every passing mile, the chances seemed to grow more and more remote that we would ever see a Gadianton again. I felt like I could breathe much easier.

During the long drive over South Pass, I happened to glance in the rearview mirror and noticed Jenny leaning her head on Muleki's shoulder. Muleki's body became as rigid as a tombstone. Jenny appeared asleep, but I knew better. Does a black widow sleep when there's a male in her web? A few minutes later, Jenny peacefully dropped onto Muleki's lap, purring a peaceful sigh. Muleki looked at my face in the rearview mirror, his eyes begging for advice on what to do. I shrugged my shoulders.

A short time later Parley looked back too, though by then both Muleki and Jennifer were asleep, or feigning such. Turning forward again, Parley let the air whistle through his gritted teeth. *Poor Parley,* I thought. I couldn't help but feel for the guy. And yet I felt sure his ego was far more bruised than his heart.

When we stopped in Farson to fill up with gas, everyone climbed out to stretch. Just outside the station's rest rooms, Parley commanded Muleki to sit in the front seat for the rest of the trip. Muleki didn't object. He didn't want to cause any more trouble than necessary during his sojourn in the twentieth century. Still, it might have been better if he *had* objected, at least for show. Parley was quick to interpret Muleki's ready consent as a sign of weakness. If Muleki had huffed and puffed a bit before he backed down, it might have been a little more satisfying to the cowboy's pride.

Instead Muleki said, "That would be fine. It must be very uncomfortable up front for you."

As Muleki turned away, Parley grabbed his shoulder. I was sure Muleki had meant *physical* discomfort, but Parley took it as meaning it must have been uncomfortable for him to watch the "goings on" in the backseat.

"Are you trying to make a fool out of me?" he asked.

"Of course not."

"You sayin' I should be jealous of you?"

"I was trying to be polite."

"I think you were trying to make me out to look like the south end of a horse, that's what I think."

The two men faced each other. Muleki adjusted his footing, taking a defensive stance. "Please," he said calmly, "don't force me to subdue you."

Jennifer ran to my side. "Jim, do something!"

Parley was laughing. "I don't think you're gonna come up on me from behind this time, hillbilly."

"C'mon, guys—" I pleaded.

But as I moved forward to come between them, the cowboy launched his fist toward the Nephite's face. Muleki twisted slightly—artfully—and dodged the swing without stepping a single inch out of his stance. Then he grabbed Parley's shoulder with one hand, his neck with the other, and tripped the cowboy into the inertia of his own swing, causing him to roll into a full flip and land flat on his back in the gravel.

Parley shook his head a time or two, then pulled himself to his feet to continue the attack, this time stretching his arms to utilize his full size and weight, intending to simply crush the obnoxious twerp. Three seconds later, Parley was once again horizontal, this time face down, close enough to the gravel to chew a few pebbles.

A couple of other motorists had gathered to witness Parley's final lunge. It was even more embarrassing than the first two. Muleki ended it with a sharp, quick blow behind the cowboy's head, which left him unconscious at the Nephite's hands for the second time this week.

Muleki felt terrible about the fight and repeated his regret several times to Jenny and me while we hoisted the groggy cowboy into the backseat.

As I was bending Parley's knees to get them in the car, I noticed something unusual about twenty yards away. A car was parked just off the highway, near a barbed-wire fence which separated the gas station from an adjoining cow pasture. The headlights were off, but the motor was running. I squinted my eyes and made out the silhouettes of four persons inside. Suddenly the headlights burst on, in bright position. The car, a weathered green Mercury Cougar, pulled onto the road and skidded away.

Muleki was too busy trying to make Parley comfortable to notice. Could it have been who I feared it was? It just wasn't possible. The Gadiantons were driving a white Impala, not a Mercury Cougar, and they were five in number, not four. Besides, the odds of finding us in Farson, Wyoming were just . . .

Parley regained full coherence about the time we reached Rock Springs. He wouldn't say a word the rest of the trip. Jenny at least had the decency to sit in back with him and tend his bruises, but I could tell by the smiles she sent Muleki that her heart was elsewhere.

As the night wore on and my passengers dropped off to sleep again, I contemplated how different this Thanksgiving vacation had been from what I'd expected. Finally, as we emerged from Provo Canyon and the highway turned into University Avenue, the events of the past three days came tumbling down upon me like an avalanche.

Brigham Young University had come to represent reality for me over the past couple of years. My home in Cody was a fantasy now—a place to relive the innocence of childhood, a place where I could gear up to face the real world while Mom cooked all my meals. Somehow, it was okay if peculiar things happened to me in Cody. But not here.

Provo was where I faced reality and set my goals. Here things were supposed to be normal. In Provo I didn't want to face my reemerging memories of an ancient land I'd visited when I was thirteen years old. I didn't want to believe I'd ever met Teancum or stared into the eyes of Captain Moroni. I didn't want to believe I'd ever walked the market streets of Zarahemla or carried an obsidian-edged sword in battle against the Lamanites. I didn't want to think about "Rainbow Rooms" in the deep recesses of Cedar Mountain. I didn't want a Nephite, a Captain of the Guard in the Palace of the Chief Judge of Zarahemla, sleeping on the floor in my bedroom at King's Court Arms. And most of all, I didn't want to believe that Gadianton robbers might be lurking in the shadows, harboring desperate motives of revenge.

I just wanted to go back to my boring life, studying for finals, arguing politics and religion with my roommates, taking girls to the movies and out for sundaes at Carousel—even if they broke my heart like Renae.

Muleki stirred in the seat beside me, seeking a better position to sleep. Glancing at him reconfirmed my loss of normalcy. He was real. The Gadiantons were real. My only hope was to help Muleki find his mysterious sword as quickly as possible. Then he could go home, and the pieces of my world could fall back into place.

I dropped by Heritage Halls and helped my sister carry her luggage into her apartment. When Jenny and I got back to the car, Parley had tossed his duffel bag in the trunk of his own vehicle and was pulling away. Jen waved good-bye, as if nothing had happened between them, though I felt sure the two would never speak again.

Then my sister took Muleki's hand and told him what a great pleasure it had been to meet him, and how she hoped he had a safe trip to Oregon, and how she wished he would keep in touch. At that point I admitted to Jen that Muleki was *not* taking the seven a.m. bus to Portland, but that he would be staying with me, at least for a couple of days. Jenny had a difficult time masking her enthusiasm.

During the short drive to King's Court Arms, I decided to warn Muleki about the obvious. "She really likes you," I said. "I've never seen her chase someone so aggressively."

"She is very beautiful," Muleki admitted. "But I'm afraid there is no place in my heart for a woman right now."

And that ended that.

My apartment was empty and silent. All around me were reminders that I was home. Lars had left a nice heap of molding dishes in the sink. Andrew's door was bolted shut with a padlock, and Benny's *Sports Illustrated* swimsuit issue was lying open on the front room floor. I kicked it under the couch before Muleki could notice.

Then I turned up the heat and told Muleki he might as well sleep in Benny's bed tonight. Tomorrow my roommates would be back, and he'd have to sleep on the floor in my sleeping bag.

"Church starts at eleven," I told him, and retired to my bedroom.

Of course, during the night, my ancient man returned, still standing behind the lightning-scarred trunk in the midst of that tiny cluster of trees. Still beckoning me forward, ever forward.

CHAPTER 7

We were late for church, as might have been expected considering the dismal hour we got home. To allow for the number of students still on vacation, our meetings were combined with the other ward at King's Court Arms, which held its services in the Pardoe Drama Theater of the Harris Fine Arts Center.

Muleki wore my blue Mr. Mac suit—the one I'd contemplated tossing in the trash after my mission. It had battle-worn knees and a badly ripped inner lining; nevertheless, the Nephite thought the raiment was beautiful and expressed much gratitude that I would allow him to wear it. "No problem," I told him, and felt ashamed that vanity prevented me from being caught dead in such a thing.

We snuck in just after the sacrament hymn and found a place in the back. Even before they began blessing the bread, I noticed Renae Fenimore seated on the stage, behind the podium, radiant in a bright-pink lace dress. Just my luck. She'd come back from Pocatello a day early to give a talk. How was I supposed to concentrate during the sacrament? Seeing her up there tangled my intestines into a snarl of painful knots. After all these weeks, I still wasn't free of her spell.

"What's going on?" Muleki whispered.

Caught up in my own troubles, I'd entirely failed to realize that Muleki's church experience had not included the sacrament.

Where he was from, the law of Moses still prevailed, as I should have remembered from when he'd refused to eat bacon.

"Like the prayer stated, we eat the bread and drink the water in remembrance of the great sacrifice of the Messiah," I explained.

I wasn't sure if it was proper for Muleki to partake. The sacrament was intended to help renew the covenants we made at baptism. Although the ancient prophet, Alma, may have baptized in the wilderness before Muleki was born, I wasn't certain if the ordinance was universally instituted among the Nephites until after Christ's coming. I almost advised him to let the plate pass him by, but as the bread arrived, I felt an urge not to interfere.

"I believe in the Christ," Muleki whispered humbly, "and I believe in His sacrifice for my sins. This is a good thing." Muleki reverently ate the bread and drank the water, each time bowing his head in prayerful contrition.

Renae's talk was on gratitude, an appropriate topic considering the season. I found it trite and overlong. Of course, if Renae and I had been on better terms, I'm sure I'd have found it brilliant and insightful.

In the hallway outside the classroom where we met for Sunday School, I couldn't escape her approach.

"Jim!" she called. "How was your Thanksgiving?"

This had to be played just right. I couldn't make it obvious that I was still pining, and yet I couldn't be rude. In this brief encounter, I had to sell the impression that I couldn't remember ever having dated her at all. Yet she had to be convinced that I still thought of her as a "dear, dear" friend.

In spite of her resistance some weeks before, when I'd come on so strongly, I was certain she hadn't shaken the flattery such attention leaves behind. How would her ego stand it to think she might have been wrong about my feelings? Oh, the subtle games that humans play. If only the rules of love were more akin to tic-tac-toe than chess.

"Renae!" I responded enthusiastically. "You look great! Loved your talk. There's someone I'd like you to meet."

Perfect delivery! What a tiger I am. If I were taking the trouble to introduce her to other guys, she would certainly wonder if my affections were all in her imagination.

"This is Muleki Jones. Muleki, Renae Fenimore."

"Hello," said Muleki.

"Nice to meet you," she replied. "Muleki, eh? Almost sounds 'Book-of-Mormonish.' *¿Habla español?*"

"I suppose I do," Muleki answered.

Renae kinked an eyebrow in confusion. "You *suppose?*"

"He does," I assured her. This gift of tongues thing was gonna get us into trouble yet.

"Your family doesn't happen to be from Mexico, do they?" Renae asked.

"No. Uh—Oregon," said Muleki.

"The reason I ask," Renae explained, "is that parents in this country don't often name their children after heroes in the Book of Mormon. In Mexico, it's different. The family I lived with as an exchange student down there had kids named Moroni, Helaman, and Nephi."

I couldn't help but fear Renae had called my bluff and was modestly flirting with my Nephite friend. Then she turned the attention back to me.

"My assumptions on Jim's name were wrong, too. I thought he might have been named after the main character in *Treasure Island,* but Jim says no."

"That's because my real name isn't Jim," I admitted. "It's Jamie."

"Really?" said Renae. "You never told me that."

Ah, my ploy was working. She was hurt that I'd kept secrets from her.

"If I'd known that," she continued, "I might have gotten into the habit of calling you Jamie. That's always been one of my favorite names."

Something about this conversation was sounding awfully familiar, as if another black-haired beauty, in some distant land, had also preferred that I go by my given name. The coincidence annoyed me. I had a bad habit of looking for hidden meanings in life, especially when it came to women. I had this fairy-tale notion that some kind of miracle would help me to identify my eternal mate. During my freshman year at BYU, I met a girl who I swore I'd seen before in a dream. Only moments later I learned that she was already engaged to some Romeo back in Colorado, whom she married that February. Since then, I'd tried to ignore déjà vu-type coincidences.

Still, I couldn't deny the fact that Renae was acting unusually warm toward me. I had to be cautious, though; she may have only been trying to solicit a sign that told her I was still on the string.

Then she pulled me aside and said, "I want you to know something. I've wanted to tell you this for quite some time. If I had known beforehand that you were Andrew's roommate, I would have never accepted his invitation to Homecoming."

"That would've been silly," I responded. "Why should our friendship change your dating habits? It just goes to prove it's a small world."

Never had another human being mastered the art of "cool" as well as I. I could tell my response was not the one she'd expected. Disarmed, she could only repeat, "Well, I just wanted you to know that."

"Thanks, that was thoughtful. But I never felt you'd done it deliberately anyway. It's nothing to worry about. I promise."

I didn't even bat an eye. What I really wanted to do was shake both her shoulders and moan, "Why, why, why did you ruin my life, you insensitive cave woman?" But I held my tongue, and she, awed by the omnipotence of my sincerity, could only hang there for a moment with an open mouth, until, finally smiling, she announced that class was beginning and we ought to take our seats.

* * *

That afternoon, Muleki and I drove over the Point of the Mountain on I-15 and entered Salt Lake County. Our task was growing more mind-boggling by the minute. In all, I counted twenty-two Smith's grocery stores in the Salt Lake phone directory. Since we had no photograph of Todd Finlay, we could only hope that some Smith's employee in one of those twenty-two stores remembered a thin man with glasses buying four three-hundred-dollar money orders in late October. Who was to say if we'd even catch this employee during the right shift, or that the person even worked for Smith's anymore?

Add to that the fact that neither Muleki nor I had any authority to be asking such questions. If I worked in a grocery store and somebody came in asking me to remember certain money orders I'd written up in October, I'd have probably called the police.

Upon reaching the first store on our list, just off 53rd South in Murray, we discovered that today's efforts had been a waste of time anyway. The department that sold money orders wasn't even open on Sundays. Driving back to Utah County, I couldn't help but express my overall opinion of this campaign.

"It's hopeless!" I whined. "I can't begin to tell you how much I would rather search for a needle in a haystack."

"We'll come back tomorrow," declared Muleki.

"I can't," I insisted. "I've got classes."

"If you understood what I was seeking," he proclaimed, "you would not hesitate."

"Well, I *don't* understand!" I cried, "I don't understand *any* of this. What makes this rusty sword so doggone important?!"

Muleki sighed. "Jim, you do not understand the evil rites that were performed when it was forged. Nor do I, but I do know that Akish, the founder of secret combinations among the people of Jared, gave it to his followers and asked these corrupted men to use it to behead Akish's father-in-law, which allowed him to take possession of the throne. It then inspired a wilderness battle that destroyed his kingdom and reduced the population to all but thirty souls. The last king to possess the sword was Coriantumr. With it, he pursued a war that wiped out every last man, woman, and child who called themselves Jaredites. This was the same blade he used to smite off the head of Shiz atop the Hill Ramah. Don't you see? Each time a kingdom has destroyed itself in my land, the sword was there."

"Men are accountable for their own wickedness," I stated. "You can't blame a sword."

"What you say is true, but the sword entices a mind already corrupted by the wants of this world to perform greater evils than it could ever imagine on its own. It feeds on the human soul like a parasite, persuading men that they can rule the world, when in reality, it wrenches from them even the power to rule themselves."

I swallowed in dismay. If this sword was all that Muleki said it was, why were we trying to find it? Wouldn't we want to be as far away from such a thing as possible? It was all so hard to digest. Yet as I thought back on my readings of the Book of Ether, Muleki's statements seemed all the more intriguing. The final conflict of the Jaredites had a subtext of pure and simple insanity—a hatred so entrenched that even when they could see the slopes of Ramah littered with thousands of the slain, they continued to fight, until finally, Coriantumr was the only soul who remained, left alone to wander in the wilderness with only the sword as his companion.

I had to consider the remote possibility that what Muleki was saying was true. What if my skepticism permitted the sword to get into the hands of some madman in the Middle East, or some despot in South America, or even some power-hungry general in the United States? Or maybe worst of all, into the hands of men already convinced of its potential—the Gadiantons?

"All right," I reluctantly agreed. "I get out of class early on Tuesday. We'll try again. But I gotta tell you, Muleki, the chances of that sword even being in Salt Lake are pretty slim."

"No," Muleki disagreed. Then he became pensive and softly uttered, "It is here."

* * *

When we got back to my apartment, Benny and Lars had arrived home from Thanksgiving vacation. I introduced them to Muleki and reported that he would be staying with us for a week or so.

As I finished making my and Muleki's dinner, I asked Lars and Benny how they'd enjoyed their Thanksgivings. It became evident that they were much more excited about events occurring *before* Thanksgiving. Lars went on and on about the UFO meeting he and Benny had attended before Benny's plane left.

"The Bernardians are like no other UFO club," Lars insisted. "Their evidences are much more profound as to why aliens visit this planet."

"Interesting ideas," said Benny thoughtfully. "They made a lot of sense."

"Has he got you hooked on this stuff now?" I asked.

"Well, I'm not ready to sell the farm," Benny admitted. "But I am convinced there's a lot about this universe that we don't understand. I was impressed, I have to confess."

As Muleki remained seated at the table, trying to master the art of coiling spaghetti on a fork, I joined my roommates on the front room couch and asked, "So why *are* aliens visiting planet Earth? And why don't they visit the *New York Times* instead of some old bass fisherman in the middle of a swamp?"

"For the same reason that Moroni didn't visit the *New York Times*," said Lars. "The world isn't ready for it. You gotta start small and grow. The Bernardians—I'm referring now to the extraterrestrials, not the club—are helping to prepare the world for the Millennium, or as they call it, the Fourth Period. I can't explain it like they do. You gotta go to one of the meetings in person. They're having another one here in Provo a week from tomorrow."

"If all this is true, why hasn't the Church come out on it?" I asked.

"I think they will," declared Lars. "I wouldn't be surprised to see the two organizations merge one day."

I laughed scornfully. "That'll be the day." Then I looked at Benny to see if my attitude was sobering him up a bit.

Instead, he added, "Nothing I heard contradicted anything in the gospel, Jim. It almost *proves* the Church is true. None of the founders are Latter-day Saints, yet they talk about the premortal world, the state of the soul after death—they even talk about the earth as a living being—"

"I could show you a scripture in the Doctrine and Covenants that suggests the same thing," interrupted Lars.

Benny concluded, "If I'd heard anything I thought was contradictory, I swear I'd have walked right out of there. They say they don't want to take anything away from what we already have—just add new insights that will give us greater happiness. Seems like a worthwhile motive, doesn't it?"

Something didn't sit right with me about this whole thing. Maybe I was just responding with the natural skepticism that everybody has for new ideas. What made me most upset was seeing such an overwhelming change in Benny. He was taking this stuff so seriously, I was afraid it would start to overwhelm all the things we had in common.

I went on, "It also says in the Doctrine and Covenants that only the prophet can add new revelations and teachings to the Church."

"Yet Harold B. Lee told us that men like Confucius and Buddha were inspired to teach many truths," Lars defended. "Latter-day Saints are commanded to seek all knowledge which is worthy and of good report, wherever they find it. There's no reason to close your mind until you've checked it out, Jim."

About then Andrew burst through the door, his arms loaded down with a suitcase, a duffel bag, and a newspaper.

"Hey, Hawkins," he blurted out even before saying hello, "I read all about your home town today." He tossed the newspaper on the counter.

"Did it hit your newspaper, too?"

"Page A-3. Bottom," he said and continued an uninterrupted beeline into his bedroom.

Benny waited for Andrew to close his door, then he leaned over to me and whispered, "By the way, Renae Fenimore called for you."

"You sure she was calling for *me?*"

"Positive." Benny winked. It was relieving evidence that Benny was still the same old Benny.

So "Operation Recover Renae" may have been working. So much was on my mind tonight that I wasn't sure if I *wanted* it to be working. Did I have time for a social life when I was busy helping Nephites find swords and roommates make reservations on the first flying saucer to Neptune?

Whatever the case, I wasn't going to call Renae back tonight. Let her stew for a while.

I went to the counter to see the paper. Muleki stood over me as I read the headline: *Police Station Held Up, Gunmen At Large.*

There was disturbing new information in the article. It reported that the white Chevy Impala the Gadiantons had used to make their getaway was found abandoned on an old dirt road near Farson, Wyoming—the town where we had filled up with gas. In the Impala's trunk a man's body was discovered. He was identified as Larry Bridenbough, a citizen of Missoula, Montana, with a reputation for drug abuse and petty theft. Bridenbough had been shot in the abdomen, no doubt during the exchange of bullets at the police station. Nevertheless, it was said that he died from *other* wounds—wounds that had been inflicted with a knife. Apparently Mehrukenah had decided that dragging along a wounded man was cramping their style. So much for honor and loyalty among Gadiantons.

The article went on to say that the police were now looking for a green Mercury Cougar that was reported missing from a ranch house only a half mile from the abandoned Impala. Apparently the other modern recruit, Mr. Clarke, was teaching them well how to survive in modern times—including the skills of hot-wiring an automobile. Later, as Muleki was laying out my sleeping bag on the floor of my room, I told him about the car I had seen at that gas station in Farson, and how it had turned on its brights and skidded away.

"As I feared, they're following us," Muleki concluded. "They've learned about this school—this Brigham Young University. They may be watching us every moment, waiting for the right opportunity to move in. Jim, I beg you, do not go anywhere without me at your side."

"But I have classes," I said. "I can hardly drag you along with me all over campus."

"You say your school is owned by the Church?" he asked.

"Yes, that's right."

"Then it is *God's* land," the Nephite concluded. "It's like a temple. I don't think they will go there. You should be safe as long as you don't wander out of its bounds alone. Still, I'll remain as close as I can."

I thought about this statement. It was true; the land upon which the university was built had been dedicated by prophets and apostles. But how could *that* guarantee anything? I felt sure every crime imaginable had occurred on BYU property at one time or another. Still, it was possible that as far gone as the Gadiantons were—so blatantly committed to evil—they might feel an actual physical discomfort there, almost like a severe allergic reaction. Despite my doubts that it would make any difference, I agreed to Muleki's terms. He closed his eyes, satisfied, and drifted off to sleep. Unable to do the same, I climbed out of bed and flipped on the screen of my personal computer.

There was still one task to perform before I ended my day. I had a letter to write. It would be addressed to Cambridge, Massachusetts. Although I had no idea what to say, or how to say it, my old comrade Garth Plimpton had to know about the harrowing events of the previous week. I'd have sent him an e-mail, but I remembered that he'd told me his personal computer had crashed and that he'd been forced to use the ones on campus. As well, Garth lived in campus housing and I knew from experience that it was virtually impossible to reach him by phone. Nope, the only way I knew for sure to reach Garth Plimpton was the old-fashioned way—with an envelope and stamp.

Maybe Garth, unlike myself, had succeeded in retaining his memories of the Nephite world. I'd never known anyone who had strived to stay so close to the Spirit. His insight regarding this escapade might be priceless. Besides, why should I have to bear this burden all by myself? After all, Muleki had accused him of being just as guilty of teenage time-tampering as I was.

CHAPTER 8

On Monday morning, Muleki carefully checked his artillery before climbing out of the car to go on campus. He'd hidden one knife inside the inner pocket of his jacket and another under the pant leg on his right shin. Since I knew the Gadiantons had guns, I wasn't sure how protected I was supposed to feel.

"As long as the Gadiantons think you still have the sword, they will not kill you," Muleki explained.

"Great," I said. "So can I at least hope to be tortured? Muleki, how am I supposed to concentrate in my classes?"

"When I return to my land with the sword," said Muleki, "the Gadiantons will follow me back. Your part will be over."

I don't remember my professors' lectures that day. This was not a good state of mind to be in two weeks before finals. Each time I came out of class, Muleki was faithfully waiting.

Since I had racquetball in the Smith Fieldhouse before lunch on Mondays, I usually went across the street for Hawaiian fast food, but Muleki wouldn't allow it since the restaurant was off campus. Instead, we ate desiccated chicken burgers at the Cougareat.

The day ended uneventfully. Hoping to close the day on a bright note, I dragged the phone into my bedroom and finally took the initiative to call Renae. She answered after only one ring. I reveled in the thought that she might have waited by that phone all night and day.

We talked for an hour about the weather, old times—it really didn't matter. I made my demeanor warm and caring, but not *too* warm and caring. Actually, my immediate frame of mind helped convey the impression I sought. It was obvious to Renae that something heavy was on my mind, but I told her I couldn't discuss it. Before the conversation closed, Renae and I had determined to try again, Friday night, with another all-out, honest-to-goodness date.

Hanging up the receiver, I could only contain myself for about a second. Then I did a Toyota jump and hollered, "YES!" Muleki rushed in from the living room, fearing my yell was a plea for help. Suddenly, I remembered my promise to let Muleki tag along wherever I went. My exhilaration started to deflate. Friday *had* to be an exception. I couldn't have a Nephite stalking ten paces behind me the whole night! Then I got an idea that would at least make things tolerable.

"Muleki, on Friday you and I are going on a double date."

"Double date?" asked Muleki.

"Dating is the way we court women," I explained. "We take them to dinner or a movie or a ball game—whatever! Don't tell me you don't date in Zarahemla?"

Muleki shook his head. "Not in quite . . . the same fashion."

"Well, I hope a modern-day American date will be the best memory you take back with you. Now, it's just a question of who." The answer was obvious. I picked up the receiver again and dialed the number of my beloved sister, Jenny.

* * *

It started snowing heavily during the night. By Tuesday morning, the stuff was coming down in flakes as big as cotton balls. Muleki had never seen snow before, except on the peaks of distant mountains. His body had yet to acclimatize in this land—in fact, he seemed to be endlessly shivering, even under the weight of my old ski parka. Yet, as we stepped out of my apartment, surrounded by eight inches of heavenly whiteness, Muleki's eyes lit up, reminding me of that four-year-old boy I'd once seen greeting his father, Captain Teancum.

The Nephite dropped to his knees in the powdery cushion beyond the front walk and tossed an armful into the air. It floated down all around him, carpeting his hair and dangling on the ends of his eyelashes.

"It's wonderful!" he cried. "If only I could carry a sack of it back to my nephews!"

"You'd have to carry a refrigerator as well," I told him.

Muleki couldn't resist the temptation we'd all succumbed to as children to open his mouth and catch a flake on his tongue. Succeeding, he savored the taste like a drop of chocolate. I couldn't help but laugh with the Nephite. Anxious to introduce him to yet another great snow tradition, I scooped up a handful and packed it for launching. But when I raised my head to scope my target, the expression on Muleki's face had changed.

He was standing as frozen as an icicle, looking at something between the buildings on the other side of the yard. He pulled his stone blade out from beneath his parka. I turned to see what had drawn away his attention, but the thin walkway, forty yards ahead, was perfectly empty. I heard only the sound of water dripping off the roof.

"Is there a problem?" I inquired.

Muleki was slow to answer, as if he hadn't heard me.

"No," he finally confirmed. "I thought I saw someone. I may have been mistaken."

Muleki declined my invitation to help scrape snow off the windshield of my car. Instead, he stood by and carefully watched the surroundings. During the drive, he remained overly wary and cautious. I was relieved when we pulled into the law building's parking lot. We'd reached campus. I think it was the first time I'd breathed since leaving King's Court Arms.

As soon as my last Tuesday class let out, the Nephite and I braved the snowy interstate and returned to Salt Lake County. The wind made conditions no less than a blizzard. Traffic jams kept us on the highway for two hours before we could again reach the first Smith's grocery off 53rd South.

At each stop, the story was the same. First they asked if we were cops, then they'd sic their managers on us. The managers always spouted store policy that no one, except the police or the individual who'd purchased the money order, could see the records. Often there was a long line of people behind us, watching us plead and argue, hoping we might drop dead so they could step over us. Every clerk we talked to had no recollection of anyone fitting Todd Finlay's description. Half of them added that even if they did, they wouldn't have been able to tell us. We struck out in Murray, Sandy, and South Salt Lake. But then, in West Valley City, we struck gold.

It was all on account of my new approach. This time, when it was my turn at the booth, I claimed that *I* had written the money orders and that I needed the totals for tax purposes. The deception worked like a charm. They opened up the books to me without hesitation, even providing a quiet corner for me to browse.

Muleki waited for me close by, in the frozen-food aisle. He looked utterly fascinated by all the varieties and colors. He interrupted me once to show me a bag stuffed with frozen corn on the cob, ecstatic to have found something he actually recognized.

Only a moment later, my finger landed on the bull's-eye. A man by the name of Todd West had purchased four three-hundred-dollar money orders on October 21st. But my elation was short- lived. In the space beside his name, where a customer was asked to write his phone number, the words "no phone" had been scribbled.

I had no option but to come clean with the lady in the service booth and confess it wasn't me who had bought the money orders. I explained that the real Todd Finlay (alias Todd West) had left his family, and that we were trying to catch up with him before the authorities did.

The clerk, a heavy-set lady with bouffant hair, was touched by my dramatization of Todd's abandoned wife and daughter. She admitted to remembering the man who'd purchased the money orders.

"A skinny man with glasses and a beaked nose. Am I right?" she asked.

"Dead on," I replied.

"He buys money orders here regularly—always breaking them up to fit our three-hundred-dollar limit on individual checks. I remember asking him why he didn't just get the whole thing from a bank. He said he didn't like banks."

"Did he tell you anything that might help us locate him?"

"No. He always writes 'no phone,' just like you see."

"The next time he comes in," I pleaded, "could you try and find out where he lives? Maybe you could tell him you've had a change of policy, and if he doesn't have a phone, he needs to write down an address. Anything that might help. We'd be forever grateful."

The lady squinted one eye, scrutinizing us closely.

I entwined my hands together on the counter. "Please. We're trying to keep him from getting into a lot of trouble."

She pursed her lips and shook her head from side to side. "Terrible thing, abandoning your family. I always wondered what drove a man to do something so awful."

"He's not well," I stressed. "We need to get him some help."

"Well, I think you boys have undertaken a worthwhile cause," she commended. Pointing at her name tag, she said, "My name is Katie. I'll keep an eye out for you. If I find out something, I'll let you know. You boys got a phone number?"

This lady was heaven-sent. I almost fell to my knees repeating, "Thank you, thank you . . . "

Driving back over the Point of the Mountain, my spirits soared. There was hope looming on the horizon that my life would soon return to normal.

* * *

By Friday afternoon, the lady at the store—Katie—had not yet called. Was it selfish to say I was glad? I'd been told that somewhere out there was a mystical sword endowed with the power to inspire universal genocide. If it was true, I hoped my descendants would say I was intoxicated with the folly of youth instead of suffering from hopeless apathy, because this night my heart was giddy beyond words at the prospect of spending the next few hours with Renae.

"What is this?" asked Muleki.

"Cologne," I answered as I arranged my hair in the mirror. "Put some on. Girls like the smell. It makes 'em crazy."

"I should want your sister to be made crazy?" he asked.

"It's the kind of crazy that nobody objects to," I winked.

Muleki picked up the green *Polo* bottle and turned it over in his hands, eyeing it like an exotic weapon—which, in a way, wasn't too far off. I was going to have to teach this guy a thing or two about the subtleties of male magnetism.

"If you insist on staying at my side tonight, you're going to have to look the part," I insisted. "Time or no time for women, I'm not going to double-date with a dweeb."

I presented the Nephite with my second sharpest button-up shirt and slacks and stood him in front of my bedroom mirror. Then I taught him the value of stick deodorant and how to apply it to the underarms without removing the shirt. He didn't like the feel of it much.

"It's slimy, like oil on a fish," he winced.

"But it smells a lot better, eh?"

"I'm not so sure."

We moussed his thick black hair—not too much, for it might dispel a girl's temptation to run her fingers through it, but enough to keep it in place. Pouring a little *Polo* into my hand, I pressed it into both palms and slapped it on both cheeks simultaneously. Muleki imitated my actions. After slapping it to his face, he staggered back a step, his eyes watering.

"It is *strong*," he said.

"You may have used a bit much. Don't worry, it fades."

Don't get the impression I felt comfortable doing this. Nephite or not, it just wasn't proper for guys to help other guys get ready for a date, and I wasn't about to make this a habit. I just wanted to say that.

We were ready. Before we left my bedroom I watched Muleki slip a knife into the sheath behind his calf. I should have known that my bodyguard's true focus hadn't clouded one little bit. Still, I wouldn't have guessed that Muleki was two thousand years old for nothin'. He was a modern-day man through and through, right off the cover of *Gentlemen's Quarterly.* All I could say as we left the apartment was, "Look out, world! Never has man nor Nephite looked so good."

"Jershonite," Muleki corrected.

It was a beautiful night, quite warm despite the snow. We drove down 9th East to pick up Jenny at Heritage Halls. As we neared Maeser Hall, where she lived, Muleki turned to me and said, "I hope we're planning to stay on campus."

"Muleki," I grumbled, "this is not the attire of a campus date. This is the attire of a classy restaurant—Magleby's or Restaurant Roy. I promise we'll stay among people—lots of people."

"That may not matter anymore," the Nephite revealed. "They are getting more desperate every day."

"We haven't seen anyone or anything out of the ordinary all week!"

"Just because we haven't seen them, it doesn't mean they're not here," he replied darkly.

My zeal for creating a memorable reunion with Renae was clouding my common sense. Of course Muleki was right. After all, the Gadiantons might have a dozen more men in their band by now.

But what were we supposed to do on campus? A campus date was something only a freshman would force a girl to endure—and only because he either lacked wheels or an imagination. I hadn't seen a movie at the Varsity Theater or gone bowling downstairs in the Wilkinson Center since before my mission.

Then Muleki got profound. "It's for the best. If this girl likes you, she won't care where she goes."

The Nephite had a point. In fact, he was a social genius! If Renae's feelings remained phony or uncertain, I'd find out real early in the evening.

I urged Muleki to knock on the door of Jenny's apartment. He objected at first; I don't know if it was out of shyness or because of his desire to get through this evening without giving her the wrong impression. He was with me tonight strictly for my protection, he explained, and he couldn't allow himself to be distracted.

"We'll be on campus," I reminded him. "Feel free to give yourself some time to be distracted."

From the car, I watched him step into the lobby of Jenny's building. He looked back at me for assurance before he knocked. After I nodded, he let his fist strike thrice on the door. I could tell Jenny had answered by the way he stood there gaping. She was wearing her ivory sweater with the glitter specks. Her blonde hair hung all the way down her back. She put her arm out for Muleki to take it. Muleki was confused by the gesture. Instead of taking her arm, he took her hand—a move perhaps a bit personal for a first date at BYU, but Jenny didn't object. In fact, she seemed to enjoy the strong grip of her Nephite warrior.

Renae had told me to pick her up at her uncle's house in the "tree streets" east of campus. Along an avenue called Cherry Lane, we found a mailbox emblazoned with the name of "Fenimore."

"Don't leave my sight, Jim," Muleki instructed before I climbed out of the car, "or I'll be forced to come in after you."

Jenny gave him a queer look, laughing once, wondering if his warning was some sort of private joke.

"Right," I said impatiently, and shut the door behind me.

Meeting Muleki's specifications, I stood in the doorway while Mrs. Fenimore fetched her niece. I waited there for several minutes, giving me enough time to adequately defeat her twelve-year-old cousin in a staredown. Finally, Renae glided down from a second-story hallway, more stunning tonight than I'd ever seen her in a black suede jacket with a lavender skirt, tan nylons, black pumps, and just the right touch of Chanel No. 5.

"Shall we go?" she invited, her eyes bright with anticipation.

I told her aunt how nice it was to meet her, and we were off. The news that we would be spending the evening on campus was either received quite well, or else both Renae and Jenny were excellent liars.

"They're showing *The Bicycle Thief* at International Cinema," Renae proclaimed. "Oh, please, let's go. It's one of my favorite movies."

Everyone agreed. There was an early showing at 6:10, which still left us plenty of time to grab a bite at the Cougareat when it let out. This was Muleki's first movie. If Jenny was hoping the Nephite's attention would be exclusively hers for the evening, she may have found the International Cinema idea somewhat disappointing. The warrior's eyes remained glued to the screen.

"The people are so *big!*" he exclaimed soon after the auditorium went dark. "Not like the house box where they're so small."

A few of the people around us looked at him like he was nuts. I think his date was reminded of how deep in the Oregon mountains he may have been raised. It was equally disturbing how he laughed at lines spoken by the Italian characters before the subtitles had come up on the screen.

"How many languages does this guy know?" Renae whispered to me.

"All of them," I answered. Then I turned to her and smiled wryly, as if to say, "Had you going there, didn't I?"

When the movie was over, we took the elevator to one of the upper floors on the Kimball Tower and found an unlocked classroom with a wide view. At first Muleki hesitated going near the window for fear he might fall, but after a moment, with his face pressed against the glass, we again watched the Captain of the Guard in the Palace of the Chief Judge of Zerahemla slacken his jaw in awe of our modern world. The Christmas season had given the city twice as many sparkling lights as usual, and as always, the Provo Temple was the brightest beacon of them all.

"There is nothing so high where I'm from," he declared. "Nothing but mountains and great soaring birds."

As he said it, I noticed Jenny at his side, looking up at the Nephite with equal awe. It was his naiveté she found so enchanting. There was nothing pretentious, nothing insincere about a single bone in Muleki's body. He seemed to have mastered the art of being childlike while maintaining a masculine grip on everything around him.

Jenny was convinced she'd found her own "Crocodile Dundee," and I could tell she wanted to stuff him in a closet somewhere before someone else could discover her secret. Muleki reciprocated her feelings only as much as was chivalrous and polite.

Perhaps my Uncle Spencer's prophecy would come true: Jenny would receive her comeuppance. Muleki was just like his father. Duty came first—nothing could stand in its way. I wanted to pull my sister aside and tell her who he really was. After all, she'd been there—she was with Garth and me among the Nephites. In fact, it was Jenny's folly which had led us into the time passageway in the first place. She'd known these ancient people, and it wouldn't have taken much for her to understand their commitments. If only her memory could be jogged in the same way as mine. Yet I knew it might be best if she didn't remember. For now, it appeared that her life was not threatened. The less she knew, the better.

After the girls declared their hunger, we took the elevator down and made our way across campus to the Wilkinson Center. Inside the ice cream parlor on the bottom floor, I read the menu aloud, for Muleki's sake. He was leaning toward the idea of getting himself a banana split, since it actually had an ingredient he recognized. While Jenny was deciding, Renae whispered in my ear a desire to go upstairs and get a pizza. I slipped Muleki enough money to cover the bill and told Jenny we'd meet later in the step-down lounge. I could tell as we walked away that Muleki was sorely tempted to follow, but Jenny had a viselike grip on his arm.

What a relief to finally have a moment alone with Renae, without Muleki breathing down my neck. Entering the Cougareat, we passed the booth where Renae and I had broken up earlier in the semester. Renae grabbed my arm and whisked us by, perhaps thinking there was no reason to relive such unhappy mistakes. When we got to the counter, the guy behind it—whose name tag said "Larry"—broke the sad news that they were out of pizza for the evening.

"What?" I cried, feigning anger. "No pizza? How could this have happened in an age of enlightened men?"

"Sorry," replied Larry.

"Oh, don't worry about it," Renae insisted. "I'll just get a cheeseburger."

"No!" I shrieked. "No lady of mine need settle for second best. If you want pizza, then you shall have pizza."

"You might try Leonardo's," hinted Larry.

Leonardo's was a pizza place just below campus.

"What do you think?" I asked my date.

"Sounds great. What about Muleki and Jennifer?"

"I sense they need to be alone for a while. We'll bring a couple of pieces back for 'em."

Renae and I escaped out the back door of the Wilkinson Center and headed hand in hand down the salt-strewn sidewalk under the power plant. We laughed another time or two, and then everything got quiet between us.

Without looking up, Renae said, "I'm glad you didn't give up on me." And then she turned to see my reaction.

I said nothing. *Let her grovel a bit longer,* I told myself.

Then she added, "I never told you, but I was engaged last summer. It had only broken off a few months before we started dating. I must have still been a little gun-shy."

In spite of her confession, I wasn't going to slip into the same trap. I replied, "Let's just take it slow, then. One day at a time. I'm in no hurry. Are you?"

A deep smile formed on her face—one so brimming with affection that it made me want to kiss it. But the fear that such a move would ultimately prove fatal to the relationship kept me from executing the attempt. Instead, I put my arm around her shoulders and tightly drew her in. Just then, I realized we'd reached the street that marked the boundary of BYU property. I hesitated, almost letting my shoe stop in mid-air over the curb.

"What's the matter?" Renae asked.

The streets were nearly empty. A few cars skirted by, tossing up slush. Up near the BYU Health Center another guy and his date were laughing, making their way home in the opposite direction. To the south, where Leonardo's was located, we could hear the faint voices of cheerful people and see the glimmer of headlights turning down 700 East.

I thought about Muleki's statement—his theory, really—that the dedicated land of Brigham Young University was a barrier against evil. It seemed absurd. The Gadiantons may have been evil, but they were evil *men*—not evil spirits or demons. This campus had certainly seen its share of evil men. It was only logical to conclude that the reason we hadn't been attacked on campus was simply because there was no one yet in Provo who wanted to attack us.

"Nothing," I replied to Renae.

The glare of the streetlights was stark against the new-fallen snow, making the night brighter and the shadows less foreboding. It was this light, finally, which gave me the confidence to step off the curb and lead Renae across the street.

It was only a block or so to Leonardo's Pizza Parlor. To get there we had to cross another parking lot—one belonging to a nearby condominium complex—and one final street.

The way was not salted like the sidewalks on campus. Renae and I laughed each time we had to save each other from falling. Nearing Leonardo's, I was thinking how satisfying it would be to tell Muleki about where we had gone. I'd offer it as proof that we could end this silly practice of his being glued to my side every minute.

Just then, a voice called out to me from behind.

"Jimawkins."

CHAPTER 9

There were three of them. They emerged from the night like sharks from murky waters, without warning and giving us no hope of escape. One of them was the modern recruit, Mr. Clarke. The other two were Gadiantons: the big-necked one called Boaz and the wizened old man called Mehrukenah.

They were wearing different clothing—shabby looking, as if from a thrift store. Mehrukenah appeared unarmed, as did Mr. Clarke, but Boaz wielded a handgun, a large one, the same kind as the one they'd given me. Draped around his massive neck was the mangy collar of an oversized gray parka. Though he'd hidden the pistol inside the coat's sleeve, I could still see the barrel, coal black and aimed straight at my heart.

Renae's grip on my arm was like a tourniquet.

"Who are they, Jim?" she whimpered.

"We are angels of vengeance," answered Mehrukenah, "though we might have been envoys of friendship."

The three of them moved in closer, pleasantly surprised to find us entirely unarmed and helpless. I wanted to look around, see if there was anyone nearby, but as I began to turn my head, Mehrukenah's voice tensed.

"Don't move a single step," he warned. "If you do, Boaz will kill you both, and believe me, I won't lose a single night's sleep for it."

"Hand them your wallet, Jim," Renae suggested.

Mr. Clarke laughed. He and Boaz had stopped about ten feet away. Mehrukenah stepped closer and smiled.

"We don't want your wallet," he clarified. "We want the sword. And we don't want any more lies."

Mehrukenah quickly drew a knife from inside his coat. It was black and sleek, similar to knives I had seen once before . . . where had it been? He noted my reaction to the blade.

"Do you recognize me now?" he asked.

Narrowing my eyes, I let his features sink deeply into my mind, again searching for a corresponding memory. From the depths of my psyche, a suppressed image broke its chains and rose to the surface. I remembered him now. We'd first seen his face in the crowded throngs of an ancient marketplace. In secret, Garth Plimpton and I had watched him purchase seven sleek obsidian knives—exactly the same type as the blade he now possessed. Like spies in a dime-store thriller, we'd followed him through the streets of Zarahemla until he entered a dark and abandoned building filled with conspiring kingmen whose intentions were to use these knives as tools of assassination against seven of the Nephites' highest-ranking leaders.

"I see you at least recognize this knife," Mehrukenah noted. "You should. You've seen it before. It was once meant to kill the notorious Captain Moroni. But, alas, it never tasted his blood."

Finally, I remembered him in prison, his jaw clenched in hatred. The conspiracy which he had espoused was all but crushed, due to a warning we had sounded. Garth Plimpton and I had pointed the finger to connect him to his crimes.

"I spat at you once," he claimed, "though it seems to me I may have missed. Not that it matters. I don't spit upon people anymore. There are more satisfying ways to express displeasure."

He was inches away now, close enough for me to count the gaps in his teeth. Abruptly, Mehrukenah shifted and seized

Renae around the neck. She shrieked as the old man dragged her between Boaz and Mr. Clarke, one hand clasping Renae's chin while the other held the knife to her throat. I started to lunge forward, but Mehrukenah only pressed the blade tighter against her skin.

"Where is the sword?" he demanded.

Renae's eyes were full of terror. Until this moment, her life had never had any events more dramatic than an exchange trip to Mexico and a broken engagement. Every shred of security in her innocent world had been stripped away in a fraction of a second. I was dying inside for her.

"You have until I count to three to answer," he said, "or I will kill her. It's that simple. *One.*"

My girlfriend was about to be murdered before my eyes! There was no way to prevent it! Had I known where the sword was, I'd have turned it over in an instant—*but I didn't!* What could I do?!

"*Two.*"

I opened my mouth to speak, to admit that I couldn't help him—to beg for mercy—to say anything that might stay his hand! But the words choked in my throat, and all efforts to dislodge them were futile. I couldn't utter a single sound. Not even so much as a cough.

"*Three!*"

"All right!" I finally blurted. "I'll tell you what you want to know."

What kind of words were these? They just came to me—the inspiration of a malevolent muse, solving nothing.

"Start talking," commanded Mehrukenah, the blade still cold against Renae's throat.

"It's at my apartment!" I cried. "In my bedroom."

Pleased, Mehrukenah lowered the obsidian knife, but he did not relax his grip on Renae. He smiled at me with satisfaction, and with a jerk of his head he indicated a white Honda Civic parked about three spaces away. Obviously, the newspapers had convinced them to ditch the Mercury Cougar and steal a new set of wheels.

"Then let's go," he said, wasting no time. "You drive, Jimawkins."

Mr. Clarke tossed me the keys, then he climbed into the Civic's backseat, sliding all the way over. Boaz stepped around and gave me a shove toward the automobile with the barrel of his gun. Mehrukenah guided Renae toward Mr. Clarke's open door and stuffed her in to sit between them, never taking the knife far enough away from her flesh to leave any doubt of his imminent threat.

Boaz, feigning kindness, opened my door on the driver's side. Climbing in, I looked back at Renae. She appeared surprisingly calm and passive. So passive I thought she might be in shock.

"Are you all right?" I asked.

"Yes," she said calmly.

Renae seemed to have mustered enough nerve to face whatever lay ahead. Mehrukenah struck me in the ear with the hilt of his knife.

"Drive!" he ordered. "She'll be fine as long as you continue to cooperate—and as long as you're telling the truth."

Boaz sat in the passenger's seat, slamming the door behind him, keeping me in the sights of his gun.

I started the car and slowly rolled out of the parking space. Before we pulled onto the street, I glanced in the rearview mirror. Above the shadowed faces of Mehrukenah and Renae I could see the BYU campus. At this moment, Muleki and Jennifer were just finishing their banana splits and beginning to wonder where we'd gone off to. Even if they concluded we were missing, I had the keys to Jenny's Mazda in my pocket. Last summer, I'd made an extra set and hidden them under the floor mat of the front seat, but I wasn't certain if I'd ever told Jenny—and even if I had, I couldn't imagine she would remember.

We were cooked.

As I stopped at the end of 820 North, preparing to go right on 900 East, Boaz turned to Mehrukenah. "What about Shurr and the others?" he asked.

"We'll come back and pick them up after we get the sword," Mehrukenah replied.

"But that wasn't the plan," Boaz informed him.

Mehrukenah glowered at his ancient comrade, but suppressing his anger, he turned to Mr. Clarke.

"Get out and find the others," he ordered. "Tell them what's going on." His eyes widened into an odd, knowing look, as if communicating some sort of clandestine intention. "Do you understand me?"

"Yeah," Mr. Clarke replied, receiving his message. "I understand you."

Mr. Clarke climbed out of the car. As we drove away, he remained standing in the street, making no immediate attempt to begin looking for Shurr, but Boaz did not turn around to notice.

These men appeared to have been staking out the borders of campus all night—perhaps even since Monday—just waiting for us to make a wrong move. As I'd feared, more people had recognized their secret signs and had been proselyted to their cause. It was impossible to be sure how many were in league with them now.

"You don't know how satisfying it is to finally be this close to you," Mehrukenah said to me. "I've always thought of you as my quetzal feather, Jimawkins—my greatest prize. When the war with Ammoron and his Lamanites was over and we were all released from prison, I searched for you and your friend for nearly a year. You see, I've always made it a point to repay my enemies. But none deserved my consideration more than you, my quetzal feather. You should be grateful that I've given you a way to repent. When you give me the sword, I'll consider that your debt to me has been paid."

I knew better than to believe that. Even if I'd had the sword to give, I wouldn't have expected him to depart without cutting my throat. Not that it mattered, because when he learned that there was nothing in my apartment even resembling a sword, I was subject to his lethal surgery anyway. Nevertheless, we continued our course toward King's Court Arms.

Mehrukenah continued, "After gaining the confidence of certain members of the Jershonite kinship, I learned that you were no longer among us—that you and your friend had gone away to a secret place—a volcano in the land of Melek with a tunnel leading upwards. Not until Rerenak had stolen the sword did I follow through with my ultimate intention of entering the tunnels to find you. Who would have thought that such a land as this could exist? And who would have thought we would find allies?"

We turned onto the street of my apartment complex and drove past the neighboring buildings. I knew they'd learned where I lived. I realized Muleki's sighting of one of them on Tuesday morning had been no illusion. I couldn't forestall the moment of truth by dragging them around town. I pulled into my parking lot and found an empty stall close to the first building.

"I'm very pleased," said Mehrukenah. "I expected you to try something stupid and force me to do something tragic in return. Thank you for not being foolish." Mehrukenah moved closer to Renae and tightened his arm around her waist. "Now, here's the plan. Boaz will follow you into your apartment. You will retrieve the sword, and Boaz will accompany you as you carry it back here. It's a simple plan, because I don't want you to misunderstand. I'll remain here with your lovely friend in case you make an error."

The glimmer of the streetlights reflected on the obsidian blade as he pressed it, once again, against Renae's throat.

"Get out of the car," Boaz instructed me.

I looked sorrowfully back at Renae, wondering if I would ever again see her alive.

"Hurry, Jim," she pleaded, unaware of my lie, faithfully believing that I could provide them with precisely what they desired.

"Yes, do hurry," repeated Mehrukenah, mocking.

How could I leave her, knowing there was nothing in my apartment to gain her freedom? It suddenly seemed so foolish not to have told Mehrukenah the truth. Maybe he would have found some value in what we'd learned in Salt Lake. My instincts told me his anger at having been deceived a second time, no matter what I had to say, would have been interpreted as deserving of grave punishment. Did he know that if he killed Renae, I would become useless to him? Unable to live with the guilt, I felt sure I would have consigned myself to die with her. Boaz thrust the barrel of his .357 Magnum into my ribs.

"Go!" he commanded.

I climbed out of the car, shutting the door. Boaz did the same.

"Let's move!" he repeated, again pulling the gun inside the arm of his parka so it couldn't be seen. I walked toward my apartment, the Gadianton at my heels.

Adding to Mehrukenah's threat, he said, "If you try anything, I'll kill you, and the girl will die as well."

The way Boaz handled the gun, it was clear he hadn't acquired much skill in its use. I might have been able to run. There was more than a good chance his bullet would miss. But Mehrukenah's knife would not miss Renae. The old man had planned this affair flawlessly.

I kept walking toward my apartment, climbing onto the sidewalk and heading around to the front of my building. As I ascended the steps toward the door, I could hear the television blaring within. When I opened it, I saw Benny and his girlfriend, Allison, seated close together on the couch, watching a horror video. Lars was in the front room too, lounging snugly in the easy chair. I could also see Andrew in his bedroom, studying at his desk.

As I entered the apartment, they all turned, even doing a double-take when they saw I had company. But then they turned back to the movie, which was at one of its more suspenseful junctures.

"You got a phone call, Jim," remembered Benny, keeping his eyes glued to the tube. "Long distance. A guy named Garth Plimpton. He said he'd call back later."

I didn't respond, but Benny thought nothing of it. As I moved toward my bedroom, Allison turned her head to give us a smile, but on the whole, everyone was completely oblivious to what was going on. Boaz remained silent and kept behind me. I opened my bedroom door and switched on the light. I'd left my computer on from the night before when I'd attempted to complete a report for my American Heritage class, but the monitor light was off. As I stepped past it I directed my attention toward my closet to pretend the sword was on the upper shelf. But with my finger I discreetly flipped on the monitor. It always took several seconds for the screen to light up. During that interim, I reached toward the closet shelf and wrapped my fingers around the bronze statue of a cavalry scout on a horse—a gift from a sculptor I'd baptized in Portland.

When the monitor light ignited, it was accompanied by a faithful hiss of static. Boaz glanced away from the closet long enough to see what had caused the sound, and his eyes were momentarily captivated by the bright blue screen. That was all the time I needed to introduce the bronze cavalry scout to the back of Boaz's head. Grunting once, the Gadianton collapsed onto my bedroom floor, dropping the gun. I picked up his weapon and bolted back into the living room.

Everyone had heard the statue strike and the body fall.

"What happened?" Benny exclaimed, then he saw the gun in my hand.

"I need some duct tape! Where do we keep the duct tape?" I demanded, throwing open every drawer in the kitchen.

Andrew arose from his studies to peer into my bedroom. The others were rushing over to do likewise. Andrew gasped at the body on the floor.

"Did you kill him?" he asked.

The duct tape was in the drawer next to the silverware. I pulled it out and fought through the crowd to get back into my bedroom. Everyone in the apartment watched as I pulled Boaz's arms behind his back and proceeded to wrap them in tape.

"Who is this guy?" asked Benny. "What has he done?"

There was no time to answer their questions, which would have only inspired dozens more. Boaz started to awaken as I finished the last of multiple wraps around his hands and began working on his ankles.

Groggily, his face to the floor, he snarled, "I'll kill you, Jimawkins! I swear it with an oath as black as the pits of hell! For this you will die!"

I picked up the gun again and left him there on my bedroom floor. As I reemerged into the living room, I looked at Andrew.

"Call the police," I told him.

"Not until you tell us what he's done," Andrew replied.

Could you believe this guy? I barely resisted a strong temptation to clobber Andrew with the same bronze statue. Instead, I slammed the arrogant putz against the bathroom door. The expression on my face was so intense that I actually saw dread in Andrew's eyes.

Through gritted teeth I hissed, "If you don't call the police, I'll break every bone in your body!"

Benny came to his rescue. "I'll call the police," he promised and went toward the phone.

I ran to the door, the gun firm in my grip. Before I rushed out, I turned back and begged everyone, "Please don't follow me! Whatever you do, *don't leave this apartment!*"

I was sweating profusely. The night air had grown much colder, and it slapped my face with an icy sting. I started down the sidewalk, trying to think rationally. What could I do? If Mehrukenah saw me coming around the corner with Boaz's gun, he wouldn't hesitate to slit Renae's throat then and there. I certainly wasn't a good enough shot to pick him off through the rear window. Everything still seemed so hopeless.

Then, beyond my wildest dreams, a figure came running toward me down the sidewalk. It was Renae! She was disheveled and crying, and she called out my name. She latched onto me, shaking out of control, unable to curb the flow of tears.

"What happened!?" I shrieked. "How did you escape?"

Through her panting and sobbing, I could barely make out what she said. "It was Muleki. It was all so fast. He pulled open the door. I pushed away. The man with the knife was yanked out of the car. They were fighting. I got out and ran."

This had to have occurred less than sixty seconds ago. I released Renae and scrambled toward the parking lot. As I stepped onto the icy asphalt, the area looked empty of life—nothing except a few snow-covered cars. The Honda Civic was still sitting where I'd parked it, but no one was inside, and the back doors were ajar.

Then I saw my sister, Jenny, kneeling behind the Civic. Striding toward her, around the other side of the Civic, I noticed her Mazda parked down the street about a hundred yards. They'd done it! They'd found the hidden key and guessed correctly the first place to look!

I approached Jenny and saw that she was holding someone. Muleki was lying quietly in my sister's arms. She looked up at me, tears streaming down her face. There was blood on the ice. Though the wizened Gadianton named Mehrukenah was nowhere in sight, he'd left his sleek obsidian blade embedded under Muleki's ribs.

CHAPTER 10

I wanted to be there when Muleki awakened. That didn't happen until mid-afternoon on Sunday. Since I wasn't a member of his immediate family, or even a distant relative, it took some fancy talking to convince the hospital staff at Utah Valley to let me stay by his bedside. Noting my determination, they sighed and shrugged their shoulders.

His wound was pretty bad. The doctor told me the blade had damaged several organs—even piercing his appendix. During any other century, Muleki would have suffered a long and agonizing death. Even in this day and age, the Nephite was pretty lucky. Mehrukenah knew the best places to stab a man. It was hard to believe that such a decrepit, saturnine figure as Mehrukenah could maintain such agility. Muleki was not an incapable opponent—I'd seen him in action. Yet in spite of that, the old wraith had struck his wound. Still, it couldn't be denied that Muleki's surprise attack had saved Renae's life.

I'd told the Provo police that the whole thing began as a mugging and soon evolved into a kidnaping. When they'd brought Boaz out of my apartment, now in handcuffs instead of duct tape, I further revealed that Boaz had admitted to me his involvement in the police station holdup in Cody, Wyoming. From the backseat of the patrol car, Boaz shouted a plethora of threats and obscenities in my direction. I was sure that when they started questioning him, he would say many things accredited to an insane man. Things about being a citizen of Zarahemla and coming up to this land through a cavernous volcano. Things which would insure his permanent incarceration in an iron-barred asylum.

Now there were only two Gadiantons left.

I'd wanted to ride with Muleki to the hospital in the ambulance, but the head paramedic decided to be a hardnose. Instead, Jenny, Renae, and I were taken to Provo's police headquarters, where homicide detectives grilled us with questions for over an hour. After we'd detailed all the events of the evening, I spelled out a description of Mehrukenah, Shurr, and Mr. Clarke. Finally, I told them I knew nothing of Muleki's background, adding that from what I understood, he had no immediate family.

During the entire interview, I would glance over at Renae and find her carefully watching me. She knew, based on what she'd heard Mehrukenah say, there was much I was not telling the police. Yet she remained silent, uncommonly trusting and loyal—though I knew she'd expect a full explanation before the night was over.

She got it about two a.m., as we sat in the Utah Valley Hospital, impatiently awaiting word on Muleki's condition. Jenny was the only other person with us in the waiting area. Unable to keep her eyes open, she'd curled up in an armchair across the room and drifted off.

Renae had heard Mehrukenah claim that he'd known me when I was younger, so I had to start at the beginning. I told her about the stone mural Garth and I had discovered along the Shoshoni River, and how it had hinted at the existence of a mysterious "rainbow room" deep inside the caverns on Cedar Mountain. I told her how the underground river had sucked us into a dark tunnel, and how we had awakened to find ourselves back in the days of the Book of Mormon. I told her about our adventures among the Nephites, and how we had prevented Mehrukenah and the kingmen of Zarahemla from assassinating Captain Moroni and others. I put it in such a way that suggested I wasn't sure if it had occurred in reality—or at least any kind of reality we were familiar with. Maybe it was a kind of vision, a gift from the Almighty designed to help a backsliding youth return to the fold. But whatever the case, that same parallel reality had invaded *our* day. I told her about the organization Mehrukenah represented. I told her who Muleki was, and used his uncanny ability to understand languages as proof. Then I told her why they had come, and what they were seeking.

Shortly after I'd finished, the doctor found us and reported that Muleki had been admitted to Intensive Care. His prognosis was excellent; however, since the chance of infection and other complications was very high, he would need to remain in the hospital for a couple of weeks. Even after he was released, the doctor predicted that full recuperation would require an additional thirty to sixty days.

We thanked him for taking the time to tell us, then Renae's uncle arrived to take her home. I couldn't read her heart as she climbed into the car and drove away. Did she believe my story? Perhaps she thought I was as insane as Mehrukenah! Maybe she would decide, even if my story was true, that it was clearly too dangerous to go on with our relationship. She needed time to sort it all out in her mind. I feared she would opt for a normal life with me out of the picture. Could I blame her? How I wished I could return to such a life! But I was in too deep now. It was because of me that the Captain of the Guard in the Palace of the Chief Judge of Zarahemla lay unconscious in ICU, an oxygen mask over his face, an IV in his arm, and a heart monitor verifying his life pulse.

Jenny was with me Sunday afternoon when Muleki awakened. His first muzzy words were, "I'm so thirsty."

I placed a straw leading to a cup of ice water into his mouth. He'd never used a straw before, but it only took a moment to catch on. He sucked the entire cup dry and started to reach over to his bedside table for more, causing him to wince in pain.

"Don't move," Jenny commanded.

"Where am I?" he asked.

"You're in a hospital," I explained. "It's a big building with lots of doctors and fancy equipment that—"

Jenny interrupted, "He's not delirious, Jim. He certainly remembers what a hospital is."

"But the wound was fatal," said Muleki. "I should be dead."

"With an attitude like that, it's a miracle you're not," chided Jenny.

"They'll take good care of you here," I promised. "Do what they tell you."

Shortly thereafter, Muleki dropped off to sleep again. Jenny and I left the hospital and returned to our apartments.

The rest of the afternoon, I received numerous visits from a concerned bishopric and home teachers, as well as from unconcerned ward gossips. Then, toward late evening, I was completely alone. My Nephite bodyguard was gone. I'd had to turn over the gun I'd taken from Boaz to the police for evidence. But the first gun they'd given me in the parking lot at Steck's IGA—the one they'd hoped I'd use to kill Muleki—was still under the mat in the trunk of Jenny's car, next to the tire jack, with four bullets still in the chamber. I retrieved it and determined to carry it with me wherever I went.

Fortunately it was winter, and I could conceal the thing inside my jacket. But what if I was forced to use it? Could I actually pull the trigger? Could I kill someone? What if I had to kill *several* people? How long would the authorities buy a plea of self-defense when bodies were piling up around me? My thoughts caused me to shudder, and I couldn't sleep that night.

Finishing out the semester seemed out of the question. Finals were about as far from my mind as the nearest quasar. I attended my classes on Monday, but I don't remember a word that was said. I was just following the routine in hopes of forestalling a nervous breakdown.

I began to think every stranger was watching me, especially the ones who stood alone on street corners. I found myself taking out-of-the-way routes to school and back to my apartment, and I made sure I got home well before dark.

Late Monday afternoon, Renae called. She wanted to know how I was doing, and she wanted to see me that night. Closing my eyes tightly, I thanked her. I needed a friend so badly.

Things had gotten relatively back to normal in my apartment. Friday night's events had been the primary topic of conversation all of Sunday. But by Monday evening, Benny and Lars were again excited about the prospect of attending the Bernardian meeting in Provo that night.

"Why don't you come?" Benny urged. "It'll get your mind off things for a while."

"You might even discover some solutions to your stress," added Lars.

"No thanks," I declined. "I've got a date."

"So bring her," said Lars. "Tonight's a big night. Mr. West will be there. He's the new president of the whole organization. Incredible man."

"Mr. West?" I repeated. "What's his first name?"

"Tim, Todd, Tom—something like that. I can't remember."

My heart starting racing like a jackhammer. Todd West was Todd Finlay's alias!

I came to my feet. "What does he look like?"

"I don' know. Kinda thin, mid-thirties, wears glasses. You heard of him?" asked Lars.

I couldn't believe it! Could he actually be the person we were seeking? If he was, how did he come to be involved in a UFO club? Lars had said that this organization had been around for some time, though it had only begun attracting widespread attention over the last few months. This was too bizarre! It had to be a different guy. And yet . . .

"Yes, I want to go to your meeting," I proclaimed.

I returned to my room and slipped into my jacket—verifying its weight to be sure the gun was still in the pocket. As I reentered the kitchen, I heard the phone ring again. I picked up the receiver.

"Hello?"

A computer generated voice came on the line. "This is MCI with a collect call from—" a female voice filled in the name, "—Katie Workman." The computer gave me several options as to how I might accept the charges. My finger searched frantically to press the "one" on the keypad, while at the same time I tried to exercise the other option by shouting into the receiver, "Yes, yes!"

Katie's voice came on the line. "Mr. Hawkins? This is Katie Workman at the West Valley Smith's store. I'm at home now. I couldn't call you from work. I don't think my manager would much appreciate knowing I was helping you."

"That's fine," I replied. "Have you seen him again?"

"Mr. West came in this morning," she admitted. "He bought two more money orders—to pay some bills, I think. He was in quite a hurry. I don't think he much appreciated it when I asked him to write an address in lieu of having no phone. Anyway, he scribbled it down quickly and left. There at the end, I had a feeling he suspected something. It wouldn't surprise me if he does his shopping at Albertson's from now on."

"Did you save the address?" I asked, unsuccessful at masking my impatience.

"Uh, yes. You got a pen?"

"Got it."

"1480 South 2344 West. I'm afraid I can't help you anymore. If my boss found out, I might lose my job."

"I don't think you'll have to," I replied. "You've already given me more than I thought I could hope for."

* * *

Renae had decided to stay with her aunt and uncle for a few days rather than sleep at her apartment in King's Court Arms. As I drove over to Cherry Lane and walked up to her door, my hand inside my jacket caressing the pistol's handle for security, I committed in my mind to end our relationship, despite my selfish need for a friend. I had to tell her I didn't feel anything for her anymore. It was for her own protection. If only she knew it was going to break my heart far worse than her own.

When Renae answered the door, already bundled up in her suede jacket and ready to go, she looked out at me on the front porch and seemed to sense what I was about to say.

Speaking first, she confessed, "I believe what you told me, Jim. I want to help, if I can."

"Renae, you don't know what you're saying—"

"Of course I do. I was there Friday night, remember? I understand the danger. That's why I want to be with you most of all. Because somebody has to look out for you. Because—"

She cut herself off.

"Because why?"

She whispered it very quietly. "Because I love you."

For a girl who'd shied away from me a month back because I was coming on too strongly, this seemed a dramatic change of policy. I knew I was experiencing the same depth of feeling. I'd known I was in love with Renae Fenimore since our very first date, but tonight just wasn't the right time to admit it. If I'd been any kind of man, I'd have told her that such feelings didn't matter, turned around, climbed into my car, and sped away.

As I opened my mouth to say exactly that, my tongue slid into the back of my throat again. Before I could loosen it, Renae had stepped past me down the front walk. I turned around and watched her open my passenger's side door. Before climbing inside, she turned back around. I was still standing on her front porch, my mouth hanging open to catch a few winter flies.

"Oh, I forgot to mention," she called back. "You don't have a choice in this matter."

CHAPTER 11

Renae was a little surprised when I announced the evening's agenda. I think she was expecting a peaceful drive to Utah Lake or around the Provo Temple in nostalgic remembrance of our first date. Fortunately, she trusted me when I said my presence at tonight's Bernardian meeting was crucial.

It was being held in the conference room of the city power building on 200 West. As we drove the Mazda across town by way of darkened side streets, Renae insisted on more details.

"I'm hoping to meet up with an old acquaintance of mine," I explained. "He could well be the Bernardians' principal speaker."

"And who are the Bernardians? What do they represent?"

"They're a UFO club," I said. "They think aliens from the second planet of Bernard's Star are visiting the earth to usher in the next stage of its evolution. Lars and Benny define that as meaning the Millennium. I know the whole thing sounds out in la-la land, but it's becoming quite popular."

"I have to tell you, Jim," confessed Renae, "I don't feel good about it. Even as you were explaining it, I . . . "

"Well, now, I don't think it's anything *dangerous*," I defended. "I've heard they don't seem to be teaching anything that contradicts the gospel."

"According to whom?" challenged Renae.

Her challenge brought things into perspective. She was right. My fanatical roommates might have twisted things any way they wanted to convince themselves nothing was wrong.

There was no parking near the building. The nearest space we found was over a block away. We walked in just before the meeting started, and found the room utterly packed—standing room only. Many people were content just to listen out in the hallway. Renae and I were lucky enough to weave ourselves into a spot along the back wall, which gave us a porthole view of the podium. I could see Lars and Benny up near the front. They'd gotten there early enough to take one of the seats.

Most of the people in the room appeared quite young: high school kids—the rebellious sort in my estimation, with outrageous hairstyles and clothing. Some kids looked conservative enough: football jocks and computer eggheads. A few older people were sprinkled among them, housewives and laborers. I even saw a couple of yuppie types with their three-piece suits and day planners. A photographer and a reporter had situated themselves close to the podium. Apparently the Bernardian furor had attracted the local press.

Smoking was not allowed in the conference room, but Renae and I were sandwiched between several people who reeked of tobacco, enough to make us nauseated. Nevertheless, there were other things that made us even more uncomfortable—particularly the conversations that were taking place around us. Lars may have insisted that the Bernardians were uplifting, but they attracted a crowd that was into everything from astrology to I Ching divination. A threesome of junior-high girls behind us were actually attempting to read the minds of several boyfriends along the far wall. Another couple to our right was discussing how Buddha, Confucius, Christ, and Mohammed were great teachers, but they had all failed to take advantage of the "full potential" of nature—whatever that meant. Three persons were seated behind the podium, two men and one woman, neatly dressed, casual, nothing threatening. Not a one of them resembled Todd Finlay, even in the cleverest of disguises. I began to think I'd misled myself, that I should take Renae by the hand and make a hasty exit. I stayed because one of the chairs up front was empty, as if a member of the panel had not yet arrived. And I couldn't deny it; I was strangely curious to see what was going to happen and what these people had to say.

The first person, a Steven Spielberg-looking gentleman with a beard and thick glasses, arose to take his place behind the podium, causing the audience to commence whistling and applauding. With a "ringmaster" smile on his face, the man raised his hands to stop the clamor.

He began by saying calmly and methodically, "What a great crowd we have tonight. We feared Utah County wouldn't have an ear for us. It's been a pleasant surprise for us all over Utah, Southern California, and Arizona to discover that the human mind is not closed. That the ancient drive to seek truth and understanding has not diminished. Nevertheless, you who came tonight are among the minority—and I should make it clear, ladies and gentlemen—you will *always* be in the minority.

"Tonight, you will experience phenomena beyond your wildest imaginations. You will witness powers of the mind which learned men throughout the world are only beginning to accept, and none to understand. Some of you may stomp out of here angry and upset, perhaps before we've even finished our presentation. Others will go home debating amongst themselves, some skeptical, others disclaiming. And some of you will come away with a precious seed of conviction that what we are saying is true and a determination to devote your lives to tapping into every glorious faculty your brain has to offer. If nothing else, tonight you will know that we are not alone in this great universe."

His delivery was magical. The crowd melted in the palm of his hand. For the next several minutes he expounded the theme and purpose of the Bernardians, which was basically to add new insights to the way people thought without diminishing their present beliefs "one iota." In fact, he declared that the things we learned tonight would *prove* the Bible was inspired, *prove* the Book of Mormon was no delusion—prove the Koran, the Vedas, the Popol Vuh, and a score of other theological volumes. He said Christian, Jew, and atheist alike would all find tonight's teachings in harmony with their own. Then he humbly introduced the next speaker, and a second gentleman arose and took his place at the podium.

This new person had a manner almost like a corporate executive, but with a flare for the dramatic, like a TV evangelist. He began by telling us a little about his life—how he had once been overweight and unhappy, unlucky in love and failing in his career. He said that one night he learned a wonderful secret, and that secret had changed him into the man he was today.

I found his presentation from there hard to follow, rather deep and abstract, but the people around us were enthusiastically nodding their understanding. He talked about how the human soul had progressed though various stages before we were born, and how it would continue to progress in the life to come until we achieved perfect "balance and harmony with the universe."

This was not at all what I'd expected from a UFO club. I thought I'd hear testimonies from people who'd seen flying saucers or who'd been abducted to other planets. Instead, the meeting exuded a peculiarly mystical and religious spirit. Then things started to get really weird.

The second man testified to having received his knowledge from a race of beings whose influence on the earth was as old as time itself. He told how ancient peoples and cultures had sung praises to them and built monuments in their name from the earliest of days. He said the time was soon at hand in the history of the world for these "beings" to show themselves in a way they had never done before. The goal of this club was to prepare the planet for the coming of these beings—"with fire and sword if necessary"—or else the very fabric of creation would be disrupted and the race who called themselves "human beings" would cease to exist.

I chuckled out loud. I couldn't believe anyone was buying this! A few people scowled at me. Embarrassed, I turned my attention back to the front.

The second man now introduced the woman to us by saying she had a very special power—the power to communicate with these beings through a sophisticated field of mental telepathy initiated by the aliens themselves. She was quite mousy looking, with straight hair and almost no makeup. Her words were shy and brief, telling us she didn't know why she'd been chosen, but that it was an honor beyond any she'd ever received.

A video projector was turned on, and we were shown a taped interview with this lady in an alien-induced trance. We were told that the voice emanating from her was that of an actual inhabitant of the second planet of Bernard's Star. It was a low, masculine drone, quite different from her natural voice.

The words and thoughts were expressed in an odd pattern, as if this alien presence was struggling to translate its thoughts into tangible concepts. The alien voice seemed unaccustomed to communicating with language, and explained that the process was "archaic" in its own culture since its kind were now able to communicate entirely through thoughts and emotions.

An interviewer on the video asked the alien several questions, which were answered via the lady. "Why was it communicating with us at this time?" "How did it travel from place to place?" "How was it influencing the universe as we knew it?" "What was the destiny of mankind?" "How did the great prophets and philosophers of the earth fit into the vast scheme of things?" "Were such prophets and philosophers indeed inspired by alien beings such as itself?"

The answers were so abstract and esoteric that I found myself straining to understand. The voice kept talking about the fabric of nature and the truth inherent in all things, the soul of the earth, and the destiny of mind and matter. The entire discourse gave the impression of being breathtakingly profound, but I couldn't help cocking my eyebrow and wondering if it was all a mishmash of mystical hogwash, made to appear profound by the theatrics of language, when in reality it was nothing more than meaningless platitudes.

There was an overwhelming air of vain pride around me. The audience put itself upon a kind of pedestal, convinced they were witnessing something extraordinary—something no one else in the world was privy to.

I supposed that on a very basic level, there appeared to be no direct contradiction to the gospel—even the thing about souls progressing from dimension to dimension. Latter-day Saints had always taught that men progressed: from an intelligence, to a spirit, to a temporal body, to a celestial body. It had just never been described in quite the same detail.

It was the next thing she said that tripped the little red "trouble" light inside me.

The interviewer asked the lady if it was more proper to pray to the "powers of the universe" or to "God." The lady, in her alien voice, said that it was not proper to pray *at all*, that prayer was an improper form of begging and did not appropriately demonstrate a correct relationship between man and his maker. It was much better to meditate, become one with the environment, and allow the wisdom of the universe to flow, unhindered, into the depths of the human psyche. A scripture in Second Nephi began repeating in my mind: "*The evil spirit teaches man that he must not pray . . . The evil spirit teaches man that he must not pray . . .*"

"Let's get out of here," I said to Renae.

She was in full agreement, relieved that I had taken the initiative. I felt ashamed to have subjected us to such a spirit while at the same time utterly frustrated that I had failed to accomplish my goal. As we fought through the crowd, the discussion turned toward dream stages and astral projection.

After breaking free into the hallway, we heaved a sigh of relief, as if there'd been no oxygen inside. Continuing to hold Renae's hand, I led the way toward the front of the building. There were two sets of glass doors leading out. The bitter cold awaiting us outside would be a welcome sensation compared to the unbearable heat in that conference room. As we pushed our way out, somebody else was pushing his way in. This gentleman was in quite a hurry, and we almost collided.

Keeping his eyes toward the ground, he apologized, "Excuse me. I'm a bit late."

The man tried to slip by. Suddenly, I grabbed his shoulder and spun him around so I could see his face.

"Todd Finlay!" I exclaimed.

For an instant, the man's eyes widened with horror.

I knew he recognized me, yet he replied, "I'm afraid you've made a mistake. My name is West. Now, if you'll excuse me, I'm scheduled to speak in two minutes. If you'll follow me, we can all join the meeting."

He tried to pull away, but my hold was firm.

"I've heard enough," I said. "I want to know where the sword is, Todd—the one I gave to you at the scene of the accident near Colter's Hell last summer."

He began to rave furiously. "I don't know what you're talking about, young man, and I advise you to take your hands off me voluntarily or I'll call someone who'll do it *forcefully!*"

He freed himself and pushed his way quickly through the inner door, disappearing down the hallway. I was tempted to pursue him, to knock his block off if I had to. Renae grabbed my arm.

"It's useless, Jim," she pleaded. "If you go after him, they'll have you thrown out."

"That sword was Muleki's whole reason for coming," I reminded her. "I have to get it back!"

"Bullying him won't accomplish anything. He obviously isn't carrying it with him."

As I stood there collecting my thoughts, an eruption of vigorous applause echoed down the hall. Mr. "West" had made his entrance.

"I know what we gotta do," I told Renae. "We have to go to Salt Lake. We have to go *now*—before this conference is over."

* * *

The drive to Salt Lake City took less than forty-five minutes. Renae chewed her fingernails most of the way.

"Don't worry about a thing," I reassured her. "We'll find his address, take the sword, drive back to Provo, and it will all be over."

This was, of course, assuming the sword was even there. It was also assuming he hadn't left a security guard, or a Doberman, behind to protect it.

Upon reaching Salt Lake, we exited the interstate at 13th South, then continued west in search of the address obtained by Katie Workman. As we approached the specified area, the neighborhood became more and more industrial. Soon we discovered that the corresponding streets were nonexistent. The closest point we found to 1480 South 2344 West was a trucking company and a field with warehouses. Todd Finlay had scribbled for Katie a line of bogus numbers.

I pulled over to the side of the road to mourn. If it wasn't one brick wall, it was another! Even if Todd went back to the West Valley Smith's, which Katie suspected was unlikely, I no longer had anyone to keep an eye out for him.

"Well?" I said, facing Renae. "Any ideas?"

"What if you turned it around?" she suggested.

"Turned what around?"

"The address. What if we tried 2344 *South* instead of 2344 *West*."

I almost scoffed at her suggestion. Then I thought about it. Maybe she had something there. Turning the numbers around *would* put the location much closer to Smith's, which seemed to make more sense. Todd may not have wanted to write down his actual address, but in his rush to comply with Katie's request, he may not have had time to invent anything more creative.

We turned north on Redwood Road and took a right at a 7-Eleven store on 2320 South. Entering a quiet residential neighborhood teeming with duplexes and tiny brick homes, my confidence in Renae's theory started rising. Only a single block later, we'd reached a street marked 1480 West.

There were very few street lamps to help illuminate the house numbers, and most residents either didn't have porch lights or simply forgot to turn them on. I decided to park in the street and search for the address on foot. Before climbing out of the car, I grabbed a flashlight from the glove box and handed it to Renae. I knew there was a brighter flashlight in the trunk. Opening it, I retrieved this one for myself.

After stealthily crossing several lawns, we found 2344 South—exactly as Renae had suggested. It was the left-side apartment of a red and white duplex. To our relief, neither driveway had a car, and there were no lights emanating from any windows. Best of all, when I knocked on the doors, I wasn't greeted by the bark of a vicious canine. There was no answer at all on either side.

Overall, the building appeared quite dilapidated: worn siding, cracked windows and duct-tape repairs. The sidewalk and driveway had not been shoveled, though frozen footprints to and from the door indicated the presence of a tenant. This seemed like a rather humble dwelling for the president of one of the fastest growing organizations in Utah. I began to wonder if I was about to make a terrible mistake, trespassing into the home of innocent people. I decided if I was wrong, I'd send the address some anonymous cash to overcompensate for any damage I might inflict.

Renae and I slipped into a dark corridor along the side of the house where a high wooden fence shielded us from the view of neighbors. There was a window there, at eye level. I pried off the screen and apprehensively tried to push it sideways to open. It slid open quite easily. The tenant had carelessly left the window unlatched.

Before climbing through, I looked back at Renae. She was shivering, and I'm sure it wasn't just because of the cold. From my coat pocket I brought out the .357 Magnum and placed it in her slender hand.

She looked at me strangely. "What am I supposed to do with this?"

"Just in case," I replied.

She tried to hand it back. "I can't use this—"

I refused its return. "Just hold onto it for me. It's too heavy to lug around anyway." I hoisted my shoulders through the window and fell inside.

No furniture obstructed my fall, but my leg got tangled up in an electric cord and I yanked an alarm clock off a bedside table. Of course, it started buzzing out of control and sent me into several unnerving moments of panic searching for the off-button. Finally, I hit it. Sighing in relief, I placed the silent clock back on the table.

Renae reached up and handed me my flashlight.

"If anyone comes," I instructed her, "signal me with your flashlight by flicking it on and off. Got it?"

She nodded, her teeth chattering. I closed the window so the current resident wouldn't find his room ten degrees colder than when he left.

Flipping the on-switch on my flashlight, I proceeded to search for the sword. The place was filthy. I don't mean cluttered filthy; I mean *filthy* filthy. The rugs hadn't been vacuumed for months. In the bedroom were bowls of half-eaten food burgeoning with mold, plus ashtrays, stale bread crusts, and torn-up newspapers. Piles of dirty clothing littered every corner—much more, it seemed, than would normally be owned by one man. He either had roommates, or frequently bought new clothes to avoid the hassle of washing the old ones.

I won't even mention how many dishes were in the sink, and I *certainly* won't mention the smell. If this was where Todd Finlay lived, I couldn't imagine it was where he slept. My nose could barely stand to walk through the place!

The mess made it difficult to look for the sword. I searched every closet and cabinet, under the furniture, and between cushions and mattresses. I dug through every shred of clothing, and even checked in the refrigerator. It just wasn't here. Maybe he sold it, I started to speculate. Maybe that's how he got the financing to build up the reputation of his fledgling UFO club.

I was beginning to conclude that we might have infiltrated the wrong house altogether when I turned to see Renae's flashlight shining on and off in desperation on the hallway wall just outside the bedroom. How long had she been signaling me? I had no idea! I'd spent the last several minutes searching through debris in the living room.

Suddenly I heard a key turning in the lock on the front door. Somebody was coming inside! I froze. What could I do?

Whoever it was, they wasted no time crossing the front room. Footsteps were already creaking across the kitchen floor!

Above my head, the hallway light flashed on.

CHAPTER 12

The switch to the hall light above my head was just around the corner. My legs could no longer wait for instructions from my brain. I leaped into the master bedroom in what must have been a split-second before whoever had entered the house turned the corner. But the footsteps were still coming, as if this person was following me by a sense of smell. I glimpsed Renae's face out the window. After sending her a quick gesture to get down, I flipped off my flashlight and slipped into the closet. The heaped-up clothing within muffled any sound I might have made. I reached the deepest corner and became deathly still as the bedroom light switched on.

I didn't even breathe. Did it matter? All this person had to do was peek inside. Some hanging shirts might have hidden my torso, but my legs were totally conspicuous. A shadow blocked the crack of light at the other end of the closet. After the shadow passed, I heard the box springs on the bed creak as the person collapsed onto the mattress.

There was silence for several moments. I almost thought whoever it was had left the room. Then I heard a sigh, long and tortured, followed by a moan.

"I can do better," said a male voice. I recognized it immediately as Todd Finlay.

But who was he talking to? Was he praying? Was there a phone in the room?

Then he repeated himself, this time emphasizing the first word. "*I* can do better."

Several seconds later he said the same thing, this time emphasizing the *second* word. "I *can* do better."

He said it twice more, emphasizing the third and then the fourth words, as if rehearsing a speech, or his only line in a play.

Again, there was silence—several minutes' worth. Finally, I heard another long sigh, and then Todd rolled off the bed and came to his feet. His shadow fell heavily across the open half of the closet again. *Todd was coming in!* I braced myself to vault forward and attempt an escape. But only his arm entered the closet—his arm, and something else. Something that he leaned against the back wall. Then he slid the closet door shut and turned off the light.

There it was—the silver-plated sword I'd held in my hands last summer. The jewels in the hilt were like the eyeshines of a cat peering back at me. We stared at each other, the sword and I. I couldn't help but shake my head. How could such an article, as sleek and ancient as it was, stir up so much excitement?

Yet somehow . . . I felt as though I wasn't alone in this closet. We were *both* hiding—me and the sword. I was hiding from Todd, and it was hiding from anyone who Todd might have thought would take it away.

I heard Todd undressing. The box springs on his bed creaked again as he climbed under the covers and attempted to sleep. The hall light was left on. Apparently Todd did not like total darkness.

So, the sword had been with "Mr. West" all along. Perhaps some other Bernardian had kept it safe and returned it to him at the convention. No, I doubted that. Most likely the object had been hidden in the car he'd driven to Provo. This whole trip to Salt Lake, the predicament I was in now, might have all been avoided if only I'd seen where he'd parked his vehicle. I resisted an urge to touch the sword, to feel the weight of it in my hand.

The very thought was ludicrous. Certainly such movement would have caused a sound and alerted Todd. Yet what was I going to do—stay here the entire night? Renae was probably still shivering outside the window, at the brink of panic.

I felt sure I could grab the sword and make a break for the front door as soon as Todd fell asleep. Renae and I could jump in the Mazda and speed away before Todd, in his groggy state, even realized what was happening. My only fear was that he kept a firearm near his bedside. He'd been a policeman, so it was certain his aim was fairly accurate. I should have taken the Magnum when Renae tried to return it. I had a much greater need of it right now than she did. I was left with no alternative but to attempt a sudden lunge for the door. My mind was in the process of rehearsing just such an action when the doorbell rang.

Todd bolted up in his bed. "Who the—!"

Was it Renae, I wondered? No, I couldn't be Renae. It was too crazy. Didn't she remember that Todd had seen her with me at the convention? She'd never get away with it!

Todd didn't seem convinced that he should answer it. The box springs creaked again as if he had settled back onto his pillow. Then the doorbell rang a second time. Finally, Todd cursed and rolled out of bed, pulling on his pants. I heard his footsteps pass the closet and enter the hallway.

Just in case this was indeed Renae's attempt to spring me, I left my flashlight behind and crawled to the other end of the closet. My fingers latched onto the sword. I hefted it into my arms. The instant I touched it, adrenaline seemed to surge anew through my bloodstream. I slipped open the closet door and took two strides toward the window. After sliding it open, I dropped the silver sword into the shallow snow and swung one leg out into the cold.

Todd's silhouette appeared in the bedroom doorway. He stood transfixed, momentarily dumbfounded as to how I might have gotten inside so fast. Then he screamed at the top of his lungs, "*Noooo!*"

He vaulted toward me. I fell out the window, grunting as I crumpled onto the frozen earth. The shadows were dark. My fingers dug around frantically in the snow until I found the hilt of the sword. Then I scrambled to my feet and hurled myself toward the street. Todd literally dove through the window's tiny opening, crashed into the wooden fence as he landed, then quickly rose to his feet.

I rushed across the lawn, half expecting to feel the fatal sting of a lead bullet as it entered my back. The bulky sword was slowing me down—it gave Todd plenty of time to take aim. As I reached the sidewalk, it actually slipped out of my hand and clattered onto the icy cement. When I picked it up again, the blade seemed heavier than before, almost as if it was desperate to remain where it was.

Renae was already in the passenger's seat of the Mazda. She'd simply pressed Todd's doorbell and run. If only I'd given her the car keys, she could have had the Mazda running by now and served as a getaway driver. All she could do was reach over and open the driver's side door to facilitate my entrance.

If Todd owned a firearm, in all the confusion he'd left it back in the room. As it was, he was bounding after me through the snow, wearing no shoes and no shirt.

I reached the car and tossed the sword onto the backseat.

"Lock your door!" I cried to Renae as I took my place behind the wheel, fumbling to plug the key into the ignition.

I turned the key. The motor fired up. The Mazda was just starting to lurch forward as Todd Finlay threw himself onto the hood, his face contorted with rage. I threw the gearshift into reverse. He tumbled off onto the pavement. I continued in reverse all the way to the end of the block and soon met the adjoining street. Todd was running after the vehicle as fast as his bare feet would carry him. As I maneuvered the car into a forward position and shifted into first, Todd caught us again, grabbing the back door—the one I'd forgotten to lock! As it began to open, the tires squealed. Todd fell again to the asphalt, rolling once, then rose again to continue his barefoot pursuit, tears streaming down his cheeks. Renae reached back to close the door as he faded into the background. I had reached a speed of fifty miles per hour in a twenty-five zone by the time we screeched onto Redwood Road. Then I directed my headlights toward the on-ramp at 21st South and Interstate 15.

With our hearts still hammering in our chests, Renae turned to gaze upon the sword lying peacefully across the center of the backseat. "So that's the cause of all the commotion?"

"That's it," I confirmed, my breathing starting to return to normal. "Hard to believe, isn't it?"

She continued gazing at it for several moments, entranced as the passing streetlights above the highway reflected on its silver plating. Finally, she faced forward, staring blankly down the interstate.

"I don't like it," she blurted.

I looked over at her, not quite sure how to interpret her words. Was she referring to an acquired taste in swords, or something else?

"It's only a hunk of metal," I assured her.

She turned to me and said in all seriousness, "Whatever we have to do, wherever we have to go, I want you to know that I'm with you one hundred percent. I'll help you in every way I can, but you have to promise me something, Jim. Promise you'll never ask me to touch it. Never."

I watched her curiously for another moment. Then, shrugging, I said, "Okay, I promise."

I faced forward, perplexed and agitated. Melodramatic reactions like hers were causing me much more anxiety than anything I'd perceived about the sword. Psychologists would have said that such reactions could all be explained by a perfectly logical mental phenomenon: If people really believe a thing possesses unusual powers, they'll begin attributing their behavior to the influence of that thing, when in reality, the power is all in their imagination. Such a simple explanation. Oh, how I hoped it was applicable here.

We pulled up in front of Renae's house just after eleven p.m. She made me promise to get in touch with her the next day. We embraced, and I thanked her for all she'd done.

"I couldn't have made it without you," I said. "Physically or emotionally."

She smiled warmly, then she waited a moment more. I think she wanted me to reciprocate the words she'd spoken to me earlier that evening. I decided not to. When I told her I loved her, I didn't want it to be out of obligation. She finally turned around to go into her house.

Driving away, I felt like a total heel. The fact was, I *did* love her. Maybe she needed to hear me say it more than I needed to wait for the right moment. Mehrukenah and the others were undoubtedly still stalking me. What if I never lived to *find* a right moment? Renae might always question how deep my feelings actually were.

I decided not to return to my apartment that night. Something inside whispered that an ambush was awaiting me there. Instead, I drove to campus and parked my car in front of the Harris Fine Arts Center. I retrieved the sword from the backseat and carried it under my coat all the way to the Wilkinson Center. The building was still unlocked due to a late showing at the Varsity Theater. I snuck into the study area west of the front doors and found a private corner, hidden from the view of anyone who might have patrolled the area in search of loiterers. I removed my coat and rolled it into a pillow. Then I curled up on the floor with the hilt of the sword snuggled under my arm.

Here in the dim after-hours light of the Wilkinson Center, with the blade only inches away from my nose, I studied the sword until my eyes grew heavy with sleep. Aside from its antiquity, there seemed to be nothing unusual about it. The surface glaze was dulled by numerous fingerprints—undoubtedly Todd Finlay's. There were a few more chips in the silver plating and tiny gouges along the blade, making the oxidized copper underneath more apparent. As I stared at it, no darkened vibes imbued my mind. If anything, I felt pity. What a shame that such a priceless artifact should be the object of so much prejudice and hatred. In a way, I felt sorry for the sword.

This was silly. I was endowing a chunk of metal with human emotions! Before long I'd be talking to it, reciting nonsensical gibberish in the privacy of my bedroom, like Todd Finlay. I shared a laugh with myself, then my eyes fell shut and I dropped off to asleep.

I was standing in the mist again, only the mist was aflame. The jungled hill was a holocaust of billowing black smoke and dying voices. The summit was discernible, but the cluster of trees, the lightning-scarred trunk, the beckoning old man—all were gone, consumed by the igneous rage.

Yet in the midst of the conflagration, something else was soundlessly watching me—a presence, hiding in the fire as easily as a shadow hides in the dark. It spoke, and the voice resonated like low mountain thunder.

"I've missed you, Jim. Serve me faithfully, for in the previous existence, we knew each other well. Welcome to my noble ranks. Welcome home. You have . . ."

". . . to go home!"

"What?" I groggily responded.

"Home! You shouldn't be here. You have to go home!"

As I opened my eyes, a student janitor was standing over me, shouting. His face was pocked with acne and his hair was in serious need of a shower. In his hand was a small carpet-sweeper.

"What time is it?" I asked.

"Almost six a.m. Have you been here all night?"

"Guess I fell asleep studying," I replied.

He seemed to buy my story, because he didn't notify his supervisor. I picked up the sword and quickly left the building. The morning was crisp and new, obscurely light—just light enough to give me the courage to return to King's Court Arms. I felt confident that the Gadiantons weren't yet desperate enough to strike in daylight, although I couldn't be sure how long this policy would prevail.

I opened the door to my apartment very slowly in hopes of muffling the squeak in the hinges. It was still an hour before the first of my roommates would come to life. The place was ghostly still—except for the hum of the refrigerator and the flashing clock on the VCR. I walked softly across the kitchen. The last thing I wanted to do was awaken a roommate and answer his baiting questions about where I'd been all night. I approached the door to my room, then suddenly I hesitated. It was a firmly established habit of mine to always close my bedroom door until I heard the click of the doorknob. Yet at this moment it was two inches ajar, allowing me to peer into the inner dimness.

I reached into my pocket and found the handgrip of my pistol. Simultaneously, I felt another inspiration. The sword seemed just as formidable a weapon, and perhaps more appropriate. Following my second inclination, I tightly gripped the hilt and held the blade aloft. After two deep breaths, I kicked open the door, filling our silent apartment with a resounding crash.

I charged inside, flipping on the light. The blankets on my bed flew in every direction. The intruder was in my bed! I lunged forward with the sword, more prepared to strike than I'd ever thought myself capable. Then I saw the intruder's face, his fire-red hair, and the freckles on his cheeks. He was backed against the wall. Upon recognizing me, he heaved a sigh of relief.

"You could have killed me, Jim! Is this the way you always greet your old friends?"

I heard my roommates stirring in the other rooms, aroused by the ruckus. As I stood there gaping, still trying to recover, the intruder couldn't help but smile. There was no mistaking that smile. It was the kind, wise smile of my comrade for life, Garth Plimpton.

CHAPTER 13

After my befuddled and grumbling roommates had wandered back to their bedrooms, I gave Garth the bear hug of his life. His arrival was the answer to a prayer I thought was too far-fetched to even utter.

His boyish features had subsided a bit, giving way to the wisdom of years. He was still an inch or so taller than me, but his skinny build might have caused people to perceive it the other way around. He wore a heavy sweatshirt with a picture of the earth and the slogan "A Planet Is a Terrible Thing to Waste."

"I got your letter Friday afternoon," Garth announced. "It began on the wrong premise—the premise that I'd forgotten our days among the Nephites. The Prophet Helaman told us the only way we'd lose those memories was by telling them. I never told."

"I still can't get over it," I rejoiced. "You're actually here!"

"Didn't your roommates tell you I called?"

As I thought about it, I did vaguely recall Benny saying something about it Friday night as Boaz held a gun against my back, but in all the excitement it had completely slipped my mind.

Garth continued, "When I didn't hear from you, I snatched up my savings and took the next flight to Salt Lake City. It arrived at eight forty-five last night. I tried to call you twice along the way—first from Boston and then from Chicago—but both times you were out. You must have had a busy evening."

"You could say that," I replied. "How did you get here from the airport?"

"Taxi. Cost me an arm and a leg. I woke up one of your roommates around midnight. He said I could wait in your bedroom. I fell asleep around two after deciding that if you weren't home by eight this morning, I was calling the police."

"But what about Harvard and finals?"

"Finals at Harvard don't start until mid-January. Don't worry. I can always prepare for finals; I can't always fly to Utah to meet a Nephite and an old friend. So where is this 'son of Teancum' you mentioned?"

"In the hospital," I answered gravely.

Garth's expression darkened. I sat him down in the swivel chair beside my computer and proceeded to update him on all the events that had occurred since I'd written the letter. I told him about our confrontation with Mehrukenah and Muleki's subsequent injury. Then I told him about Todd Finlay and the Bernardian meeting that Renae and I had attended the night before.

"The sword you mentioned in your letter—" Garth wondered, "is that the same instrument you almost used a few minutes ago to chop off my head?"

I nodded. "We got it back last night. By the skin of our teeth, I might add."

Garth stood to get a closer view of the object, now sitting at the end of my bed.

"Like I told you in the letter," I continued, "Muleki believes it was forged by the Jaredites using wicked spells and black magic. Then it got passed down from wicked king to wicked king. Muleki thinks it inspires evil wherever it goes."

I sincerely hoped Garth would put an end to such bunk here and now. Instead, after musing over the concept a moment, he replied, "The Nephites had the same kind of traditions, only they did it with articles they considered sacred. The Liahona, the Urim and Thummim, the Sword of Laban—they passed these relics down from generation to generation until the time of Moroni, and then even into the hands of Joseph Smith. King Benjamin was still wielding the Sword of Laban in battle five hundred years after Nephi brought it across the ocean. It's an age-old policy of Satan that whenever the Lord establishes something good, he'll mock it by setting up a wicked imitation. I think what Muleki believes should at least be respected."

That wasn't what I wanted to hear. Oddly, Garth seemed to feel the same aversion toward touching the object as Renae had.

"Now that you have the sword, what are you gonna do with it?" asked Garth.

That was an easy question. "Get rid of it!"

* * *

We took a shower and changed our clothes before driving down to the hospital to return the sword to its rightful bearer. Garth showered first. After I had finished and stepped out, Andrew marched past me, whining about the amount of hot water we'd used, and slammed the door.

Benny and Lars were already up and dressed. They were both sitting at the breakfast table with Garth. From my bedroom where I dressed and shaved, I overheard snippets of their conversation. They were telling Garth all about last night's Bernardian meeting while he politely listened to every word.

As soon as I emerged from my bedroom, Benny asked me what I thought of the talk given by Mr. West.

"I didn't stay that long," I replied.

"Really? How could you miss the best part?" Lars asked.

I couldn't continue to let them wallow in Todd Finlay's deception. The Bernardians had to be exposed; better now than after it was too late—especially for Benny.

"Todd West isn't his real name," I said. "It's Todd Finlay. He's a former police officer from Wyoming, suspended for insubordination and suspected of dealing drugs."

Benny and Lars glared at me open-mouthed.

"I'm sure those are lies," Lars declared.

"I knew him in Cody," I continued. "I personally met the wife and daughter he abandoned."

"More lies!" Lars turned to Benny. "They concocted the same kind of lies about Joseph Smith."

"Do you put this man in the same category as Joseph Smith?" asked Garth.

"In the particular realm of understanding that he's chosen to pursue, yes!" Lars replied.

Never, until this moment, had I realized how twisted the thinking of Lars had become. I'd always considered his explorations into the unknown as innocent exercises of the mind. Maybe in the beginning they were, but somewhere along the line his love for the "twilight zone" had risen above his testimony of the truths that God had already given.

"Lars, what would be my motive for lying to you about this?" I asked.

"Because of your need to defend what you've been brainwashed with all your life—the principle that tells you if somebody thinks differently from you, they need to be dragged back into the fold," Lars responded.

"That's not true," I insisted. "I'm only telling you who 'Mr. West' really is."

Garth added, "If what you've told me about the Bernardians over the last ten minutes is accurate, it sounds like some kind of

New Age organization bordering on the occult."

"The occult? Satanism? You're full of it!" scoffed Lars. "Nobody is performing blood sacrifices or conjuring up demons."

"That's not the way Satan works in the beginning," Garth explained. "First he determines where we're most vulnerable, usually an area of vanity—like wanting to know things that no one else knows—then he lures us with something that seems perfectly harmless. If we let him, bit by bit he'll lead us into the vortex of out-and-out witchcraft. Do you follow what I'm saying?"

Lars wouldn't respond, but Benny admitted, "Not entirely."

"Put it this way," said Garth. "Satan's church is like a bicycle wheel. There's a whole variety of spokes that can bring you to the center. One spoke might be astrology, another might be drugs, and another might be bizarre psychic powers or Ouija boards. Ultimately, Satan's goal is to use one of those spokes to bring us as close to the center of the wheel as possible. He's an expert at disguising his best methods and means."

Lars laughed. "Are you saying just because a guy reads his horoscope in the newspaper, he's one step away from becoming a devil-worshiper?"

"No," Garth replied. "But if he feels that his horoscope starts coming true day after day, and if he starts following its counsel, how much more likely is he to turn to astrology in a time of crisis, than he would be to turn to prayer and fasting? That's the danger."

"What a crock!" Lars accused. "Philosophies like that create the kind of prejudice and fear of knowledge that end up inciting people to burn each other at the stake!"

"I desperately hope not," said Garth. "The Lord commands us to learn and discover everything we can in this life. There's nothing wrong with wanting to know the mysteries of the universe or the human mind. The problem comes when we desire to use that knowledge for our own gratification, rather than to build the kingdom of God."

Lars snorted in derision. "I should have learned by now that if someone insists on ignorance, there's nothing I can do or say." He made a hasty exit into his bedroom.

Benny continued to sit across the breakfast table, staring at his soggy bowl of Raisin Bran. He shook his head back and forth. "I don't know which end is up anymore. All the lines seem so thin."

"What lines?" I asked.

"The lines between truth and error. It doesn't seem like I can depend on anything anymore. Not even the Church. Not after the stuff Andrew brought up last week."

"What stuff was that?" Garth inquired.

I told Garth about Andrew's discourse on doctrinal controversies, particularly the contradiction on plural marriage that he had pointed out in Jacob 2:24 and D&C 132:38.

Garth smiled. He spoke to Benny patiently, with absolutely no condescension. It was moments like this that reminded me why Garth Plimpton was one of my heroes.

"Benny, I promise you, the Lord is the same yesterday, today, and forever. Those two scriptures no more contradict each other than the law of Moses and the higher law of Christ. They were teachings given to different men under different circumstances and in different times. If a parent commands a little child not to play with matches, and then commands a teenager to light the campfire, is that a contradiction? It's only a question of preparedness—one is ready and one is not. If you read Jacob 2 closer, you'll notice in verse 30 that right after Jacob calls plural marriage a sin, he suggests that the rule may have exceptions."

Benny nodded. He accepted Garth's explanation, but it failed to lift his spirits. "How many more questions am I going to have to struggle with? How many more controversies are there?"

"The closer we get to the Second Coming, the more confusing it may all become," Garth replied. "The answer is to live the commandments, repent, follow the prophets—anything to keep ourselves in close proximity to the Spirit. And above all else—stay in the mainstream of the Church."

"But I still don't understand," Benny complained. "Why was I so easily deceived by the Bernardians in the first place? I'm not suffering from this great vain desire to have knowledge and power. I could care less about being smarter than everybody else!"

Garth hesitated, choosing his words carefully. "I couldn't tell you. But if it were me, the first thing I would do is see if there was anything in my life that might be driving away the Spirit. Anything that might be leaving me vulnerable. But like I say, you're the only one who could know for sure."

At that moment, the doorbell rang. In barged Benny's girlfriend, Allison, as usual not waiting for anyone to answer.

"Surprise, surprise!" she called over to Benny. "I decided to drive *you* to school today. Ready to go?"

Benny looked dumbstruck. The coincidence that Allison had entered at this exact moment seemed remarkable. Without anybody needing to say a word, it became clear what might be amiss in Benny's life. In all the months since Benny and Allison had started spending more and more time together, I'd never allowed myself to suspect anything negative about their relationship. I didn't want to know. I decided it wasn't any of my business. Benny looked to see our reactions, then he turned away. He fidgeted a moment more before deciding to stand. Allison was now frowning as well, intuitively uneasy about what might have been said before she made her appearance.

"Is everything okay?" she wondered.

"Sure," Benny replied. Without looking at her face, he retrieved his coat from the closet. The door closed behind them, and Benny and Allison were gone.

Garth and I ate breakfast quickly, then I returned to my bedroom to get the sword. I didn't feel comfortable carrying it out in the open. I had to find some way of disguising it.

Sitting in my closet was the guitar I'd purchased shortly after my mission. My intention had been to master the instrument by this Christmas, but I only ended up completing about a lesson and a half. It had been gathering dust ever since. I decided it was time to put my investment to a practical use—well, at least the case part. I tossed my guitar on the bed and was pleased to discover that the sword was just the right length to fit inside the case.

As we were preparing to leave the apartment, the phone rang. Garth stood behind me as I picked up the receiver.

"Hello?"

"I want to speak with Jim Hawkins," wheezed a voice on the other end of the line. It was Todd Finlay.

"This is Jim," I confirmed.

"Jim!" he exclaimed. He sounded on the verge of tears. "We need to get together this morning. I need to talk to you. We need to talk in person."

"I'm not able to do that," I replied.

There was silence on the other end for several seconds.

"I want the sword, Jim. I have to have it back. Please. You don't understand what it means to me. I'll do anything if you'll agree to hand it over without any trouble."

"I can't do that, Todd."

He grew angry. "What is it to you? It means nothing to you!"

He sounded like a junkie desperate for another hit, as if he was dependent upon the sword for his very well-being. How serious *was* this addiction? Would he die without it? As he spoke, I had the impression that he was literally suffocating.

"Todd," I said, my voice sympathetic, "you've become mixed up in something beyond your control. Something I fear the sword has inspired. I've given you a chance to get out, and get out fast—"

"Fifty thousand dollars!" he cried. "It's everything I have. It's all yours if you'll just give it back to me."

Fifty thousand dollars? Was he serious? It's not that I was tempted. It was just that . . .

"I can't," I insisted.

His voice became shrill and harsh, no less than insane. *"You're a dead man, Jim Hawkins! I'll kill you if you don't give it back! You AND your girlfriend! I'll kill you all!"*

I hung up the phone. Todd's voice was loud enough that Garth had heard the death threat quite clearly.

I turned to him, smiled, and shrugged my shoulders.

"Typical of my life these days," I said.

CHAPTER 14

Garth and I arrived at Utah Valley Hospital shortly before nine a.m. I carried the guitar case with its ancient cargo all the way to ICU. Muleki was awake when we walked into his room. His breakfast tray was sitting in front of him as he busily enjoyed a hospital Danish.

"Jim!" he called out enthusiastically. "I've missed you."

Upon seeing Garth enter the doorway behind me, his face brightened even further.

"The spotted boy!" he exclaimed. "I remember you. You're Garplimpton!"

Garth stepped over to Muleki's bed.

"And you're Muleki, son of Teancum. You know, when we first met, the first thing you said to me was that if you looked as pale as I did, you'd cake your face in mud and wash it off over and over again until your face was brown."

Muleki blushed. "I was an outspoken child."

I dropped the guitar case at the foot of Muleki's bed, unlatched the buckles, and lifted the lid, displaying its contents to the Nephite. Muleki looked down at the silver-plated sword, and up at me open-mouthed, shaking his head, unable to believe it could be true.

I nodded.

The Nephite was so ecstatic he nearly tore his stitches trying to sit up. "How? How did you do it?"

I told him all the events of the previous night. I told him how I'd slept on campus because I feared an ambush was waiting for me at my apartment.

"It's important to follow such instincts," Muleki commended. "But remember, the longer you possess the sword, the harder you must concentrate if you're to be sure the inspiration comes from the correct source."

"I don't *want* to possess it any longer," I said. "I'm turning it over to you."

Muleki tensed. "You can't leave it with *me!* Not here! Not while I'm like this!"

"What else am I supposed to do?" I asked. "If I hold on to it, it's just a matter of time before Todd Finlay or the Gadiantons spot a moment of vulnerability and steal it back, leaving me in some back alley with my throat cut."

"You're right," Muleki agreed. "If you fooled them last night, I fear not even daylight or crowds may stop them now."

"I could hide it," I suggested. "Someplace where no one would look."

"No," Muleki objected. "They may be watching you, even if you're certain you're alone. But even if you could hide it, there's no safe place. The sword has a way of attracting an owner for itself—always the wrong kind of owner."

I could see where this conversation was leading. I didn't like it.

"Muleki, I came here to get rid of this," I declared. "I'm sorry for what happened to you. To make up for what I've done, I've gotten your sword back and laid it at your feet. I can't do any more than that."

"You *must* do more," said Muleki. "Because of my wounds, I can't carry it back to my land. You're the only one I would trust to complete the mission."

"The mission can wait sixty days!" I cried.

"Two moons is a long time," said Muleki. "So much evil can occur. We can't take the chance. Not even I would want to possess the sword for more than a few days."

"What are you saying?" I asked. "Are you suggesting that I go back to the year 50 B.C.?"

"No," said Muleki, and I felt a wave of relief. "You must not go through the caverns. The way will be heavily guarded by the men of Gadianton."

My relief was short-lived as he added, "You must go to the Hill Ramah as it stands in *this* day and time. Find the coffer at the highest summit point and place the Sword of Coriantumr within it."

"What's that supposed to accomplish?"

"The Jaredites used their evil rituals to curse many swords, though none were as powerful as the one wielded by Coriantumr. After the last battle, Ether walked among the dead, gathering all the accursed swords together. He buried them in a spot of ground that he had blessed. Here the curses were lifted and the swords returned to the dust. The only sword Ether was unable to find was Coriantumr's. The king kept it with him until the day he died among my ancestors, the people of Zarahemla. Petty sorcerers kept it hidden for generations, unable to grasp its full potential. Then Gadianton discovered it. It must not fall back into his hands."

"Let me get this straight," I said. "You're asking me to go to the last battleground of the Jaredites—a place I'm not even sure exists in our day—and climb to the top of a hill to find a sword-filled box that's about twenty-five hundred years old? What makes you think the box is even there anymore? Who knows how far earthquakes and erosions have carried it? We might have to dig up an area the size of a football field. You're asking too much, Muleki!"

"Please, Jim. I'm begging you. Without you, the mission will fail. All the efforts of Judge Helaman, all the years I've spent trying to destroy it, will have been in vain."

I couldn't believe what I was hearing! The doctors must have done something to Muleki's brain. Did he know who he was talking to? This was a job for heroes and prophets. I felt about as far from either of those designations as an ant from the surface of the moon.

Garth spoke. "One thing is certain, Jim. You can't stay in Provo. Based on what I've heard, it would be suicide. The only way to end this affair once and for all might be to do exactly what Muleki suggests. You won't do it alone, Jim. I'll be with you every step of the way."

"But we don't have any money," I tried as a last resort. "If we're going to travel, we need money. I only have about two hundred and twenty dollars until the end of the semester."

"I've got another hundred and fifty," said Garth.

Muleki directed us to the closet where his clothes were hanging.

"Reach into my coat pocket," he said.

Garth did as he requested and retrieved the pouch I'd seen on Thanksgiving—the one that had contained the gold nugget he gave to my brother. Garth dumped the contents into his hand. There were two nuggets left. I had no more excuses.

I hung my head. Sighing, I announced, "All right. I'll go."

Tears welled up in Muleki's eyes. But he was still gravely concerned by my lack of enthusiasm. "If you are lukewarm about this quest, Jim, you will surely fail."

"I'm fine," I assured him. Then, less confidently, I mumbled, "I'll be perfectly fine."

Muleki added another warning. "The power of the sword will grow more and more intense as it nears the land of its creation. This will make the going harder for you, but it will make it easier for your enemies."

"Great," I said sarcastically. "As if things aren't bad enough. As if the wolves aren't crashing through the windows already."

Muleki suddenly looked very weary, though he insisted on using the last of his energy to grip my right hand in both of his. Looking into my eyes, he offered one final word of advice.

"Stay close to the Lord, Jimawkins." He looked at Garth. "Hold as tight to His principles as ever in your life, or the sword will destroy you as mercilessly as it did Shiz under Coriantumr's hand."

I swallowed. This was crazy! What had I gotten myself into? I wanted Muleki to release my hand, but he held on for a moment longer. Finally, his weariness caused him to let me go. The nurse came in to remove Muleki's breakfast tray. When she saw his weakened condition, she shooed us out immediately, scolding us for having forced him to exert himself.

"The sword," muttered Muleki as we were walking out of the room.

I'd almost left it on his bed. My determination to get rid of it had sunk into my brain to the point that I almost left it behind. As I shut the guitar case and lifted it into my arms, Muleki smiled peacefully.

"God be with you," he whispered.

* * *

"This is like old times," Garth said. "You and me fighting against overwhelming odds."

I nodded, my spirits depressed and showing no signs of lifting. Garth frowned. I knew he'd always depended upon my sense of humor to lighten even the most stressful moments. Not finding my sense of humor cocked and ready concerned him a great deal. It must not have seemed natural. I'd always found something to laugh about, no matter how serious the situation. In the past, I had been convinced that it made life's pains infinitely more bearable.

After Friday's events, I'd begun to question my whole outlook on life. It was my levity that had gotten me into the most trouble in life. It was this same reckless levity that led me to step off campus even after I'd been warned of the danger. Because of it, Renae's life had been threatened and Muleki lay recovering in Intensive Care. Because of it, the mantle of Muleki's burdensome quest had been laid upon my head.

As we arrived back at King's Court Arms, I parked in the south parking lot. I'd never parked here before. I was determined not to do anything the way I usually did it in case anyone might have been watching, lurking. Cautiously, I vacated my car with one hand on the butt of the Magnum. My paranoia was infectious. Garth also found himself watching for sudden movements near the corners of buildings and checking the source of every sound.

When we were safely inside my apartment, Garth began reciting a checklist of things we needed to accomplish before leaving Provo. First we'd pack, then I'd try to reach as many of my professors as possible to let them know I was leaving town on an emergency. Then we'd find a local pawn shop to buy Muleki's gold. If all went smoothly, we'd be out of town by sundown.

Andrew was the only one home for lunch. He listened curiously to our conversation and devoured some leftovers. "Where is it that you're going?" he inquired.

"New York," I answered him. "Palmyra, New York—"

Garth interrupted, "I don't think so, Jim."

"Huh?" I responded. "We're going to the Jaredite battleground, right? I always thought the Hill Ramah and the Hill Cumorah were the same hill."

"Yes," Garth confirmed, "but the hill where Moroni gave Joseph Smith the gold plates may not be the same hill where the last battles took place. Latter-day Saints have always assumed it was the same location, but the Book of Mormon doesn't say that. In fact, Mormon 6:6 states that Mormon went to Cumorah and hid up all the records *except* the gold plates, which he gave to his son, Moroni."

"So what are you suggesting?" I asked.

"I'm suggesting that if we want to find Ether's coffer, we need to go to the place where the last battles took place, not the place where Joseph found the plates."

"But how come the hill in New York is called Cumorah if it's not the same Cumorah as in the Book of Mormon?"

Garth went on, "Some think Oliver Cowdery named it that. The Angel Moroni never called it Cumorah, nor did he say it was the same hill where his people fought their last battle. Joseph Smith never said it was the ancient Nephite or Jaredite battleground, either."

"The 'two-Cumorah' theory, eh?" chimed in Andrew. "You should know, folks have been shooting that one down since the 1960s."

"It seems to make sense. Most people who study the matter usually conclude that the hill in New York can't be same hill mentioned in the Book of Mormon. Actually, I'm not sure if Nephites ever set one foot in New York—or even in the United States, for that matter."

"The speculations of men," Andrew scoffed, swallowing another bite of lunch. "If you want to 'hold to the rod,' you'd better stick with what the Lord had to say."

Garth shrugged. "The Lord has never really spoken on this matter. Joseph Smith himself was left to speculate. In the Nauvoo periodical called the *Times and Seasons*, he suggested that Zarahemla might be in Central America."

"But he also said that Manti was in Missouri," Andrew countered, "and that Zelph, a skeleton found in Illinois during the Zion's Camp march, was a white Lamanite who fought during the last great struggle of the Nephites and Lamanites. That sounds like Nephites in the United States to me."

"Neither of those statements can be clearly attributed to Joseph Smith," Garth replied. "It was written after he died. Sometimes we can unwittingly turn traditions into doctrine. We have to be careful of the source."

"How come I've never heard about this 'two-Cumorah' thing?" I demanded.

"Well, I think there are more important things in the gospel to worry about than that," said Garth. "To me, the biggest piece of evidence that the Book of Mormon never took place in New York is that never once in the entire scripture does it mention snow, cold weather, ice, or anything else that you might expect from an ancient New Yorker."

I thought of a solution. "Maybe the majority of it took place in Central America, and then, at the end, the Lamanites drove the Nephites up to New York."

"That's over three thousand miles," said Garth. "This was a battle involving a quarter-million Nephites—and who knows how many Lamanites. Why travel so far, crossing hundreds of rivers and encountering other potentially hostile tribes, just to fight a battle? The Book of Mormon tells us about an expedition traveling all the way from the land southward, through the narrow neck, and discovering the last battleground of the Jaredites—all in a matter of weeks. If we assume Limhi's expedition went all the way to New York in search of Zarahemla, it would have taken years—if not their entire lives."

"Then how did the gold plates get to New York?" I asked.

"Well, there appears to be a gap of thirty-seven years from the time of the last battle until Moroni wrote his final entry," said Garth. "That leaves plenty of time for at least *one* Nephite to travel to New York. I think a prophet like Moroni eventually would have departed from the wicked land where his people had been destroyed and traveled to a place where he could continue preaching the gospel, finally depositing the plates at the end of his life right where Joseph Smith unearthed them. Or he may have put them there as a resurrected being. To me, it really doesn't matter."

"So where *is* Cumorah?" I finally asked.

"Good luck with that one," Andrew interjected. "Folks have proposed more sites than Brigham Young had wives."

"Well, let's look at the facts," said Garth. "It has to be a prominent landmark—much more prominent than the tiny hill in New York. It has to be within a day's journey from a large and ill-defined body of water which Ether called the Waters of Ripliancum and which Mormon called a land of 'many waters, rivers and fountains.' It has to be small enough for an injured man of eighty years—Mormon—to climb to the top and enjoy one last night with his son and twenty-two other Nephite survivors of the first day of battle. Yet it also has to be high enough for Mormon to view hundreds of thousands of bodies on the plains and hillsides below. It must be near the eastern seashore, near the narrow neck, and in the midst of a volcano and earthquake zone. In the studies I've read, the only place that seems to fit all these criteria is a hill north of the Isthmus of Tehuantepec and south of the Papaloapan water basin in the state of Veracruz, Mexico, called *El Cerro Vigia.*

"Mexico?!" I exclaimed. "Are you suggesting we take a plane to Mexico?"

"No," said Garth. "Not a plane. A silver sword would never get past an airport's metal detector. If what Muleki says about its potential for being stolen is true, there's no way I'd leave it in the hands of baggage handlers, either."

"So how are we supposed to get there?"

"We drive," said Garth.

"Drive?! How far is this place?"

"I'm not sure. At least three thousand miles."

"In Jenny's Mazda?!" I shrieked. "Garth, I wouldn't trust that wreck too many more times to get me to Salt Lake and back! It's got over 90,000 miles on it. The tires are nearly bald!"

"Do you have a friend with a better car?" he asked.

"Not anyone who would let me drive it for *six thousand miles!*"

Garth thought about this for a moment. "I'd talk my mom in Rock Springs into letting us use her Chevette, but it's in a lot worse shape than your Mazda. Unless you can think of a better idea in the next couple of hours, I'm afraid we'll just have to risk driving Jenny's Mazda—and pray the Lord is behind us."

CHAPTER 15

Since there was far less chance of Garth being recognized, I gave him the pistol and sent him out alone to complete the last-minute shopping. On his list were motor oil, coolant, enough junk food for two days, and adequate maps to get us as far as El Paso, Texas. While he was gone I rolled and tied the sleeping bags, packed my duffel bag, and contacted my professors. I explained that I had a personal crisis that required my immediate attention. They agreed to let me take "incompletes" in lieu of grades. I was to contact them when I returned to find out how to make up my finals. The only bugger was my stats professor, who wanted more of an explanation than I was willing to give. He agreed to my terms only if I took the final for his class by the first week in January. I agreed without hesitation. I'd have agreed to anything. Under the circumstances, January seemed a millennium away, and finals in general seemed like the most insignificant and trivial aspect of my life.

I still couldn't believe I was actually going through with this. You don't just wake up one day in Provo, Utah, and decide before lunch that you'll be driving practically to the Yucatan Peninsula.

After Garth returned safely from shopping, I asked him, "Have you been to this hill before?"

"No, but I've seen pictures of it," he replied. "It's just above a small town called Santiago Tuxtla."

"Do you know how to get there?"

"Not really. But I'm sure we can buy a detailed map of Mexico at the border."

My confidence was waning. "Have you ever even been to Mexico?"

"No, I haven't," Garth confessed. "But don't worry. We'll be fine. I still speak fluent Spanish from my mission in Guatemala. If worse comes to worse, we can always ask someone for directions."

Personally, I'd never been out of the continental United States. My impression of Mexico was formulated strictly by old western movies and postcards from Acapulco. I'd always imagined the Mexican frontier to be a wasteland of cactus, gila monsters, and roving bandits.

"Are there any special laws we need to know?" I asked. "What would we do if Jenny's car broke down?"

"Take it to a garage, I suppose," Garth answered.

"But the car is Japanese," I pointed out. "Will they have Japanese parts?"

"I don't know."

"And what if we get into trouble? Do you know anybody down there who we could call?"

"Not a soul," admitted Garth. "But, remember, Mexico has plenty of Latter-day Saints. It shouldn't be too hard to find Church members."

I groaned. "This trip may be the most ludicrous thing I've ever done—and that's sayin' something. I hope we know what we're doing. I can just see myself rotting in some Mexican prison until I'm eighty. My parents, my family—nobody will know where to find me."

Garth scoffed, "It's not like we're going to Mars. Retired folks drive their motor homes around Mexico for months on end."

"That's *old* people," I pointed out. "They're not gonna bother them. It's the young people they need to work the salt mines."

"Don't sweat it," said Garth. "I admit, it would be better if we took along a person who knew the territory, but I don't see how we could find someone on such short notice."

I thought of Renae. Hadn't she mentioned that she'd been to Mexico as an exchange student? A second later, I dismissed the idea. It was out of the question. Nevertheless, I realized it might be advantageous to at least call her for information. Maybe she could give us the names and phone numbers of people who might come to our rescue. I called both her uncle's house and her King's Court Arms apartment, but I couldn't locate her. I left the same message in both places: "Leaving today for Veracruz, Mexico. Wanted to know if you could give us helpful hints. Call me as soon as possible."

Afterwards, I called Jen. Somebody in my family had to know where I was. But as soon as she picked up the phone, I couldn't get a word in edgewise. She was terribly frightened.

"Jim, there are people following me. I can't leave my apartment. I can see a man right now through my kitchen window, standing under the tree across the street. He's been there ever since I came home from class."

"Have you called the police?"

"What would I tell them? They haven't done anything yet. I don't even know how many there are. Two different people followed me home from the Jesse Knight Building."

"You mean they were on campus?"

"Yes," she confirmed.

This was the most disturbing news of all. I'd hoped the BYU campus was a kind of impregnable safety zone. It occurred to me that the Gadiantons' modern-day converts might not feel the same discomfort on dedicated ground as an oath-bound

Gadianton like Shurr or Mehrukenah. Jenny could be abducted at any moment.

"You need to get out of Provo," I told Jenny. "They'll use you to get at me. I'm leaving town tonight. I have something they want desperately."

"Where are you going?"

"Mexico."

"*Mexico?* Not in *my* car you're not!"

"Jenny, please. It's not by choice. My life is in danger!"

"Why Mexico?"

"It's a long story. I'll tell you when we get back."

"You'll tell me *today*," she demanded. "Because if you're taking my car, I'm going with you."

"You can't," I told her. "It's too dangerous."

"And it's less dangerous *here?*"

I closed my eyes tightly. Her point was indisputable. How could I have placed the people I loved in such precarious circumstances? The stress would have been so much more endurable if it was only my neck on the line.

"Call your professors, pack your bags for two weeks, and sit tight," I told my sister. "We'll be over to get you in fifteen minutes."

* * *

It was actually in less than fifteen minutes. I tossed the guitar case, sleeping bags, luggage, and groceries into the trunk. Then I put the pedal to the metal all the way to Jenny's apartment, screeching to a halt in the parking lot behind her back door. Immediately, I saw the man she'd mentioned. He was leaning against a tree, standing shin-deep in snow. He watched us knock on Jenny's back door, looking concerned as we were allowed inside.

Jenny had actually finished packing—an amazing feat, I thought, for any woman in that length of time. Her clothes, makeup, shampoo—all of it was piled into one suitcase.

She was ecstatic to see Garth, and left some lipstick on his cheek. He blushed bright red. As Jen went to her bedroom to fetch her coat, he turned to me and remarked, "She's really grown up, hasn't she?"

It occurred to me that this was quite a noteworthy reunion. Ten years ago, the three of us had stood together upon an ancient land. Even if Jenny had no memory of it, she still seemed to feel an odd sense of nostalgia. Greetings were short-lived. Before we could leave town, we had to sell Muleki's gold.

As we emerged from Jenny's apartment, the man under the tree was quick to notice. He signaled to someone and began approaching our vehicle. Another man came out from around the corner of the building. I drew the Magnum out of my jacket and aimed.

"Keep back!" I warned.

They both stopped abruptly. Jenny climbed into the back-seat as Garth hurriedly looked for a place in the trunk to stuff her suitcase.

The second man smiled. "What's the matter? I just need to ask you a question."

I cocked the gun, and they froze. They were both wearing heavy coats. They might have easily been concealing their own firearms. But keeping a bead on them prevented such weapons from being drawn. I didn't relax my aim all the while I climbed into the driver's seat and started the engine. Our trunk had been so badly organized that Garth was forced to toss the guitar case behind the front seat to allow room for Jenny's suitcase. The strangers watched our tires kick up the icy slush as the Mazda pulled back onto 900 East.

We drove toward south Provo, where an assayer in a local pawn shop had promised to look at our gold and make an offer.

"Why are you bringing your guitar?" asked Jenny.

"There's no guitar in it," I admitted. "It contains an ancient sword. That's what these people want to take from me."

"What are you doing with such a thing?" she asked, hoisting the guitar case onto the seat and proceeding to open it.

"The sword has been cursed," Garth explained. "We're traveling to Mexico to destroy it."

"You've got to be kidding me," said Jennifer. "Cursed? Destroy? Sounds like something out of *Lord of the Rings*."

Jenny opened the case. Her gaze was transfixed for several moments by the glittering jewels and glossy silver. In the rearview mirror, I saw her hand reach out to touch the cold surface. As I recalled Garth and Renae's repulsion, I thought of shouting out a warning, but I'd have felt ridiculous. After all, I'd hefted the object at least a half dozen times, and felt no different whatsoever.

Jenny's fingers closed around the hilt. She gripped it for a good ten seconds. Then she released it with a gasp, looking up at Garth and me with widened eyes, as if it was the first time she'd ever seen us.

"What's the matter?" I asked.

"Pull over!" she cried.

Responding quickly, I pulled into the gutter a half block from University Avenue. Then I turned around and demanded, "Are you all right?"

She was smiling, looking at Garth, and then back at me with eerie wonderment.

"I'm fine," she proclaimed.

I reached back, shut the guitar case, and replaced it in the foot space behind the seat.

"You shouldn't mess with this," I told her.

"But I remember it all now!" Jenny announced. "I remember the cave, the Rainbow Room, the underground river." Her eyes darted around, as if she were seeing the images in her mind as clearly as sights outside the car. "I remember the jungles, the people, the Lamanites—all as if it were yesterday! *It really happened!"*

Garth and I considered her carefully. Not even *my* memories had been restored so instantly. They had filtered in slowly, over the course of a night and a day.

"Did the sword *tell* you all this?" I asked.

"I don't know," said Jen. "It just rushed into my head, like a gust of wind-like a geyser." A second later she looked dizzy. She sat back and touched her palm to her forehead. "I feel a little . . ."

"What's wrong?" asked Garth.

"Just a little nauseous."

Clearly, if the sword could give, it could also take. Why hadn't anything like this ever happened to me? I'd handled the hilt for much longer periods and never felt so much as a chill. Maybe I was immune to its supposed power.

"Go ahead and drive," Jenny instructed, closing her eyes and breathing deeply.

I pulled back into the street and told her, "I don't want you touching it anymore."

"Don't worry," she said. "I won't."

* * *

At the pawn shop, my sister still felt a little lightheaded. Garth asked for a chair behind the counter. She sat down while we waited for the nuggets to be priced and weighed. I stood by the window, watching for predators.

Finally, the assayer offered three hundred dollars for our nuggets. "The grade isn't very high," he said. "I'm afraid I can't pay any more."

I almost objected, knowing pawn shops weren't famous for

their generosity, but time was running short. We couldn't waste a day shopping around for the best price.

So our total finances to reach Veracruz, Mexico, including the seventy-five dollars Jenny had in her purse, were seven hundred and thirty-three dollars and twenty-five cents.

When we got back in the car, Jenny asked if we could see Muleki before leaving town.

"I'm sorry," I replied. "We just don't have time."

Garth noted Jenny's disappointment. Clearly she harbored some tender feelings for the Nephite. I got the impression that he found her affections disappointing. He turned away and shook his head, seemingly scolding himself for imagining that a girl like Jenny might ever feel something for a guy like him. All our years growing up, I'd never suspected that Garth harbored any secret feelings for my sister beyond a simple friendship. He was too wrapped up in his studies for women. Apparently Garth Plimpton had changed.

The changes had been physical, as well. He was hardly the gawky, no-shouldered kid I remembered from grade school. It occurred to me that some girls might actually find him handsome—though it was apparent that he still viewed himself as the same nerdy misfit he'd been growing up.

We neared the on-ramp for Interstate 15. Just as we were about to make a clean escape from Provo, Garth blurted, "Hold it, Jim. Did you bring your birth certificate?"

"You never said I needed it!"

"I got mine," said Jenny.

"How is it *you* were so inspired?" I asked her.

"I wasn't inspired," replied Jen. "Everybody knows you can't get into Mexico without a birth certificate or passport."

Groaning, I turned the car around and headed back toward King's Court Arms. This was exactly what I didn't want to do. The light was fading fast. I even considered swimming the Rio

Grande like a wetback and meeting the others on the opposite side. I pulled into the south parking lot one last time. I handed Garth my pistol and told him to stay with Jen and watch the sword. After carefully studying the shadowy corners of all the buildings, I made a mad dash into the complex.

As I burst through the doorway of my apartment, I was alarmed to see Renae Fenimore seated in a chair at the counter, bundled up in a warm sweatshirt, a pair of jeans, and her black suede jacket.

She heaved a sigh of relief and came to her feet. "Thank goodness you're still here! I was beginning to panic." Her suitcase was on the floor beside her.

"What are you doing?" I demanded.

"My uncle dropped me off, and Benny let me in to wait. Your message said you were headed for Mexico tonight. You're going because of the sword, am I right?"

"That's right—but I wasn't asking *you* to go with us!"

"I didn't figure you were. That was my own decision."

"Don't be ridiculous," I scoffed, and went into my bedroom to grab my birth certificate from my top dresser drawer.

She followed me. "Jim, it's okay. My professors are all cooperating. My uncle's not too keen on the whole thing, but he knew there was nothing he could say—"

"Well, *I* have a say," I retorted. I picked up her luggage and started back out the door. "I'm taking you home."

She followed me outside. "Jim, I was an exchange student in a town called Poza Rica. It's only about six hours from Veracruz. I know that area especially well. I have friends there who can help us. It would be stupid for you to go without me. You don't even speak Spanish."

"An old friend of mine is coming with us. He speaks it just fine."

"Does he know Mexico?"

I turned to face her. "Renae, I've already endangered your life twice in the last week. The odds are running against us. I couldn't live with myself if anything happened to you."

"Did you ever think I might feel the same way?" she asked.

I stood there staring. "But," I stammered, "I need you to be here when I come back. I need to know you're safe."

"Then your only hope is to let me come along." Her expression darkened. "They know where I'm staying, Jim. My aunt saw a man watching the house this afternoon."

If Jenny was in danger, certainly Renae was in the same predicament. I realized I had no choice. I had to bring her. Besides, she was right that Garth, Jenny, and I alone stood a good chance of getting completely lost in Mexico. Her knowledge might save us an infinite amount of time, as well as save our lives.

So there would be four members in this expedition. As I thought about it, if this journey had even half the hazards Muleki had warned us about—if this was to be a struggle more dangerous than any I had ever faced—there was no mortal fellowship I would have wanted to be with more, or from whom I could have gained greater strength and endurance, than the one I was with now: my kid sister, my best friend, and the girl I loved.

Call it the "Fellowship of the Sword." Indeed, as Jenny suggested, I felt a strange kinship to Frodo, the humble hobbit from Tolkein's trilogy. Like him, it was my quest to carry the One Ring to the eternal fires of Mordor. And all the while, the evil, penetrating eye of Sauron would be watching my every move, eagerly awaiting the moment when he could crush me in the grip of his terrible hand.

CHAPTER 16

Garth reported that several cars had driven past the parking lot very slowly while we were gone. I introduced Renae and Garth as quickly as I could, then pulled our vehicle back into the street.

No sooner had we reached the first stoplight when two automobiles deliberately pulled into the lane behind us—a blue Suburban with silver trim, and a gray Cavalier. Since it was now twilight, I couldn't make out the passengers' faces, but there were four silhouettes in each vehicle. They followed us all the way to Center Street, keeping a modest distance of fifty or so yards. At the intersection with University Avenue, the Suburban pulled into the other lane to hide behind a pickup full of high school girls. I did some fancy swerving in and out of the traffic all the way to the interstate. By the time we reached the on-ramp, I was confident that I'd shaken off the Cavalier, but I wasn't so sure about the Suburban. The sky had darkened; all I could see in the rearview mirror were headlights.

Our fuel gauge read less than a quarter tank. I'd planned to fill up before leaving town, but now the risk was too great. Gadianton patience had certainly been worn to the breaking point. Any stop—even for a few minutes—would assuredly draw them to move in. How far could I get on a quarter tank? Hopefully, we could fill up when I turned off the interstate at

Spanish Fork, another ten minutes up the road. It was the last fuel stop I recalled before Price, Utah—a hundred miles away.

We also had to find a way of organizing the trunk so Renae's luggage and the guitar case could fit in it. For now, the case was sitting upright in the middle of the backseat, with Garth fighting at every turn to keep it from falling on Renae's head.

We took the exit at Spanish Fork. There was a vehicle following right behind us. As we passed near a streetlight, I recognized it clearly as the blue Suburban.

"We have to find a way to shake him," I told everyone. "I don't think we have enough gas to reach Price."

"Duck into the city," Garth suggested.

The municipal center of Spanish Fork was west of the highway. I took Garth's suggestion, driving through residential neighborhoods at dangerous speeds and knocking my passengers about as I screeched around corners. Somehow, that bulky Suburban remained on my tail. You'd think such a crazy chase through city streets would attract the police, but even though we forced two other cars off the road, no one came to our assistance. Where was a cop when you needed one? Upon returning to the highway, I still hadn't shaken the mystery car, and now the fuel gauge looked even worse. As we climbed into Spanish Fork Canyon, the headlights of the Suburban continued shining through our back window.

I floored the gas pedal, but the Mazda was just too gutless on this terrain. I couldn't get it to exceed seventy miles an hour for any stretch of time. Just as the road curved downhill, another upward slope impaired our acceleration. Jenny leaned over to see the gas gauge again and gave me a concerned glance. It was now sitting just above empty.

"Don't worry," I told her. "It always goes fifty more miles on empty."

My words gave everyone hope, but to be honest, with the gas

pedal floored like it was, I couldn't believe the tank was going to give us much more than twenty-five. I started to think we should have just taken our chances and filled up with gas in Provo or Spanish Fork. Maybe my instincts were wrong. Maybe they wouldn't have tried anything in a public gas station. But surely they wouldn't hesitate to attack a stalled vehicle on the side of the road. I'd made a terrible mistake.

The landscape began to broaden. I was able to increase the speed to ninety. The Suburban did likewise. We left every other vehicle in our wake. Soon our gas gauge was reading *below* empty. It was just a matter of minutes, I thought. I felt the pistol in my jacket. Soon I would find out if I really had the nerve to use it. The car choked once, then regained power—the first symptom of a dying engine.

We came over a short rise and passed a darkened car on the side of the road. Instantly, its flashing red and blue lights burst into action. Yes! Never had I imagined that a police siren could sound so wonderful. And our luck didn't end there! Before the patrolman could pull onto the highway, the Suburban passed it as well. Somehow the officer decided that the larger vehicle was more deserving of a ticket.

My passengers erupted into applause and hoots of joy as we watched the Suburban pull over and the highway patrolman park behind him. They were fading well into the background as our car again choked for gas.

Lights appeared ahead—and not a moment too soon. We rolled off the highway on our last pocket of fumes and pulled up beside the gas pump of a country station called Cedar Haven. I felt certain that the inspiration of some crazy entrepreneur to build a place of business in such a remote locale was for no other reason than to save our lives this night.

I quickly started to fill the tank while Garth rearranged the trunk to accommodate all our luggage. Thankfully, we even found a spot for the guitar case. The tank seemed to take forever to fill. I gave up at an even ten dollars, and hung up the hose. Then I paid the man and we screeched off again into the night. The Suburban did not reappear.

We continued down the highway past Price and on toward Green River. Garth sat in front with the map. We saw no further evidence of our pursuers. I began to wonder if they'd turned around and driven back to Provo. Perhaps they'd astutely determined that it might be better to find out exactly where we were going rather than try to follow us in the dark. The only people who knew our destination for sure were my roommates and Renae's uncle. I began to fear they might be in danger. The Gadiantons, and perhaps even Todd Finlay, would certainly try to interrogate them. I decided to find a gas station in Green River to call and warn them.

It was ten thirty-five p.m. when Benny accepted the charges on my collect call.

"Where the heck are you?" he asked.

"I'd better not tell you any specifics," I said. "I wanted to warn you—people might be coming by the apartment, asking where we've gone."

"Somebody already came," Benny reported. "One of your classmates."

"Classmate? Who?"

"I didn't catch his name. He wanted to know where you were. He said you guys had planned to do a class project together this evening. Andrew told him not to expect you; that you'd gone all the way to Mexico to a hill called—now how did he pronounce that?—*El Cerro Vigia.*"

I groaned inwardly. It was too late.

"*Another* one called for you, too," added Benny. "I don't know what he wanted. Lars spoke to him."

"Is Lars there?" I asked, hoping for more details.

"Not at the moment," Benny replied. "When are you coming back?"

"A week. Maybe ten days. Listen, Benny. Don't talk to *anyone*. And don't tell anyone else where we've gone."

"You might be interested to know," Benny continued, "the Bernardians canceled all their meetings until further notice. It's as if all the head honchos just packed up and left. Lars is pretty upset. I wanted to thank you, Jim, for what you and your friend said this morning. I know it's kind of personal to tell you, but Allison and I saw the bishop tonight. Everything's gonna be okay. I love you, man."

"You take it easy, Benny. I'll see you later."

At almost the same moment, Renae got off the phone that stood opposite of mine.

"Nobody's been by my uncle's house," she said. "I told him not to talk to any strangers at all until I come back."

"The news wasn't so good on my end," I admitted. "Andrew told them everything. Still, I think we're at least a good three or four hours ahead of them. We've just got to keep moving."

We continued on into the night. Garth predicted we'd cross the Mexican border sometime the next afternoon. Around Moab, I had trouble keeping my eyes open. Garth took over the wheel and steered us on toward Cortez, Colorado.

As we drove south, the reflection of snow on the shoulders of the highway grew thinner. I only slept twenty minutes that whole night. The worst deterrent to a sound sleep was listening to Jenny in the back and that endless snore which would one day drive a husband crazy. She was the only person I knew who could make a snore sound effeminate—a crisp, clipped little mew. Renae, however, seemed to be sleeping without any trouble at all.

We reached Cortez at two a.m. and turned sharply south, traveling through the Navaho Indian Reservation with its ghostly silhouettes of towering mesas brooding over us like primeval gods. I knew this area was rife with legends of Indian mysticism and black magic. I was grateful when we reached Gallup, New Mexico at three-fifty a.m. At last we merged with a new interstate and proceeded on toward Albuquerque.

"You doin' all right?" I asked Garth.

He stretched his eyelids wide. "I was drifting off pretty badly about an hour back, but I seem to be okay now."

"Don't take any chances," I told him. "We can't afford to stop, but we especially can't afford to wreck."

The New Mexico sun was just beginning to rise as road signs announced our arrival in Albuquerque. At this moment, the only sound worse than Jenny's snoring was the growling in my stomach. We spotted the Golden Arches and pulled off the highway to enjoy hot breakfast biscuits from McDonald's.

Afterwards, I told Jenny it was her turn to drive. She sternly objected.

"I can't drive here—not on an interstate! Semi-trucks like to crowd out little cars like mine just for amusement. Let me drive when we get back on a normal road."

"That won't be until we reach Mexico," I said.

"And believe me," added Renae, "if you hate crazy drivers, you'll want to drive in Mexico as little as possible."

"This is a long trip, sis," I concluded. "You gotta pull your weight."

Reluctantly, Jenny took her place behind the wheel. Garth sat beside her. I was sure I'd now be able to enjoy several hours of uninterrupted slumber in the comfort of Renae's lap. However, not ten minutes after we'd changed interstates and continued our southward route toward El Paso, Texas, I was jolted as the car lost power and began slowing down.

I sat up. "What's the matter?"

"I don't know!" cried Jenny. "The engine just shut itself off.

Didn't I tell you? This always happens to me! It's a curse!"

The Mazda rolled onto the shoulder and came to a stop. Jenny tried the ignition several more times. It wouldn't turn over. I asked her to move aside and give me a shot at it, but my efforts made no difference. I popped the hood and Garth and I climbed out to investigate—not because either of us knew anything about engines, just because it seemed like the appropriate macho-type thing to do.

The two of us glowered at the engine, still humming from the sound of churning steam in the radiator. Of course we couldn't make heads or tails of anything. I tried grabbing this or that to see if it appeared loose. All I got for my efforts was a greasy hand.

"Well," I said to Garth. "This might be the end of the line."

"Don't give up the ship 'til it's sunk," he replied.

Garth and I left the girls with the car and marched across to the other side of the interstate, setting our sights on a construction warehouse about a quarter mile in the distance that we hoped had a phone for calling tow trucks.

While holding apart a barbed-wire fence so Garth could crawl through it, I added to my pessimism by saying, "Even if it *can* be fixed, it might exhaust all our finances."

"Have more faith, Jimbo," was Garth's response.

That was a hard thing for me to muster at the moment. I felt like if God were truly behind us, why were we experiencing all these hassles?

At the warehouse, a caretaker in overalls was nice enough to let us call the nearest tow company. He even got on the line to give the switchboard lady directions. She promised that a truck would be by to rescue us in about forty minutes.

We thanked the gentleman in overalls and made our way back across the fields and fences to our dead Mazda 626. But as we climbed the rise to the asphalt surface of the interstate, I saw what I thought had been impossible.

Parked behind our Mazda was a bright blue Suburban with silver trim.

CHAPTER 17

In spite of an oncoming barrage of northbound traffic, including two or three semi-trucks, I bolted across the road to reach our Mazda and the Suburban. I only vaguely remember the sounds of brakes screeching and cars honking as vehicles swerved to keep from running me over. Even more vague is the memory of Garth's voice calling out something from behind which sounded like, "False alarm!"

All I knew was that I had to reach our car—save Jenny and Renae! How could I have left them alone on the highway? I hoped one of them had seen me place the pistol in the glove box last night and was presently using it in self-defense.

As I drew nearer, it was clear that was not the case. The hood of the Mazda was still sitting open. My sister and one of the men from the Suburban were looking over the engine. He was an older man—perhaps Mehrukenah in a cowboy hat. There were others still inside the Suburban, but I didn't take the time to count.

"Hey!" I shouted across the highway.

Jenny looked up at me, alarmed by the tension in my voice. The man in the cowboy hat perked up as well. As I crossed the southbound side of the interstate, again causing a few tires to skid and horns to honk, I realized this man was not a Gadianton. He must have been a proselyte to their evil cause.

"Get away from there!" I growled upon reaching my car.

The man in the cowboy hat threw up his arms and backed away from the engine.

"Just seein' if I could help," he defended. "Pardon my neighborliness."

"What's the matter with you?" Jenny asked me angrily.

The man stomped back to the blue Suburban. I realized his other passengers were a mother and a flock of wide-eyed children.

"See if I ever help anybody on the highway again," the man called back.

He climbed into the Suburban and drove away. I noticed the license plate was from Texas, not Utah. Jenny was scowling at me.

I shrugged sheepishly. "I thought it was the same car that followed us last night."

"Don't be stupid," scoffed Jenny. "The one last night was *dark* blue, and it didn't have luggage racks."

I heard Renae laughing uproariously in the back seat. Garth arrived, also laughing, as well as scolding me for almost getting flattened by traffic. An hour later, as the tow truck arrived, I thought about that poor offended Samaritan and how he'd stomped off in the cloud of steam that came out of his ears, and I was finally able to laugh at myself.

The tow truck charged us forty-five dollars, which fully obliterated a quarter of everything I had left in my personal account. The driver dropped us off at a generic garage with a tobacco-spitting owner and mechanics who hadn't washed their overalls in at least five years. They did a quick inspection of the problem and announced that the fuel injector belt had snapped and needed to be replaced.

"How much is that gonna cost?" I asked.

"The part itself's only about twenty dollars," the owner replied. "But the labor's gonna run you at least another seventy-five. See, they gotta dig quite a bit to get to it."

I sighed drearily. "Fine. When will it be done?"

"Well, it's a dealer part so we'll have to run uptown to get it. I got all these other cars ahead of you. I'm afraid we're not gonna be able to start on it until tomorrow morning."

I tried to moan and complain a little more to rush things along, but to no avail. We were stuck in Albuquerque, New Mexico, for the night in a neighborhood where the mayor was clearly not a resident.

The good news, if you could call it that, was that a dive called the Sandia Motel was only a half block away. Under the watchful eyes of at least a dozen street urchins, we toted our luggage down the block, across the street, and into the office. Each room was thirty bucks a night—another five if we wanted to view the current triple-X feature movie. Needless to say, we saved the five bucks. I tried to save more money by suggesting we get only one room and hang a blanket between the beds for privacy, but the girls adamantly objected. Inside the girls' room we did an inventory of our remaining finances. Renae had added another ninety dollars to the pool. After paying the repair bill, we'd have approximately five hundred and thirty dollars left to make it to Veracruz, Mexico.

The day passed slowly, and boredom reigned. About five o'clock we ate supper at a nearby Skipper's Fish and Chips. As we walked back to the motel, I noticed two young boys—street urchins from the gang we'd seen earlier in the day—standing near our motel room doors. Upon seeing us, one signaled to the other and they both made a hasty retreat.

Garth and I discovered that they'd tried to break into our motel room. Though the effort was unsuccessful, I made a vow to never leave the sword unattended again. Muleki's warning that it had a way of attracting new owners seemed to be accurate.

That night, Jenny and Garth ventured out again to do some window shopping while Renae and I watched the network's selection of sitcoms in my room. I admit, it felt a little awkward being alone in a motel room with a girl. Not that I had any ideas. I guess I just wondered how I'd have explained it if my bishop had burst in. It might sound corny, but I felt more comfortable sitting in one of the chairs across the room.

When Garth and Jenny returned, my sister announced that she had a present for me.

"There's a little antique shop a couple blocks from here. I thought you might find a use for this."

She brought her gift out of a paper sack and thrust it forward. It appeared to be some kind of leather scabbard and belt.

"It was only fifteen dollars," said Jenny. "The lady said it was Chinese, though I don't think she believed it was very old. I figured it might make the sword easier to tote around."

"If you have to, you could keep it on your person at all times," added Garth.

"But I'd look ridiculous," I said.

"No," countered Renae. "You'd be in Mexico. Mexicans expect Americans to look ridiculous."

I took the silver-plated sword out of the guitar case and carefully slipped it into the scabbard. Then I strapped the belt around my waist. "What do you think?" I asked.

"You look like a Samurai warrior," said Renae.

I felt a rush of pride. Now I understood why Genghis Khan felt invincible—so much so that he conquered all the lands between the Pacific Ocean and the Black Sea. *I could do the same,* I thought. *In fact, I could go much farther . . .*

These thoughts couldn't be good. I felt conspicuous and placed the sword and scabbard back into the guitar case.

"Thanks," I told Jenny while I was still fighting some weird feelings swirling in my head. "It could come in quite handy."

After the girls retired to their own room, I suggested to Garth that maybe *he* should be responsible for the sword. "I don't know if my spirituality is quite up to par."

He shook his head. "Even if that's true, I don't have your stamina." He put his hand on my shoulder. "Like Muleki said, the most important thing for us is to stay as close to God as possible. If the powers of that sword are as real as I suspect, our only defense is going to be righteousness. We need to truly understand what it means to strive for perfection in every way—in our thoughts, our words, and our actions."

That night I lay awake for quite some time after Garth had fallen asleep. I couldn't get over how attached I was getting to the sword. It frightened me a little. Somehow the ancient weapon gave me a sense of security. I was grateful Garth had declined my offer. In reality, I didn't want anybody else to touch it. The sword was *mine.*

I shook off these feelings. At least I had the presence of mind to know the feelings were wrong. But as sleep overtook my thoughts, and I drifted into a dream about Roman legions on the field of battle, I wondered if I'd always be able to shake them off so easily.

* * *

The mechanics at the repair shop didn't declare our car "good as new" until after one o'clock the next day. Their bill was ten dollars higher than they'd estimated. Albuquerque inflation, I'm sure.

So twenty-nine hours after our breakdown, our Mazda was again carrying the four of us toward Mexico and the Hill Cumorah. Renae commented how lucky we were that our automobile had broken down in the United States.

"All cars in Mexico are Fords, Chevys, Volkswagens, and Nissans," she recalled. "I'm not sure they've ever seen a Mazda."

I didn't feel lucky at all when I heard that fact. Who knew what part would wear out next? I had visions of being stranded in some podunk Mexican town, waiting two months for some three-dollar factory-made bolt to arrive in the mail.

Also, if our Mazda was going to stick out like a sore thumb, it wouldn't be hard for the enemy to spot it either. If my hunch was right and Mehrukenah's gang was indeed following us to Mexico, our delay in Albuquerque had given them plenty of time to get ahead of us. By now they might have set up lookout posts all along the way. We continued down the interstate toward El Paso, Texas. About the time we passed a New Mexican town named "Truth or Consequences," Garth peeked at the speedometer.

"You're going eighty miles an hour," he notified me.

"We're fine," I explained. "These are long stretches. If there's a highway patrolman, I'll spot him a mile away."

"That's not the point," said Garth. "We're striving for perfection, remember?"

"Garth," I said tiredly, "I think the Lord would approve of me trying to make up for lost time."

"I don't believe that," Garth declared. "I think the Lord would want us to obey the law of the land."

"Are you serious?"

"As a heart attack," he replied. "If we're going to be as righteous as possible, we can't make up our own rules along the way. Latter-day Saints can be guilty of that sometimes. Pornography and profanity are wrong, unless we find them in good movies and music. Stealing is wrong, except when pirating computer disks or videotapes. Cheating is wrong, except on our income taxes. Gambling is wrong, unless it's a state-supported lottery—"

"I can't believe this," I whined. "You're straining at gnats."

"If you've been speeding all your life, it becomes a pretty big gnat. You believe murder and suicide are wrong, don't you? Then how can you continue to speed, knowing that statistics have been compiled for decades proving that excessive speeds can cause either?"

"You're saying if I speed, I'm a potential murderer? Give me a major break!"

"God can't look upon sin with the least degree of allowance," Garth proclaimed. "Do you really understand what that statement means? If we want to keep God's spirit as close to us throughout this trip as possible, we can't indulge in things we know are wrong."

"He's right, Jim," agreed Renae.

Great, I thought. Now he had the women on his side.

"All right!" I grudgingly agreed. "I'm dropping down to sixty-five."

"Please, don't do it grudgingly," Garth pleaded. "How many people find themselves forced to strive for utter perfection and know how it feels—even if it's just for a week?"

"But no one can be perfect," I said.

"Maybe we can't be as perfect as Christ. But if eventual perfection wasn't an achievable goal, why have the Atonement or repentance in the first place? We can do it for a week, Jim. Even if we can't, we have to try harder than ever before in our lives. Our success depends on it. This is a great opportunity. Think of it as a great blessing!"

I'd never felt that a blessing could be so much of a curse. Not only did we have to putt down the highway at a turtle's pace, but we couldn't even play the radio for fear a song with questionable lyrics would come on. This was ridiculous! I'd heckled every anti-rock-and-roll talk I'd ever been forced to listen to. It was just music!

I was of the opinion that if people were afraid of being influenced by somebody else's sins, maybe they shouldn't read the paper or watch the news or read Shakespeare—or even *live life*! Only one argument in my life had ever come close to changing that opinion. It was a statement by my favorite mission companion, Elder Bigler. Yes, he admitted, we couldn't avoid the sinful influences of the world, but did we have to pay money to see and hear them firsthand?

But even that argument didn't hold water after a while. I was always of the opinion that knowledge was power. Seeing life in all its shades of black and white could only make me a stronger person in the end. Maybe that outlook wasn't true for everyone, but I felt certain it was true for me.

"If I don't hear some kind of music," I shouted, "I'm going to go nuts!"

Garth's prescription came in the form of a cassette tape of *Saturday's Warrior*. I rolled my eyes in ultimate revulsion.

"Anything but that! Please! Anything but that!"

He tried Michael McLean.

"Help!" I chirped. "Will somebody help me *pleeeeeasssse!*"

As I glanced in the rearview mirror, I noticed that Renae was frowning. She looked disappointed in me. That shut me up. I moped in silence. Later, they tried cassettes of Kenneth Cope, Felicia Sorensen, and even an upbeat rendition of Primary songs by Brett Raymond.

It was somewhere around Las Cruces, New Mexico, that my spirit finally started to break down a little. I couldn't admit it to anyone, but I was actually enjoying the songs. I began to wonder what arrogance within me had caused my outbursts. What was it about me that made it so necessary to tear down things that obviously gave other people so much pleasure?

The feeling didn't stop there. It spread deeper. I began to wonder why I did so many similar things in other circumstances. Why did I spend so much energy justifying my weaknesses rather than admitting them and finding a solution? It seemed such a hopeless part of my personality. Did the sickness have a cure?

As Brett Raymond sang the lyric, "Whenever I touch a velvet rose, or walk by our lilac tree, I'm glad that I live in this beautiful world Heavenly Father created for me," I felt a tear come to my eye. Nobody saw it. The girls were napping in the back, and Garth had aimed his attention down the highway. Discreetly, I wiped the tear away. When I felt my composure had been fully regained, I spoke my first words to Garth since my temper had flared.

"You know," I began, "when I was a little kid, I thought everything was totally black and white. I remember being so hurt, so disappointed when I realized that everything was gray. As I've grown older, it seems I've been just as disappointed and struggled just as hard against the awareness that everything is really as black and white as I first thought it was."

"You're right," Garth agreed. "There are only two forces at work in this world—black and white. Only people are gray."

CHAPTER 18

As we approached El Paso, Texas, I got my first up-close view of a foreign country. The interstate ran parallel to the Rio Grande for a short span. On the American side of the river, industry was booming—high-tech factories and mirror-polished office buildings. On the Mexican side, the hillside revealed only dilapidated adobe dwellings and bedrock roads. The contrast was quite disturbing.

"Since we're taking our car in, we should get Mexican car insurance," Renae suggested.

"I think we're gonna have to risk it," I said. "Money's a little tight."

"That's not a smart thing to do," said Renae. "An accident in Mexico is considered a criminal as well as a civil offense. Even running into a fence, you could go to jail."

My phobia of Mexican prisons resurfaced.

"Lead the way," I conceded.

We took the next exit and drove around the downtown streets of El Paso until we found a sign reading *Palm's Mexican Insurance*. We purchased seven days' worth, expending our resources by another fifty dollars. In return, I was handed a lime-green sticker and advised to put it in my window. If I didn't, Renae said I ran the risk of having a Mexican driver deliberately ram into me in hopes of receiving a payoff. Already, Mexico was sounding like a really charming place.

We also bought a three-dollar tourist map. Upon returning to the car, Garth and I took a moment to locate Veracruz. It was a big oil port on the Gulf of Mexico, way down where the country's landmass makes its eastward bend toward the Yucatan Peninsula. My finger pinpointed our final destination—Santiago Tuxtla. It looked to be a blink-and-miss town about a hundred miles south of Veracruz, near a big lake called Catemaco, maybe thirty miles inland from the ocean. We still faced two thousand grueling Mexican miles. According to Renae, there was no such thing as an interstate in Mexico. From here, the going might get very slow.

Renae pointed down the block at a sign that read *Exchange Rate: 2875 Pesos.* "We should exchange our money over there. You'll always get a better rate on this side of the border."

I traded four hundred dollars and received in return over a million pesos.

"I'm a Mexican millionaire!" I raved.

Foreign currency was a whole new experience for me. The bills were multi-colored and the coins were fat. This was gonna take some getting used to. My whole perception of the value of things was severely distorted.

I handed Garth half our pesos and provided Renae with the remainder of our American green, about one hundred and thirteen dollars. Garth stuffed the greater portion of his money into the bottom of his shoe.

"Of course, you know," I teased, "the odor you're giving that cash will make it very difficult to spend."

Renae also advised us to enjoy one last American meal, so upon spying a nearby Pizza Hut, we accordingly gorged ourselves.

"Two things to remember to avoid getting sick while we're down there," Garth instructed, lapping up a string of pizza cheese off his chin. "First, remember to ask if the water is *purifi-*

cada. A lot of places won't purify it, so be prepared to drink a lot of soda pop."

"And second," continued Renae, "don't eat anything that grows in, or on, the ground—carrots, potatoes, that kind of stuff. Mexican farmers sometimes use human excrement to fertilize the soil."

Such conversation served to make our meal all the more palatable.

After dinner, we hopped back on the interstate and soon found ourselves in the midst of several spaghetti-twisted on-ramps and off-ramps. One of the off-ramps was preceded by a sign that said *Mexico: Ciudad de Juarez.* After crossing the Rio Grande, we took our place behind a fast-moving line of cars passing through what appeared to be a row of toll booths. I noticed to our left that the line to get *out* of Mexico went on for a mile.

"Everybody take out your birth certificates and passports," Garth warned.

But when we reached the row of booths, the border guard just took one look inside our Mazda and waved us through.

I glared at Garth. "Looks like I didn't need it after all."

Garth shrugged his shoulders. "Well, I know we'll need them to get out."

Now I was officially, for the first time in my life, inside a foreign country. We'd watched the climate grow warmer and dryer with every mile as we drove southward. Here there was absolutely no evidence of winter. It felt rather peculiar to be sweating in December.

The first thing that struck me was how old the cars were, some scrap heaps literally held together with nothing more than tape and twine. I don't think I'd ever seen so many Volkswagen Bugs. Every tree along the thoroughfare was painted white about four feet up the trunk. I thought maybe it was to ward off some kind of insect.

"What's the matter with the trees?" I asked Renae.

"It's decorative," said Renae.

"Painting a tree is decorative?"

"They do the same thing in Guatemala," added Garth.

A moment later, we found ourselves floundering in the bustling streets of Juarez, Mexico. This place was a circus! Bumper stickers telling other cars they were driving too close was a sadly missed commodity.

"We need to find the Pan-American Highway," said Renae. "You're gonna have to ask somebody for directions."

As we hit a stoplight, a bony-looking man on a bicycle rode up to my window.

"You look for souvenir?" he asked. "Eh, souvenir?"

He leaned closer and grinned at me wryly, flinching his eyebrows. "You look for young girls? Pretty girls?"

He noticed Jenny and Renae in back. "Maybe hotel, eh?"

The girls bristled with offense. "Drive on," Renae insisted.

"We're looking for the Pan-American Highway," I told the man.

"Souvenir?" the man repeated.

"No," I said. Then slowly I repeated, "We're-looking-for-the-Pan-American-Highway."

The man gave no indication of understanding a word I was saying. Garth leaned over to translate my question for him, but the man had already pedaled away from the car and was riding on ahead saying, "You follow! You follow!"

"Don't follow," said Renae as the light turned green. "He only knows enough English to con the tourists. He just wants you to follow him so you'll feel obligated to pay some money. If anything, he'll get us more lost than we already are. Then, if you don't pay him what he wants, he might smash a dent in your hood and ride away."

"Who *can* we ask then?" I said in frustration.

"Pull over here," said Garth.

I stopped at the curb. Garth opened his window, speaking in Spanish to a couple walking down the sidewalk. The only word I recognized was *Panamericana.*

Cordially, the man and his girlfriend pointed toward the east.

Garth waved his thanks. "*Gracias.*" He turned to me. "Take a left—not at this street, but the next one. You'll know it because it's a 'one way.'"

The filth and poverty I saw over the next few blocks left me speechless. I'd never seen anything like it. I guessed this was what they called 'culture shock.' Streets were chokingly thin. Everything looked dilapidated. *Everything.* There didn't appear to be a stainless, sturdy building in sight. And bright orange and blue paint just didn't look right on stucco and adobe.

My sheltered existence in the western United States was grossly apparent. I'd never really seen a slum before. Oh, there were a few bad places in Portland, but nothing like this. And yet despite the poverty, the people themselves looked remarkably clean and well dressed—especially the girls. I might have thought it was illegal for a women to wear pants. I never saw a girl in anything but a dress, and the school children were always in uniform.

Advertising was posted everywhere! On telephone poles, fences, buildings, sidewalks, trees—you name it. Most of the time the posters were faded or torn, having hung in the same spot for a decade. And just like in America, massive billboards along the Pan-American Highway shouted at us all the way to the city limits. Half of them were hailing the slogan "*¡Solidaridad!*" which Renae translated as "Solidarity!"—a political slogan of the Mexican government to unify all of Mexico's states into a solid national unit.

"Are they on the verge of revolution or something?" I asked.

"Not necessarily, but that is a continual threat in many Latin American countries," explained Renae. "Mexico, though, is one of the more stable."

American industry south of the border was alive and well. Everywhere I turned were businesses touting American-made products from Coca-Cola to Kinney Shoes.

We pulled in for gas at a Pemex station. Actually, *all* the gas stations were called Pemex—short for Petroleum Mexico. As we stopped our car, it was immediately surrounded. Two eager boys took a tin can filled with soapy water and sent a wave across my windshield, afterwards vigorously wiping with towels. I was impressed. Few places in the U.S. gave you this kind of service anymore.

Sales people approached all four windows, peddling various kinds of jewelry and food. Jen couldn't resist the charm of a five-year-old girl distributing tiny packages of Chiclets gum. She bought four of them for an American quarter. The guy at my window displayed a plate stacked with skinless, dripping fruit, brilliantly colored in red, yellow, and green.

"What's this stuff?" I asked.

"It's called tuna or *atun*—the fruit of the cactus flower. If you want one, ask him 'How much?' *¿Cuanto cuesta?*"

The man said five hundred pesos. Wincing, I replied, "No way!" and shooed him off. He was persistent, but the gas tank was full, so I paid the attendant thirty thousand pesos and prepared to drive away.

"What about the boys who did your windows?" Renae asked me.

"I have to pay them, too? I thought they were just being nice."

"Nobody here is just being nice," said Renae. "This is how they feed their families."

I handed one of the boys a fifty peso coin. He looked very disappointed.

"What more does he want?" I wondered.

"Jim, fifty pesos is less than two cents," Renae informed me.

She handed him a one thousand peso coin. He looked significantly happier and went on to the next windshield.

"Are we gonna have to pay everybody who so much as waves hello?" I asked.

"As many as we can," said Renae, "or you'll make enemies real fast."

We continued down the Pan-American Highway. My eyes were darting from place to place with such wonderment, Garth almost insisted that he do the driving. This was indeed a different world, a world as different to me as the world of the Nephites.

We passed the Juarez Airport, or *Aeropuerto*, and set our navigational sights on the city of Chihuahua, two hundred and fifty miles into the Mexican interior. The sun was dropping into the Mexican desert, providing the sky with a bright and friendly blanket of red, and making me finally feel relaxed and welcome for the first time.

But the feeling only lasted another ten miles. A little farther into the desert, in what I'd have termed the middle of nowhere, there was another inspection post. A line of a half dozen cars was moving through it a lot slower than the one we'd been through already.

"Maybe this is where we'll need our birth certificates and passports," said Jenny.

As we neared the front of the line, I noticed a station wagon parked about a hundred yards up the road. *Strange*, I thought. The car didn't appear to have any connection with the official vehicles or personnel who talked with the drivers. A man was leaning on its hood, wearing dark sunglasses. He seemed to be studying all the cars that drove by. As our Mazda reached the inspection station, the sunglasses man unfolded his arms and took several steps toward us for a closer look.

The man in the inspection booth asked me, in a heavy Mexican accent, for my tourist card.

"My what?"

Renae spoke to him in Spanish for a moment. In the course of the conversation we learned, to our utter dismay, that we would have to go all the way back to the original border post and show our birth certificates and car registration in order to get a tourist card. Such was the required ticket if we wanted to get any farther into the country.

The sunglasses man was still watching us as I turned the Mazda around and aimed it back toward Juarez. Nobody else seemed to notice the man or care. As I looked across the desert, this appeared to be the only road leading into the Mexican interior for hundreds of miles in either direction.

My paranoia started stirring. If the Gadiantons had successfully deciphered Andrew's information and determined our destination, there were only four or five major border crossings that they would have to be concerned about. If I'd been them, and if I had enough manpower, I'd have positioned lookouts at each of those crossings. I started to wonder how foolish it may have been to come into the country the way we'd come. Maybe we should have crossed at some totally obscure location like Del Rio, Texas, or Nogales, Arizona. For that matter, maybe my earlier idea of swimming the river wasn't so absurd.

I decided to shrug him off. The man in sunglasses could have been standing there for any one of a thousand reasons. Besides, if he was the enemy, why wasn't he following us back into Juarez? It was aggravating enough having to drive all twenty miles back to the border. I'd never been all that patient with bureaucracy—even in America. But in Mexico, I had no idea who to complain to.

Renae apologized. "Sorry. I've never driven a car into Mexico, so how could I have known?"

We waited in the line of cars a full hour to get back through to the American side to get a tourist card.

"This is it for your firearm," said Garth. "If they search our car and find it, we can kiss this trip good-bye."

"What if I took my birth certificate and registration and hiked up to the border post by myself, without having to drive through?" I wondered.

"I think it's too late," said Renae.

She was right. We were in the far right lane of a six-lane line of cars. This conveyor belt was moving no direction but forward, and there was no way to turn around.

"What do you suggest?" I asked.

"Toss it into the river," Garth replied.

Sighing, I stuck the .357 Magnum into an old McDonalds sack and threw it into the shallow, gray waters of the Rio Grande.

After passing through the border and then turning around to come back, we waited in another line for twenty minutes. At last I presented my birth certificate and Jenny's car registration. All I got in return was a tiny slip of paper that said "Tourist Card." *What a waste of time!* I thought. I'd driven all the way back there for this? Nevertheless, when we reached the interior inspection post again, that piece of paper was our magic golden ticket. We passed right on through.

The station wagon with the man in sunglasses was no longer there. My suspicions about him being a Gadianton spy were obviously a mistake.

The drive to Chihuahua would have to be executed under a darkened sky. Earlier in the day, Renae had expressed some concerns about driving in Mexico at night. Her reasons soon became dramatically clear. The highway was comfortably divided for the next few miles, but then it combined into a single two-lane road. Not only were the lanes cardboard-thin, there was no shoulder if we wanted to stop. The asphalt seemed to have been laid across the desert without any consideration for making it level with the surrounding ground. Thence, there was an eight-inch cliff on either side of the road! One false move would send an automobile hurling into the desert like a tumbleweed. To make matters worse, there were no reflectors or painted lines to tell you where this cliff began. Since a greater portion of the road was in disrepair, there was often no center line either. None of these obstacles seemed to slow down Mexican traffic though, which at night consisted of mostly semi-trucks and buses.

In short, it was a total nightmare! My muscles constricted every time headlights drew near and whizzed past. Our average speed was about forty miles an hour. I learned quickly that the term *peligro* meant dangerous, because signs used the word to define highway conditions at almost every turn. Needless to say, nobody slept for the next two and a half hours.

About halfway to Chihuahua, I stopped the car in a one-horse town named El Sueco to catch my breath. There, as we sat parked in front of the white picket fence of a small church, I got out of the car and walked around a bit, taking in the soothing sound of Spanish music coming from someone's nearby radio. Everyone else got out to stretch as well.

"Do you want me to drive?" asked Garth.

"No," I quickly replied. My nerves were frazzled enough by my own driving. I didn't need them to frazzle worse trying to "backseat drive" somebody else.

Renae noted a sign on the roadside that read *Neuvas Casas Grandes*, with an arrow indicating a right turn at the next intersection, about fifty yards ahead.

"The Mormon colonies are off in that direction," she said. "I've never been there, but I . . ."

I didn't hear the rest of what she said. I was too busy watching a certain station wagon make a careful approach, spot us, and then ease on the brake, as if the driver was verifying that we were precisely who he thought we were. I assumed the man in sunglasses was still its pilot, though it was too dark to tell. The station wagon idled for several seconds. I was about to step up to the driver and ask him what he wanted, but then he abruptly hit the gas, whipped past us, and sped away. Garth had been watching the phenomenon as well.

"Who was that?" he asked.

"I don't know," I replied.

So the station wagon *was* following us. Nevertheless, I decided not to alarm the others yet. Something compelled me to open the trunk. I just wanted to make sure the sword was still in the guitar case. It was, along with the scabbard Jenny had bought me in Albuquerque. I decided to keep it up front with me for the rest of the journey. I don't know why. It just made me feel more secure. I tied it securely around my waist and climbed awkwardly into the front seat.

"A bit bulky, isn't it?" asked Garth.

I shrugged. The sword fit perfectly under the dashboard. I didn't feel like it was in the way at all, but even if it had been, I'm certain I'd have endured the discomfort.

As we left El Sueco, I realized I wasn't feeling the same tension as I had during the first half of our drive to Chihuahua. The road had not improved, but somehow I was able to navigate the obstacles with much more deftness and precision. A good portion of the highway still lacked a center line, but I could almost sense a natural barrier which kept me from going off the edge. My speed increased to sixty-five.

"The sign says seventy kilometers per hour," Garth remarked.

"But that's only forty-five *miles* per hour!" I grumbled.

"Perfection. Remember?"

I slowed down, and sometime between then and the end of the Millennium, we arrived at the city limits of Chihuahua.

CHAPTER 19

It was midnight, and everyone was of the opinion that nothing in this world could feel as glorious right now as a soft, cool bed in a clean hotel. Renae had led us to believe hotel prices in Mexico were cheap, but from our initial investigation, her assumption was sadly inaccurate. Renae's experience in Mexico was limited to an area much farther south, where touring gringos were few and far between. Chihuahua was still reasonably close to the border, and hotel owners were all too aware of the liberality of American spending. Room costs were about the same as in the United States—if anything, they were a little higher.

The highway was divided the last few miles into Chihuahua, as well as along the main strip through town, giving us a wide-angle view of all the hotel signs. As we began checking each of them out, we soon understood how they got away with such inflated prices. It was simply a matter of supply and demand. We couldn't find a single vacancy anywhere in the city—to say nothing of finding two adjacent rooms. It was worse than finding lodging in Las Vegas on a weekend.

After checking a dozen places on the main strip, we plotted a course for the older part of the city. After coming up empty at two more prospective inns, and after facing the embarrassment of having to back up twice on one-way streets, we spotted the flickering white neon sign of the Hotel Apolo.

The couch in the lobby should have been our first clue of the hotel's condition. It was worn to paleness and the springs had collapsed, making the only possible seat in the very middle. The manager was a squalid-looking geezer with nose hair comprising most of his moustache. For a room with two double beds, he quoted us a price of ninety-eight thousand pesos (thirty-five bucks). Our exhaustion bound us to his offer.

I paid the man and signed my name and address to the register. The manager took his pen back and added the number ten under my name, handing us the corresponding key. After climbing a flight of creaking stairs, we braved the dim and peeling hallway in search of a door with a number matching our key. The decal on the door had long since been torn away, and the number "10" was drawn in with a pencil. Jenny turned the knob and entered first. Two seconds later, she shrieked and reeled backward, caught by Garth. A cockroach with the wingspan of a sparrow was scaling the wall above the rust-stained porcelain sink.

"Look! The National Bird!" I said rudely.

I did a karate-style kick, adding the appropriate yell, and crushed the beast under my shoe. Its carcass stuck there a moment, then dropped conveniently into the drain. Putting my hand on the hilt of my sword, I did an oriental bow for Renae and then for Jenny. But when I went to wash its remains down the pipes, no water came out of the faucet.

Garth went into the bathroom to investigate the shower. He called out to us, "The water doesn't work in here, either."

"These beds are disgusting," winced Renae. "I don't think I can sleep on this blanket." She leaned down to smell it. "I take that back. I *know* I can't sleep on this blanket."

"Let's get our money back," Jenny insisted.

The four of us marched down to the manager, our eyes ablaze, but he didn't seem influenced by them a bit. In Spanish,

Garth told him our opinion of the situation. He responded and shook his head.

Garth turned to me. "He says he can't give us all our money back. Only half."

I stomped around the lobby. "I can't believe this! Of all the dishonest—!" I turned back to Garth. "Tell him we'll take it out of his hide!"

"Let's just take half the money and go," suggested Renae.

The manager spoke again.

Garth interpreted. "He says he has two other newer rooms which actually adjoin, though they're quite small. We can have them for 'only' fifty thousand pesos more."

"Do they have running water?" asked Jenny.

Garth asked the question and the manager replied. This time Renae translated. "He says the city shuts off the water supply during certain hours of the night. It should be fine in the morning."

"Let's see these other rooms," I grumbled.

The manager dropped a different pair of keys into my palm, and we headed back up the stairs. The newer rooms were at the very end of the same hallway as room ten. They weren't much larger than rabbit hutches—one single bed in each room, but they did smell slightly newer. At least the blankets looked fresh. With our revulsion only slightly tempered, we agreed to endure the night. Renae even haggled the price down twenty-five thousand pesos.

"Next time," Garth said, "we need to insist on seeing the room before we hand over any money."

Garth and I went down to retrieve our luggage. We decided it might be best to park the car a few blocks away, where the neighborhood looked a bit more private and secluded. Garth took the bags up while I went to park the car.

Though it was after one a.m., the town hadn't seemed to slow down much. A good deal of traffic was still honking in the streets and the sidewalks were fairly crowded. As Renae promised, people sent me some pretty strange glances upon seeing the sword and scabbard around my waist. I started to worry that carrying such a weapon unconcealed might not only look ridiculous, it might be illegal. I decided while out in public it might be best if I cloaked it somewhat under a towel or sweater.

I noticed a few Christmas decorations here and there—strings of tinsel and colored lights in a couple of windows. Actually, my walk back to the hotel was quite refreshing. I even stopped a moment in front of the nightclub neighboring the hotel to listen to Phil Collins' "Land of Confusion," playing inside on the stereo.

The lyrics were tame enough. I didn't feel I was violating Garth's appeal for perfection. The song made me feel comforted, like I wasn't as far from home as I might have imagined.

When I returned to my room, Garth was asleep in my sleeping bag on the floor, his Spanish edition of the Book of Mormon—the same one he'd dragged with him everywhere since his mission to Guatemala—sitting open under his hand. What a guy. He'd left me the bed. I dropped down on the mattress, the cold steel of the sword in its scabbard still tucked under my arm. Rock music from the neighboring nightclub seeped up through the floorboards. I didn't care. I was so tired I could have slept through BYU's halftime marching band.

* * *

I awakened sometime around seven. The music was gone. Jenny's chirping snore, audible even through the thin walls of the adjoining room, was the only sound.

I had "cotton mouth." I recalled seeing a purified water dispenser at the top of the stairway, so I got up and went out into the hallway, still toting the sword and scabbard. I proceeded toward the stairway in my bare feet, feeling every speck of sand and dirt from the unvacuumed strip of faded carpet that ran down the center. Passing by the infamous room ten, I was surprised to see that the door was open. Hadn't we locked it before we went back down to complain to the manager? Maybe he'd found another sucker.

As I looked into the room, my eyes widened. The place was a shambles. Furniture had been overturned; the mattresses had been flung off the beds; someone had even tried to rip the sink out of the wall—either that or my karate kick had a delayed reaction. This room was only five doors away from ours. I couldn't believe we hadn't heard anything. The four of us must have been awfully tired; either that or all the music and ruckus from the bar downstairs had led our subconscious to think nothing of it.

Not quite sure how to interpret this situation, I continued walking to the end of the hallway and got my drink from the dispenser. Maybe the manager had taken our complaints to heart and decided to start remodeling early this morning.

I felt an urge to go downstairs and see if the manager was still awake. As the front desk came into view, nobody was there. The registry was sitting open on the counter. The last page—the one I had signed—had been torn from the book. I looked around, a feeling of dread coiling inside me. I considered calling out; maybe the manager would emerge from a back room.

Then I noticed the streak of dried blood on the carpet behind the counter. I heard a noise. Glass fell and broke in the back room, followed by a muffled groan.

Drawing the silver sword, I moved carefully behind the counter. Taking a breath, I charged into the back room, fully prepared to assault whatever I might find. The manager was lying gagged and hog-tied in the middle of the floor, his hair still damp with blood from a blow to the head. Pieces of a smashed lamp he'd just knocked over lay strewn across the floor. I untied his gag. He mumbled something to me in Spanish, but of course I didn't understand. I proceeded to untie his other knots. The instant he was free, he got to his feet and stumbled into the lobby to get to the phone, all the while pressing the wound on his head with his palm to soothe what surely must have been a terrible headache.

As the man dialed the phone, Garth descended the stairs, greatly concerned. "What's happened?"

"The manager was attacked last night," I said. "I don't know what time."

Garth started asking the manager questions. He answered until somebody came on the other end of the phone line.

"What did he say?" I demanded.

"He said five men attacked him. He thinks it was around four a.m. He doesn't know what they wanted."

"Did you see our old room upstairs?"

"Yes, I did."

"They were trying to find us, Garth. They know we were here." I grabbed the registry off the counter and showed him the torn page. "The only reason we're still alive is because we changed rooms. The manager didn't correct the registry. They must have clobbered him before he could tell them about the switch."

Garth examined the book. "But how could they have followed us? How did they know to check this hotel? To find us, they would have had to check the registries of almost every hotel in Chihuahua."

The manager was talking into the phone a mile a minute, still pressing his palm to his head.

"Is he calling the police?" I asked Garth.

"I think he's calling a relative. Maybe the owner of the hotel."

"Wake up the girls, and let's get out of here."

The manager didn't seem to connect us with the attack, so he said nothing as we vacated the hotel three minutes later. I ran to retrieve the car. Parking so far away might have also been a factor that had saved us. The Gadiantons must have figured we'd already left. Thus, there was no reason to search every room.

Our car was still sitting untouched in its quiet corner a few blocks away. How I wished I knew enough about Chihuahua to find a back road connecting us with the Pan-American Highway far beyond the city limits, but perhaps even that would have been futile. Who knew how many people Mehrukenah and Shurr had working for them now? There might have been spies setting up ambushes all the way into Mexico City—maybe even to the Hill Vigia!

As I pulled up to the front of the hotel, Garth tossed the luggage into the trunk. The girls climbed into the back, still looking bleary-eyed and disheveled from their rude awakening. We found the Pan-American Highway again and proceeded through the rest of the city. I looked for alternate routes. I didn't see any. A large hill with the road cutting through it seemed to mark the city's southern boundary. Just beyond this point, the first car—a gray Cavalier with Utah plates—was patiently waiting. It pulled into the lane behind us. I didn't recognize the driver. He had long black hair and a thin beard. Like the man I'd seen yesterday, his eyes were hidden behind a pair of sunglasses.

Giving this situation the benefit of the doubt, I pressed on the gas pedal. Sure enough, the Cavalier matched our speed. I still felt confident. The divided highway beyond Chihuahua appeared relatively clear of traffic, giving us an empty speedway across the hilly plains. But it wasn't half a mile later when two other cars pulled in behind the Cavalier. One of them was the station wagon.

"I think we're in for a chase," I announced.

My passengers gripped any and all handles in the car. I increased my speed to ninety-five miles an hour. The other automobiles had no trouble keeping up. Now I noted *four* cars behind us.

A gold-colored Camaro led the pursuit. It sped up beside me in the other lane. The big-shouldered driver smiled as he passed. The Camaro pulled into the lane in front of me. Suddenly the Cavalier accelerated and came up alongside. The station wagon then tightened up the gap from behind.

Their intentions were obvious. I was about to be locked into a deadly vise-grip on three sides, allowing the other cars to carefully decelerate and force my Mazda to come to a stop. How could I prevent this? I couldn't lose them by going any faster. I slammed my fist on the dashboard. "Gutless piece of garbage!"

The Cavalier was in position. As I'd predicted, the Camaro began to slow down. My passengers were breathless with fear. There seemed to be no escape. The moment they succeeded in forcing us to stop, the villains would undoubtedly climb out of their cars and surround the Mazda. They'd see the sword at my side and smile with satisfaction. Then they'd slit our throats. Who would stop them in the middle of the Mexican desert?

I thought about the sword and the strange power surge it had given me the night before as I tried to navigate the hazardous highway. For some reason, it was not inspiring me at this moment. But why? Did it know who surrounded our car? Did it *want* me to be defeated? I had a feeling that this was not the case. It didn't seem to care who its owner was, as long as that owner was devoted. I would not be inspired unless I *asked* for the inspiration. No longer would its services be freely given. I had to request them.

Where were these thoughts coming from? It was as if the sword was speaking to me. But that was insane! Nevertheless, in the next instant, I found myself wrapping my fingers around the cool metal hilt while my other hand remained glued to the wheel. Suddenly, my mind began flowing with confidence and my limbs surged with energy.

The Cavalier misread our rate of deceleration and slipped past us several yards. This was my chance. With flawless precision, I grabbed that space behind the Cavalier and escaped the vise.

Two more enemy cars had joined in the chase. That made six altogether. Where were all these vehicles coming from? They were trying to close in from behind again, this time with the object of pinning me into the left lane.

Ahead of us I spotted a turn-around space between the divided highway. I veered the Mazda sharply and crossed the lane, separating us from the enemy vehicles entirely, though I was now facing oncoming traffic. A Mexican farmer with a pickup full of cabbage was heading right at us! I saw the farmer's eyes widen in horror as he gripped his steering wheel and swerved into the other lane at the last second. A head of cabbage hit the hood of our car and rolled over the top. Jenny shrieked.

The enemy vehicles were still speeding beside us in the southbound lanes. The Cavalier had unintentionally taken the lead, blocking the Camaro and allowing me to pull a few yards ahead. As the Mazda came up over a rise, I was startled by the blasting horn of an oncoming semi-truck as it was passing a Volkswagen Bug.

"Watch out!" Garth hollered and shrank in his seat.

I made a split-second decision to play chicken with the Bug instead of the semi and switched lanes. The Volkswagen's driver hit the brakes, allowing the semi to pass him. In the nick of time, I veered back into the inside lane. The Volkswagen skidded into the brush growing in the median.

Just ahead, the road converged into a single two-lane highway again. I dodged another Mexican farmer and found myself back on the same roadway with the enemy cars. They were about ten yards to the rear. The Camaro was closing in fast. As it tried to pass, I swerved into the center, forcing him to stay where he was and continue eating my dust.

Where would this end? My gas gauge was back to its familiar quarter tank. At these speeds, I could only keep going for another fifty miles. Something would have to happen well before then if we had any hope of escape.

Just as we rounded the next corner, a *seventh* vehicle appeared, waiting just off the highway. As our convoy approached, it pulled into the road, blocking both lanes of traffic. This time there was no mistaking the car's identity. It was a dark blue Suburban with silver trim.

CHAPTER 20

Our hopes for deliverance looked grim. With six vehicles in hot pursuit and the blue Suburban—whose occupants were certainly Mehrukenah, Shurr, and Mr. Clarke—blocking the road ahead, what options did we have?

My fingers continued to grip Coriantumr's sword. I found myself reaching inside it, as if reaching beyond the silver-plating and into the copper fibers themselves. My right hand seemed almost welded to the metal—indeed, the two had become one—my left hand turned the steering wheel sharply to the right.

Our tires kicked up a cloud of dust. We skidded into the driveway of some sort of ranch with rusty tin warehouses and fence lines of wood and stone. A Mazda 626 was not built for this kind of treatment. Two of its wheels lifted off the ground—so high I thought the car would flip—but my passengers shifted their weight and somehow we came back down on all four tires. After fishtailing a time or two, I guided the car between two of the warehouses. The Camaro stayed with us, nipping at the Mazda's bumper all the way. Four other vehicles were close behind it.

Three Mexican boys sitting on the fence watched the chase with intense excitement. There was a gate up ahead. Ranch hands were in the process of closing it, but upon seeing our stampede of automobiles, they leaped out of the way.

I hit the unlatched gate and sent it sprawling backward, opening the way for everybody else and leaving a hefty dent in my hood. One of the enemy vehicles, trying to thread through the gate while driving alongside the station wagon, smashed into the right post—a log with the circumference of a telephone pole—and buckled up like an accordion.

I veered left. The remaining vehicles pursued us down a roadway that was little more than two tire tracks in the middle of a pasture. Several massive Brahma bulls watched intently, chewing the cud, not concerned enough to get out of the way. The station wagon made an error in judgment while dodging a bull and high-centered in a ditch. Only the Cavalier and the Camaro remained in the chase.

Fifty yards farther, the tire tracks connected again with the highway. A second gate obstructed the pathway, but I figured one good dent deserved another. We crashed through it. The thin and rotting cross-posts snapped like Popsicle sticks, leaving little more than a few more scratches to the Mazda's paint job.

Nevertheless, the explosion of wood greatly frightened the driver of a top-heavy semi-truck with an open roof, its wooden sides bulging with a full load of scrap metal. It coughed a cloud of black exhaust like a barreling locomotive. The driver hit his brakes, attempting to dodge the flying debris and oncoming cars. We heard a horrible screech—like the death-knell of a great hulking monster—as the truck began to tilt, overturning on its side, and sending a thunderous wave of twisted metal across the asphalt. I thought we were going to be crushed, but when the dust had cleared, it revealed a highway completely cut off to traffic. And the only vehicle south of the debris was our Mazda.

There was no way for the Gadiantons to get around. The strewn metal and a strip of rocky terrain prevented passage around the right; a muddy riverbed blocked any passage around the left. I knew it would be impossible for them to backtrack. There were no optional roads! Unless the Gadiantons wanted to go hundreds of miles out of the way, they'd have to wait several hours for the mess to be cleared.

The driver of the truck hoisted himself out the driver's side door, now facing skyward. He began frantically waving his hands and assaulting the Gadiantons with an arsenal of Spanish obscenities as they vacated their own vehicles to climb around the mess and ascertain our position.

We sped away, stopping to look back only after we reached the top of a rise that overlooked the accident, about a half mile ahead. When I looked back, I saw a man standing in the middle of the highway on the south side of the overturned truck. It was Mehrukenah. His fists were clenched. Once again we'd slipped out of his grasp.

* * *

"I think I was safer back in Provo," Jenny commented some time later.

Renae had taken over as driver, with a hell-bent desire to get as far away from Chihuahua as possible.

Exhausted, I gazed out across the Mexican frontier, hilly and treeless, yet abounding in brilliant green grasses and shrubbery similar to Joshua trees. There were many small houses and farms, some so meager it was unbelievable that people lived there. Stone fences crawled all the way up the mountainsides, no matter how steep, and appeared as tiny lines scissoring the prairie. Stacking all those rocks must have taken decades.

For the next hour, no one spoke. Everyone's nerves remained on edge. Garth, behind me, seemed especially tense.

"You all right?" I finally inquired.

"No, I'm *not* all right," he snapped.

I had no reason to think his animosity was directed at me, but I thought I'd better make sure.

"You're not mad at *me,* are you?"

"Something is wrong, Jim. Horribly wrong."

"Not anymore," I contended. "Even if the Gadiantons finally get through, there are so many trails and highways between here and Veracruz, it would be virtually impossible for them to track us—unless they have a hundred more lookouts we don't know about—"

"It's not the Gadiantons I'm worried about anymore," Garth interrupted. "It's *you,* Jim."

My jaw dropped. "Me?"

I looked over at Renae and back at Jenny. Fortunately, they were both staring at Garth with the same bewilderment, though I suspected Renae was waiting for Garth to confirm something she already feared.

"What happened back there wasn't natural, Jim. You're not a Hollywood stunt driver—not unless there's a part of your life I don't know about. How were you able to maneuver like that?"

"I have to be a Hollywood stunt driver to execute a few simple moves?"

"You grabbed the hilt of the sword, Jim. Why?" Garth demanded.

"I don't know. It gave me confidence, mostly."

"Did you make a conscious decision to ask for its help?"

I laughed nervously. "Garth, what are you accusing me of? You're treating me as if I was a criminal!"

"Then I'm right? You asked it to support you?"

"Not in so many words," I admitted. "I just knew it could help me drive better. I can't explain why—I'm sure it's psychological."

"After all you know about the sword—after all you've seen, and everything Muleki has told you—you still think it's *psychological?!*"

"Of course. Isn't everything psychological? If we *believe* something gives us power, can't we sometimes gain real power from it?"

"Yes!" Garth clamored. "It's called faith. All the power in the universe is controlled by it, and the blessing hand is either God . . . or it's not God. You exerted your faith toward something which was *not God!*"

"Now, don't get all hellfire and damnation," I huffed. "If the sword has power, I've just proved it can be used for good instead of evil, right?"

"Wrong!" Garth thundered. "It wasn't ordained to that end. It was ordained for evil. To use it any other way goes against its very nature. If I were wrong, there'd be no harm in experimenting with witchcraft or black magic. Many people are fooled into thinking those powers can be used for good, but it can't be done."

"The fact is," I said deliberately, "if I *hadn't* used it, *we'd all be dead right now!*"

"Maybe you're right," Garth agreed. "Maybe we would be. But when death is staring you in the face, the source we look to for help is not an inanimate object. It's our Heavenly Father."

"Joseph Smith used seer stones, didn't he? Correct me if I'm wrong, but those are inanimate objects, are they not? What's the difference between that and what I did?"

"The difference is that Joseph Smith always knew the power through which the stones operated. They were tools to help his faith in God, and eventually he didn't need them anymore. Like the Liahona in the Book of Mormon—its power was entirely predicated upon faith in God. Like the priesthood itself! If one attributes its powers to himself, or to anything other than God, amen to that power. The sword was the sole object of your faith, Jim—not God."

"But we're alive!" I reminded him. "Our survival was a *good thing!* Are you saying our survival was evil?"

"If by our survival the sword has gained your unyielding devotions, then the answer is yes, Jim," Garth replied.

They were all staring at me, their eyes burning holes in me from every angle.

"Okay! Fine!" I angrily exclaimed. "I won't ask for its help anymore! Will that make you happy? Is that what you want?"

Indignation boiled inside me; I felt bitterness toward every person in the car. They were all against me! I'd saved their lives—and what was my reward? To be pronounced a cheater! A person possessed!

I looked over at Renae. She was gripping the steering wheel as intensely as a Catholic rosary, struggling to keep her attention fixed on the highway, but failing to stop a tear from burning a trail down her cheek.

"What's the matter with *you?"* I barked.

She turned to me and glowered.

Jenny put her hand on my shoulder. "This is not you, Jim. You're not acting like yourself."

"Of course I am! You think because I'm angry, I'm some sort of demon?"

Garth sat forward and asked point-blank, "Jim, can you give me the sword?"

A variety of sensations erupted within me. How can I describe them? Every inch of my flesh was pulsating. I shivered. I felt cold, and yet my palms were sweating. It was so important that I didn't hesitate, so important that I fool them.

That I *fool them?* Why had I thought that? Who was I trying to fool? *What was the matter with me?*

I began untying the scabbard from my waist. Then I held one end of the sword in each hand and thrust it toward Garth. My old comrade was looking into my eyes, not at the weapon.

"Well? Are you going to take it?"

"No," Garth replied. "Keep it. I just had to know if you could do it."

A few minutes later, my conscience was burning. Profusely, I begged forgiveness from everyone in the car. I told them how sorry I was for acting like such an idiot, and how I had no idea what came over me. Once again I tried to hand Garth the sword, only this time I did it with sincere contrition. Again, he refused.

"I'd take it in a minute if I felt it was the right thing to do, Jim. I don't think it is. I believe when Muleki singled you out in the hospital as the only one he fully trusted to complete this mission, he did it deliberately. I can't tell you why, I just know his choice was right."

I laid the sword in the space between my seat and the passenger's side door. I looked over at Renae. Her right hand was at her side as she drove, so I took it in my own hand and held it gently. She continued to watch the road, but she smiled, compressing my palm with equal tenderness. I leaned back and closed my eyes, wondering about what Garth had said. Why *had* Muleki chosen me? Garth was certainly more spiritual. Maybe he wouldn't have chosen me at all if he'd known Jenny and Renae were coming—they weren't fooled for a second by wrong voices. I couldn't think of a single advantage I had over any of them.

Maybe it had something to do with the way righteousness was channeled. Garth placed much of his faith in his knowledge—in his personal power of reasoning. In a way, that was *his* seer stone. It would be so until he could one day tune his instrument more perfectly to receive the pure intelligence of God unbounded, as had Joseph Smith. As for Renae and Jenny, their seer stones were intuition and emotion. By exercising them in righteousness, they could one day partake of the same promise.

And me? I guess I was somewhere in the middle—and constantly plagued by questions. Maybe that was *my* seer stone.

Skepticism forced me to gain a testimony in areas others took for granted. It made the going a little slower, but at least the road was perfectly paved.

One thing was for sure: I still had many skepticisms about the sword. I couldn't bring myself to fully liberate the notion that it was all in my mind. Maybe in this instance, my doubts were a gift that made it subtly more frustrating for the sword to tie an enduring knot. I certainly didn't feel the same fear toward it that everyone else did. Could my nonchalance in this instance be a strength? I couldn't decide.

We passed through a town named Delicias and were reminded of the grumbling in our stomachs. Unfortunately, this part of Mexico had no drive-thru restaurants to speak of, making it difficult to eat on the run. We found a tiny eatery just off the road called the Caballo Locho, where I ordered pancakes. Though they lacked maple syrup, the corn syrup they offered was unexpectedly good.

Garth sat beside Jennifer, translating every item she pointed to on the menu. She enjoyed his attention, but she also seemed to be fighting any feelings that might be developing. Now and then she'd mention Muleki's name to remind herself of her devotions, and I would watch the light fade in Garth's eyes. I started to wonder if my old comrade had secretly harbored a crush on my sister for years.

Garth and Jenny ordered *huevos rancheros*—basically eggs and salsa—and Renae had *huevos queso norteno*, a sensuous-smelling cheese, egg, and tortilla dish that made me regret having played it safe with pancakes.

Outside, a kindly old gentleman squeezed us some oranges with a manual juicer. The oranges were green instead of orange and not as sweet as the ones from Florida or California, but it felt stylish to be drinking fresh-squeezed juice from a roadside stand. Each of our meals, including the juice, was less than two dollars. At last we were far enough from the border to enjoy true Mexican prices.

Just beyond Delicias there was a monument in the middle of the road—a smashed car on a pedestal. It might have been a Volkswagen Rabbit; the chassis was so twisted it was hard to tell.

"Mexicans make statues out of wrecked cars?" I asked.

"Only the worst ones," Renae revealed. "They believe it encourages drivers to be more careful. You'll see those kinds of monuments all over Mexico. Also, whenever you see a wreath of flowers along the road, it means an accident occurred there in which somebody was killed."

"How gloomy," I commented.

"Family members consider the memorial as sacred as the grave site in a cemetery," said Renae.

We filled up with gas again at the local Pemex and paid some boys another thousand pesos for washing our windshield. We then continued on toward Jimenez and Torreon. The road remained in fairly good condition, though once we had to slow down to traverse a short stretch that was six inches under water.

Garth spent much of the afternoon talking our ears off about the ancient ruins of Mexico—Palenque, Monte Alban, Chichen Itza, and perhaps the greatest of all, Teotihuacan with its massive Pyramid of the Sun. He told us that some LDS scholars felt they had about eighty percent of the Book of Mormon's sites locked down. I was curious to see how time would bear them out.

Near every town there were roadside stands selling fruit, pistachio nuts, wood carvings—everything under the sun. I finally tasted the cactus fruit they called *tuna*. Its sweet juices were tasty, but I had to spit out so many seeds that it just wasn't worth the effort.

All the poverty made me depressed at times. Most people would offer us some kind of menial service to earn a few pesos, even if it was just shining our tennis shoes, but a good number of people just begged. They'd seemingly trained themselves to spot Americans from a mile away. Sometimes their open palms were thrust in our windows the moment a town's speed bumps forced us to slow down. Each time I refused I felt terribly guilty, like maybe I wasn't as good a Christian as I thought. But if we'd given money to everyone who asked, we'd have been penniless by evening. We were most generous to the handicapped—the blind and the lame. Renae claimed that handicapped people in Mexico received little if any government compensation. Since they couldn't work, they got no social security when they grew old. What they earned by begging was generally all the money they ever saw.

It wasn't so much that Mexicans were illiterate and unlearned. Renae insisted that Mexico was quite educated compared with most third-world countries. A college education was not uncommon, but neither was it uncommon to see an attorney plowing a field, or an engineer driving a cattle truck. There just weren't enough jobs to support the professional working force.

Nearly every community boasted a magnificent Catholic cathedral, rising up from the shabbiness of a town like a glistening oasis. Even in the poorest places one could find tall statues of Mexican heroes and fiery white effigies of the *Cristos* looming down from the tops of the highest hills.

Despite their circumstances, the people actually appeared happy and humble, making the best of life in spite of the package it came in. What a contrast to America's poor, I thought, who so often seemed angry.

I felt blessed for having been born in a wealthy and healthy nation. But at the same time, the humility of an old woman I saw standing in the mud, selling rugs and necklaces day after day in the endless struggle to feed her family, made me wonder if her chances of reaching the celestial kingdom might be greater than my own. My temper was prone to flare if my steak was cooked medium-well instead of medium-rare. In the eternal scheme of things, was my station a blessing or a curse? I found some comfort in knowing that it was still in my power to decide.

CHAPTER 21

The sky was just starting to dim as we passed through the town of Fresnillo. We'd come so far south now that the days were a few hours longer. Upon reaching Zacatecas, we discovered our first fast-food restaurant—El Pollo Chicken. Thus, our dinner consisted of barbecued bird, french fries, and of course a stack of corn tortillas, just to stay true to the culture.

My experience with roads into Chihuahua had made me leery of driving at night, but the roads here seemed considerably better, so we opted to go a little farther before seeking a hotel. An hour and a half later, we found ourselves navigating the narrow cobblestone streets of San Luis Potosi.

San Luis Potosi was a magnificent town—even at night. It was one of the oldest colonial cities in Mexico, and its architecture boasted arching colonnades and plenty of "Romeo and Juliet"-type balconies. The first hotel we discovered was the Hotel Filher.

As I entered its lobby, I imagined I could hear all the ghosts of its first hundred years singing hearty songs of welcome. We stared up in awe at the lofty ceiling and the filigreed walls of its various levels, further dignified by expansive murals of old Mexico—the conquistadors and Catholic friars, Aztec cities and glorious revolutions. The handrails of the upper floors burgeoned with tropical plants whose weeping vines cascaded down to the floor below. The wide staircase was divided into two walkways that spiraled inward as it climbed, finally joining at a platform between the floors and then dividing again for the final ascent.

At the risk of sounding like a travelogue, I'll add that the price was surprisingly affordable—thirty thousand pesos less than the cockroach-infested dive we'd tenanted in Chihuahua—and the rooms five times as nice. Also, the water worked, which was a pleasant contrast.

The clerk was a fine-trimmed gentleman with a cheerful smile. In perfect English he told us that the Filher was actually a three-star hotel. The reason it wasn't four-star, and remained inexpensive, was because they hadn't added all the possible modernizations—carpeting, new paint, and the like. For that I was grateful. It was the colonial authenticity that made it enchanting.

I advised Garth that it might be best if we signed pseudonyms to the registry. For our room he signed Eduardo Ramirez. For Jenny and Renae's room he signed Louisa Ortega. It was just a precaution. I actually didn't expect to see Gadiantons again until we reached the Hill Vigia. If we were very lucky, perhaps we'd beat them there as well. We ordered a wake-up call for six a.m. to try and maintain our lead. The only way they could pass us now was if they drove all night. Certainly even Gadiantons needed sleep—and on something less bumpy than a Mexican highway.

I parallel parked our car in a small gap between a new Ford Fiesta and an older Scirocco about a block west of the hotel. There was a plaza nearby with stone benches and massive trees projecting so many branches that I'm sure I'd have deliberately lost myself in them as a kid. San Luis Potosi was the first Mexican town I'd seen that had made a serious effort to put up Christmas decorations. The park was aglow with lights. I won't say it looked like Christmas on Temple Square, but it was impressive enough in its own right. The lights were arranged to create shapes and figures—the Virgin Mary, the Christ Child, a donkey. Yet somehow it all seemed out of place. Maybe it was the humidity. I just couldn't put Christmas and ninety-degree weather in the same scenario.

We carried the luggage up to our rooms. In spite of our weariness, Jenny and Renae were determined to enjoy an ice cream soda, or its Mexican equivalent, in the hotel's restaurant before retiring. I was agreeable. Our muscles were so stiff from driving that we sorely needed a moment of recreation. What a waste of Mexico to only see it from the highway! The girls insisted that they needed twenty minutes beforehand to take a shower and do whatever it is that girls do. As we waited for them in our own room, I lay back on the soft twin bed and let my face absorb the coolness of the breeze blowing through the curtains above our balcony doorway. All these nights of lost sleep were catching up with me. I'm sure I would have passed out entirely if I hadn't found it so amusing to watch Garth try and get ready for his date.

He gave himself a towel bath and washed his hair in the sink. Then he carefully shaved every stubby hair on his chin and combed every crimson lock on his scalp, all the while whistling and humming the theme "I'm Gettin' Married in the Mornin" from *My Fair Lady.*

Once he turned to me and asked, "Do you have any . . . um . . ."

"Aftershave?" I guessed.

He looked embarrassed, as if he'd asked a female store clerk where to find the underwear.

"Yeah," he replied.

"In the end pocket of my duffel bag," I told him.

As he began slapping the stuff on his face in front of the mirror, he became aware that I'd been smiling at him from my bed the whole time.

"Is it that obvious?" he asked.

"Yes, it's obvious."

"Is it okay?" he wondered, as if I were Jenny's overlord.

"Hey, I wish you the best of luck in the world."

Garth sat on the end of my bed. "What does she see in Muleki, anyway? Doesn't she know he could never be happy here? And I *know* she could never be happy there—not living as a Nephite. There's just no way!"

"You'd be surprised where Jenny might be willing to live. But . . . I think you're right. Still, I gotta warn ya, she's not an easy catch. Many a noble knight has died of a broken heart trying to slay hers."

"Maybe they haven't used the right weapon."

"Maybe not. What's yours?"

"I was hoping you could give me some ideas."

"The only one I don't think anyone has used is fortitude."

"Fortitude?"

"Yep. If Jenny lets you get your foot in the doorway, don't leave. I've seen her use some pretty harsh pesticides to get rid of boyfriends. The guy who wins Jen is going to be the bug who keeps coming back for more."

Garth nodded thoughtfully, then pursed his lips and repeated, "Fortitude."

Of course the girls took twice as long as they'd promised, so I had plenty of time to change my clothes and throw on a little aftershave myself. I also covered the sword a bit by tying a sweater around my waist and letting it hang, preppy-style. When the girls finally knocked on our door and met us in the hallway, neither of us doubted that it had been worth the wait. Amazing what a shower, a dab of makeup, and a touch of perfume can do for a girl, I thought. Renae looked outstanding, easily the most beautiful creature I'd ever seen.

Both girls held out their elbows to be formally escorted down the stairs. Garth was so busy gawking at Jenny that he nearly missed his cue. We guided our princesses gracefully down either side of the staircase and into the dining room. There was no ice cream, but the hostess highly recommended a fruit bowl that included mango, papaya, pineapple, watermelon, walnuts, raisins, coconut, and a special whipped topping. The dessert was celestial, but it nearly did me in. Any other date would have thought me very rude as I struggled to keep my eyes open. Renae just put her arm around my shoulder and kissed my cheek.

The hostess suggested that we might want to see the colonial church before we left. We were a bit reluctant, but she went on to describe its grandeur, saying the carvings were some of the finest in Mexico and the ceiling in the rotunda was ornamented with pure gold. It was built in the late sixteenth century. I couldn't imagine anything that old in the New World. The pilgrims hadn't even landed yet! She said this church was only a couple of blocks from the hotel.

Enraptured by the description, Jenny and Renae begged for an additional fifteen-minute reprieve from the day's anxiety to take a glance at the edifice. In spite of my interest, I was just too tired. Garth sighed and agreed to be their escort. I climbed the stairway back to my room, this time with Renae doing the guiding. Outside my door, I embraced her and whispered good night. I think she'd have let me kiss her as well, but half asleep as I was, I decided our first kiss should be something I fully remembered.

I gave her my room key to give to Garth, and told her to make sure everyone was back at the hotel and in bed in half an hour or less, or I'd call out the cavalry. Then I shut the door, turned off the light, unbuckled the scabbard and sword, dropped it to the floor, and fainted onto my bed.

The ancient man behind the lightning-scarred trunk was beckoning more fervently than ever before, his face deathly white with terror. The sword was in my hand. I tried to climb through the jungle to reach him, but the sword became so heavy I could go no farther. Then suddenly the sword took on a will of its own. Still gripped in my fingers, it lifted itself high overhead, and an instant later, swished through my neck with the ease of a guillotine.

I sat up abruptly in bed, gasping for breath, my fingers grasping my throat. It took a few seconds for it to sink in that I'd been having a dream, and that dream was over. When reality finally settled over me, I sighed deeply and closed my eyes. When I opened them, my focus fell on Coriantumr's sword, still in its sheath right where I'd dropped it, the jewels in the hilt continuing to watch me. Maybe it was laughing at me.

I don't know what made me think that.

It was faintly light outside. I threw off the covers and set my feet onto the cold stone floor. Now that I was facing the other end of the room, I could no longer fail to notice that Garth's bed was empty.

I stretched my eyelids to make sure I was interpreting things correctly. Sure enough, the covers were unruffled. It hadn't been slept in at all. Panic started rising within me. I actually stood and walked toward the bed to make sure he hadn't fallen off the other side and was sleeping along the wall.

The phone rang. I looked at the thing strangely. It had to be Garth, apologizing that he'd stayed up the whole night talking with my sister in the hotel lobby. Not such a terrible thing. I'd committed similar crimes. Nevertheless, as I reached for the receiver, I decided to punish him with a good tongue-lashing anyway.

"Hello?" I responded.

"Front desk," said the heavily accented voice. "You request six o'clock wake-up?"

"Yes," I replied. "Thank you."

I opened my mouth to ask him if Garth was in the lobby, but he hung up too quickly. Still dressed in yesterday's clothes, I rushed into the hallway, continuing to tell myself there was as yet no reason to panic. I stopped at the girls' door and pounded several times—a little louder than may have been necessary. The door was locked, or I might have stormed in. Instead, I continued down the staircase, fully expecting to see Garth and Jenny asleep in the lobby's loveseat, nestled in each other's arms. The lobby was empty except for the young desk clerk, who stared at me with obvious consternation.

"Have you seen my friends?" I asked. "Americans?"

"Americans?" he repeated. "No, I not see."

I leaped back up the stairs, five at a time, and reached Jenny and Renae's doorway again. After knocking even louder, I called out both their names. No answer. I ran downstairs again and demanded a key to their room. Upon entering, I could see plainly that their beds hadn't been slept in either. *Now* my panic was justified.

I returned to my room one final time and found the sword on the floor. Without bothering to cover or shroud it, I restrapped it around my waist. Then I rushed back down to the lobby for the third time. The desk clerk was still quite attentive to my behavior.

"Where is the church?" I demanded.

He didn't understand.

"The church!" I cried. "The Catholic church!"

"Ah, Catholic!" he repeated. He pointed out the door and to the left.

I charged outside and bolted down the narrow cobblestone street. It was early and there was very little traffic, except for an early-bird cabdriver in a Volkswagen Bug. He offered me a ride as I ran. I ignored him and reached the end of the block.

The spires of the four-hundred-year-old sanctuary loomed above me, silhouetted against the new morning sky. A flock of pigeons parted as I ran into the courtyard. Though I'm sure it was disrespectful, I darted from one statue or fountain to the other in hopes that my companions might be hiding behind them, perhaps hurt or afraid. I reached the church's towering doors; they were chained and padlocked.

Breathless with terror, I ran back toward the Hotel Filher and paced wildly back and forth on the sidewalk outside. What else could I do? Where else could I look? The cab driver decided not to bother me further, deciding it was best to leave a loco gringo with a sword to himself.

The car! It was my last hope. I hurried up the street toward the plaza where I'd seen the Christmas lights. As I rounded the corner, I saw the Mazda still parked in the street, wedged between the same Fiesta and Scirocco. But even from a distance I could see that its trunk was sitting open, and there was broken glass in the street.

The triangular window behind the rear door on the driver's side had been smashed. All the maps and other papers from the glove box were strewn about. The trunk had either been picked or pried open. The jack, spare tire, and the carpet that had covered them were lying on the plaza lawn.

Had the circumstances been different, I might have interpreted all this as the work of local vandals, but the note left propped on my steering wheel removed all doubt as to who was responsible. I reached in and grabbed it, reading the words with horrified apprehension.

Found your friends. Sorry you weren't with them. Had to kill one to set an example. Other two are safe for now, but will not be so after six o'clock tonight. At that hour we will trade their lives for the sword. We are waiting at the Pyramid of the Sun in the place you call Teotihuacan. I'm told the park gates close precisely at six. If you are not there, we will add their blood to those of the thousands of victims already sacrificed upon its steps.

I look forward to seeing you again, my quetzal feather.

Mehrukenah

CHAPTER 22

I sat on the ground with my back to the Mazda's hubcap for what must have been fifteen minutes, drinking in the devastation. The note with Mehrukenah's words, though certainly not his handwriting—perhaps it was Mr. Clarke's—was crushed in my fist. I was too numb with shock; I couldn't cry, I couldn't mourn. How could I have thought it was safe for them to go sightseeing? Did we think we were tourists?

Now one of the people I cared for most in this world was dead. To twist the knife even deeper, Mehrukenah hadn't told me who it was. The horror of guessing the answer was indescribable. My sister Jenny—I couldn't bear it. And Garth—the best friend I'd ever had. Renae, my love . . . I was shaking all over and I couldn't stop. I thought of Mehrukenah. How could such a soul have been allowed to come to earth and receive a tabernacle of flesh? My teeth clamped down, clenched with thoughts of the sweetest, bitterest hatred. I wanted vengeance. Revenge would feel so good.

I realized my hand was gripping the hilt of the sword. I removed it as if from a hot stove. The instant I did, my emotions were released. Tears trickled down my face. Around me the residents of San Luis Potosi were coming to life. Street vendors were setting up their wares; laborers were making their way to work. Determination welled up inside me, and I felt strong enough to stand. After breathing deeply a time or two, I started back to the hotel to get everyone's luggage. There was much to do this day. I couldn't let my emotions distract me. I wasn't sure how far it was to the Pyramid of the Sun. Garth had mentioned that Teotihuacan was near Mexico City. I knew that was still six or seven hours away.

But what would I do when I got there? Would I simply hand over the sword, and expect them to automatically make good on their promise to release Garth and Jenny, or Garth and Renae, or Renae and Jenny? A Gadianton's promise was worthless. If I showed up after the ruins had closed, it would be an easy matter to kill us all on the temple steps like any of the thousands of Aztec sacrifices from centuries past. If I were a true soldier, I might have ignored the plight of my loved ones and gone on to Cumorah without them, knowing our cause justified the losses. But I was *not* a true soldier. I couldn't lose them all. I just couldn't lose them all.

What did it matter to us in the twenty-first century if the world of 50 B.C. experienced a little more pain as a result of my returning the sword? I could live with that, couldn't I? After all, these people had been dead for two thousand years already! Their pains were part of history. I'd never know their anguish or see their turmoil. Nothing in my world would change.

Or would it?

I thought about Muleki. Though he was still healing in a Utah hospital, I knew that he soon expected to return to his people, as if past and future were one and the same. I couldn't do it. I just couldn't hand it over. I knew in my heart that if I gave Mehrukenah the sword, I would stand accountable. There had to be another solution. It would come to me. I had full faith that it would come. But for now, my only concern was to reach Teotihuacan. I had eleven hours.

I loaded our luggage and shut the trunk tightly, grateful that it still locked after all the tampering. Then I started the car and drove through the cobbled streets of San Luis Potosi until I again connected with Highway 57, which would take me through Queretaro and on into Mexico City. The traffic became gradually more congested, and the population grew denser and denser. Beyond Queretaro the road was permanently divided, which made the going considerably faster.

At about one o'clock I finally reached the toll gate of Mexico City. Getting through it cost twelve thousand pesos! A short ways farther I stopped at a roadside stand and bought a bag of Mexican potato chips and an apple soda. For now, this would have to suffice as both breakfast and lunch.

My tank was on empty again. I found the nearest Pemex station and pulled up to the pump marked "Extra." As I was waiting for the tank to fill, the station attendant stepped up to my window and began speaking in Spanish. I kept repeating, "*No hablo español, no hablo español!*" Nevertheless, he kept right on yakking, seemingly determined that I follow him around to the back of my car. I got out and let him lead me around to the license plate. He pointed at it frantically, waving his arms. I knew he was trying to tell me something was wrong, but what? I shook my head in frustration. The attendant finally threw up his hands and walked away. What had it been? Was I parked incorrectly? Was the car somehow damaged? Had I run over somebody's foot? I felt so desperately alone.

Before I pulled back onto the highway, I found Teotihuacan on the map. It was about thirty miles north of Mexico City. There was probably a shorter way to get there—some way that would have allowed me to avoid Mexico City altogether—but I was too afraid of making a wrong turn. This was one of the largest cities in the world—twice the size of anything in the United States. Some of the hillsides were as steep as "Y" mountain behind BYU, yet they were terraced all the way to the top with housing. I felt if I didn't stick to the major highways, I'd lose myself among these twenty-five million residents and never find a way out.

Mexican drivers around here were absolutely insane. The cars in all five or six lanes of traffic insisted on traveling seventy miles an hour despite being almost literally bumper to bumper. If a vehicle wanted to cut in front of me, it did so without hesitation, giving me two choices—either let it in or crash.

It was two hours before I realized that I'd made a mistake. The tourist map was so confusing! One page had a blown-up schematic of the streets of Mexico City, but it didn't give the streets any names! I knew at some point I had to cut across to reach Highway 80 and then Highway 130 to Teotihuacan, but I had no way of knowing what the crossover highway was called, or where I needed to exit Highway 57. If only I could find someone who spoke English!

I wandered aimlessly through the suffocating congestion of downtown Mexico City. Finally, I found another major highway. But soon I found myself headed southeast toward Puebla. Once again, I pulled over to the side of the road to study the map. I had only three hours left to figure out this maze and reach the ruins.

My face was still buried in the tourist map when I heard a rapping on my window. A Mexican policeman was standing outside, looking in. He was fat and wearing sunglasses. If not for his Latin features, he'd have perfectly fit the stereotype of a backwoods southern sheriff. I glanced back and saw that the lights on his patrol car were flashing. His partner was still sitting behind the wheel. I'd been so preoccupied, I hadn't even noticed them pull up!

I rolled down my window, and the policeman began speaking to me in Spanish. Shaking my head, I told him I didn't understand. He paused for a moment, then spoke to me *again* in Spanish. Couldn't these people get a clue?

"I don't understand you!" I cried. "*¡No hablo español!*"

The officer nodded and stepped back to the patrol car. I began fearing for the sword and tried to discreetly cover it over with a dingy towel from the floor. The officer's partner, doubly overweight and also wearing sunglasses, emerged and came forward. This one had learned some English.

"You are driving illegally," he said.

"I am?"

"Your license plate ends in six. Today is Saturday. Fives and sixes may not drive."

"I don't get it," I replied.

"It is the law of Mexico City. Pollution control. Autos which end in certain numbers may not drive on certain days."

Now I knew what that guy at the Pemex was trying to tell me. "I'm sorry," I said. "I wasn't aware—"

"You cannot drive today. There will be a fine. Your car will be impounded until morning."

"*What?!* You can't! I have to be somewhere at six o'clock! It's an emergency!"

"The fine is three hundred thousand pesos," he said, unfazed by my pleading. "You must follow us."

"Please! How can a foreigner be expected to know your driving laws? You don't know what you're doing!"

"Follow," he repeated, and stepped back to his vehicle.

I sat there nonplussed while the patrol car rolled ahead of my Mazda and waited. I hesitated, then I did as I was directed. *They can't get away with this*, I thought. Was there no justice at all in this country? During any moment of this trip, I'd never missed America more than I missed it now.

The patrol car pulled onto a new street and started heading in the opposite direction. I decided I'd have to make a break for it. I rehearsed it in my mind. At the next intersection I would twist the steering wheel to the right and punch the gas pedal. It didn't matter that I might go to jail. Nor did it matter that I might be shot. But then suddenly the patrol car pulled over again and waved for me to do the same.

The English-speaking officer walked back to my car. He directed me to step out. I left the sword covered on the passenger's seat, greatly fearing that if they noticed it, they'd impound it as well. The officer was carrying some paperwork written in Spanish. He spread it out on the trunk of his patrol car.

He pointed to a paragraph. "Here is where the law is written. This is where it says the law includes foreign cars."

This seemed rather stupid. Did he think I had any way of reading it?

"I believed you the first time," I said.

The officer continued glaring at me, as if there was something I was supposed to do. Finally, he looked back at his partner and shook his head, as if to say, *"This gringo is not very bright."* At that moment, his true intentions popped on in my head like a light bulb.

"Can I . . . give you some money?" I inquired.

The officer looked relieved, as if shouting in his mind, *"Finally!"* Nevertheless, he continued playing out his role. Shrugging his shoulders, he replied, "Well, I don't know. How much do you have?"

I thought hard. What would be the least amount I could offer without insulting his intelligence? Since the official fine was three hundred thousand pesos, I figured one third of that amount should suffice.

"One hundred thousand pesos?" I meekly suggested.

The officer seemed pleased. Clearly I had proposed much more than he'd expected, but there was no way to retract my offer now. I reached into my wallet—careful not to let him see how much there actually was—and pulled out two fifty thousand peso bills.

He took them quickly and stuffed them in his pocket.

"Can you tell me how to get to Highway 130?" I asked.

"You still may not drive today," he said. "But we will not impound your car. If you try to drive, the police will stop you again. We will follow you to the nearest hotel."

These guys were operating one heck of a racket. I wondered if the government ever saw a dime of collected fines. Bribery seemed a way of life. Who could you trust in a country if not a policeman? No wonder the injured manager in Chihuahua had called the hotel's owner rather than calling the police. It was becoming apparent that the Mexican people avoided confrontations with the cops at any cost.

I started my engine and headed back toward the heart of Mexico City. About a mile later, I saw a sign indicating Highway 80, which I knew connected with highway 130 to Teotihuacan. When I looked in the rearview mirror, the patrol car was no longer following. They must have decided not to bother with me anymore and turned off. My only fear now was that another patrol car would spot my license plate and I'd go through the same thing all over again. My finances were desperately thin as it was! I merged with the traffic on Highway 80, careful to avoid any official-looking vehicles. I felt like I now had firsthand knowledge of what it would have been like for someone to try and escape from behind the Iron Curtain.

It was five o'clock when I passed through the toll booth at the city's boundary. I dreaded the possibility that someone would stop me again. I had only sixty minutes to reach the ancient ruins. Fortunately, I passed through without any problems and heaved a sigh of relief.

The congested city soon gave way to open country and agriculture. Only a short distance later, I passed a sign with an emblem of a pyramid. Teotihuacan was only seven miles away.
A half mile farther, I found a secluded spot off the road and

parked. If I was going to come up with a plan, it had to be now. As I looked over at the sword on the passenger's seat, the temptation to hold it in my hands and ask for its inspiration was very strong. I could almost hear a voice within the metal calling out my name.

Instead, I bowed my head and said a prayer to God.

* * *

I continued on toward the ruins. At one point the road divided. I had the choice of either going to *Piramide de la Luna* or *Piramide del Sol.* I recognized the similarity between the words "lunar" and "solar" easily enough. It was clear which road would take me to the Pyramid of the Sun. Nevertheless, I took the road to the Pyramid of the Moon.

The ancient edifices loomed above the trees long before I reached the parking lot. It was hard to believe an ancient people, using nothing but backbone and sweat, could have constructed anything so massive. The people in the distance climbing the pyramids' steps in their variegated clothing looked like candy sprinkles on a sundae.

As I pulled into the parking lot, it appeared that the majority of the cars were already pulling out. In a few minutes the park would be closing. I found an empty stall, cautiously climbed out of the Mazda, and surveyed the area. As might have been expected at a tourist attraction, there was a row of vending booths along the walkway leading toward the ruins. A man leaning against one of the booths met my gaze. He then ran down the flight of stone steps and into a wide roadway that ran from one end of the park to the other. According to the sign, it was called the Avenue of the Dead. I felt sure his intention was to reach the Pyramid of the Sun at the southern end and warn the Gadiantons of my arrival.

I opened my trunk and retrieved Mehrukenah's elongated package. It was wrapped in two towels and bound with string. After hoisting it in place under my right arm, I proceeded down the stone staircase and entered the Avenue of the Dead, ignoring the vendors' pleas to have me look at their wares.

The ruins of Teotihuacan covered about eight square miles of ground—an area that I was told was larger than the ancient cities of Athens or Rome. All around me were the crumbling and weather-worn remains of great palace walls and wide platforms flanked by lesser pyramids and temples. Tall stone pillars projected upward in many places, having once supported a mighty roof. The Pyramid of the Moon was behind me now, and the Pyramid of the Sun—the mightiest edifice of them all—was about a half mile ahead, its facing of volcanic rock towering over two hundred feet toward the clouds.

Peculiar feelings filled my breast. This seemed to be a place of great righteousness as well as great evil, perhaps each phase flourishing centuries apart. Garth had told us that Teotihuacan meant "City of the Gods" or "The Place Where Men Become Gods." Perhaps that name had once had the proper implication. Perhaps this site was once an actual dedicated temple. But later its purposes were savagely corrupted, and thousands of lives were sacrificed for rulers who thought to make *themselves* gods on earth.

A uniformed gentleman—no doubt the equivalent of a park ranger—passed by me, shouting to tourists in Spanish and in English that the ruins were closing. The place was nearly empty anyway. Merchants who'd set up their jewelry and ornaments on blankets in the middle of the park busily gathered their wares into baskets and suitcases, pausing only to attempt one final sale to camera-toting tourists. No one stopped me. Since there was also a parking lot just south of the Pyramid of the Sun, it was only natural for the rangers to assume that this was where I was headed.

Still toting my towel-wrapped package, I started down another flight of steps which brought me into the ancient city's central plaza, positioned directly before the staircase of the great pyramid. I could see about half a dozen figures standing at the summit. Except for them, the surface of the pyramid was clear of tourists. As I proceeded to climb, I noticed a ranger standing on the ground near the southwest corner. He watched me, making no effort to remind me that the park was closing. Obviously he'd been well paid to allow this rendezvous to occur without interference.

I continued to climb the pyramid's narrow steps and soon found myself panting. Nevertheless, I refused to stop and rest. The landscape began to stretch out in all directions as the vastness of all the various ruins of Teotihuacan became apparent.

As I neared the top, I began to recognize the faces of those awaiting me. Mehrukenah and Shurr were among them, as well as three of their minions—including one who appeared to be Mexican. Indeed, the Gadiantons seemed to find friends wherever they turned.

Two more figures were seated about ten yards away, at the edge of the pyramid's eastern face. Their hands were bound behind their backs, and gunny sacks had been draped over their heads. By their slender builds, I had to conclude I was looking at Jenny and Renae. There was no staircase on that side. The fall would certainly be fatal if one of the thugs standing nearby happened to give them a shove.

"Welcome!" greeted Mehrukenah. "I'm so glad that you could make it. I trust you had a pleasant journey?"

"Jenny? Renae?" I called to the figures under the gunny sacks. They didn't answer.

"Perhaps we can relieve you now of that sword." Mehrukenah reached out his hand to take it from me.

I knew full well that he was armed, likely with a dagger

under his vest. I knew the others were armed as well. Nevertheless, I demanded, "Release them first. I want to see their faces."

Mehrukenah feigned offense, then he grinned. He saw no harm in playing along with my request. "Of course. I wouldn't want you to feel we were dishonest in our end of the bargain."

He directed the thug to remove the gunny sacks. As he did so, Shurr and the others had a difficult time suppressing a fit of laughter. When the gunny sacks were lifted, the faces of Jenny and Renae were not revealed. Instead, the faces of two very frightened Mexican girls were unveiled. They had obviously been abducted for this very charade.

"Then again," laughed Mehrukenah, "honesty in bargains was never one of my stronger traits."

"Well, it's almost always been one of mine," I replied, "but today I thought I needed a change of pace."

Pulling back the corner of one of the towels, I exposed the leafy stub of a three-foot branch.

CHAPTER 23

The taunting cachinnations of the Gadiantons ended. As Mehrukenah realized that his precious sword was not in my hand, his smile changed abruptly to a scowl. The double-crosser was not accustomed to being double-crossed. He stepped forward and yanked the towel-wrapped branch out from under my arm. Unexpectedly, he swung it at me and clobbered the side of my head, under the ear. The old man packed quite a wallop. I fell onto the jagged stone of the pyramid's summit and shook off the disorientation, my hand massaging the bruise. Mehrukenah flung the branch away with a cry of anguish. It flew out over the edge and struck a stony shelf about a hundred feet below. Then Mehrukenah stood over me, his corroding teeth a-grinding and his eyes full of fury. He thrust his palm in front of my face, its tendons rigid.

"I could raise this hand over my head, and the throats of your sister and lady friend would be slit from ear to ear," he seethed.

I glanced down toward the valley floor, where Mehrukenah's signal would be received. South of us was the lot where I would have parked if I hadn't followed the road around to the Pyramid of the Moon. I thanked Heavenly Father for my inspiration. If I'd tried to park there, I'd have never made it this far. Thugs might have snatched away the towel-wrapped package and likely killed me even before discovering my ruse. The blue Suburban was there, along with nine or ten other cars, many of which I recognized from yesterday's chase. These were the only vehicles still in the parking lot. The drivers stood around, looking up at us, awaiting the very signal which Mehrukenah was threatening. Most likely, Jenny and Renae were imprisoned in the Suburban.

"But you won't," I replied to Mehrukenah. "Not now. If you did, I promise you would never see the sword again."

"Then I'll kill your lady friend! Perhaps bargaining for the sole survivor will make you a little more reticent."

"You've already murdered Garth. If that didn't humble me enough to bring the sword, what makes you think killing another will?"

I struggled to appear unconquerably fierce, but inside my emotions were near collapse—my heart felt as though it might burst. I knew full well that if I *had* brought the sword, sending the signal would have been exactly what Mehrukenah would have done. Immediately thereafter, the old wraith would have used his blade to slaughter the two Mexican girls, and lastly, he would have killed me. Why else would he have chosen Teotihuacan for this rendezvous, if not to pay homage to the edifice by letting his weapon spill the first blood on these steps that it had tasted in many generations?

"Where is it?!" he thundered.

"It's safe," I replied. "Hidden in a place where no one would find it for a thousand years."

Mehrukenah pulled a dagger from a sheath strapped under his shirt and placed it against my throat.

"If you don't take us there immediately, I'll kill you this very instant."

I smirked at Mehrukenah. "You're ranting, old man. Don't act like a fool. I know full well the only thing you'd love more than killing me is to feel the weight of Akish's creation in your fist."

Mehrukenah studied my face, then his expression relaxed. The wizened Gadianton chuckled. He turned around and continued to feign amusement, glancing back at me and shaking his head. Stopping sharply, he presented another idea.

"I could torture you. It's an art form which I've mastered well. You would retain no secrets."

"Maybe," I concurred. "But maybe I've made arrangements that would make that ineffective as well."

I was bluffing, of course. But he pondered the statement nonetheless.

"Why waste the time?" I continued. "It's really not necessary. I'm perfectly willing to turn over the sword, as long as I can be assured that you'll fulfill your end of the bargain. You must allow the three of us to depart in peace. I've already lost my best friend. I won't lose anyone else. The sword isn't worth it to me. I can't stomach being around it a moment longer."

Mehrukenah paced, never entirely taking his eyes off mine, trying to read my thoughts. He glanced at Shurr, his partner in intrigue. Gadianton's brother looked resigned to my view of the matter. The bloody ceremony they'd been planning atop this pyramid was a trifle compared to finally obtaining the sword. Shurr communicated his opinion to Mehrukenah with a nod. Mehrukenah turned back to me.

"What do you propose, Jimawkins?" he requested, narrowing his eyes.

"The way I see it, we have to find a way to deliver the sword into your hands, while at the same time guaranteeing our deliverance to freedom. I think its obvious we don't really trust each other—am I right? So we're gonna have to do this on terms that we can both agree to."

The muscles in Mehrukenah's neck were pulsating. He didn't like this arrangement at all. He'd never tasted compromise, and he didn't like its flavor.

"I'm listening," he said shortly.

"First, let the *señoritas* go," I insisted. "You have no need of them."

Mehrukenah ordered their bonds to be cut. This was an easy concession. Such hors d'oeuvres for his sacrificial appetite could be recaptured at the snap of the finger. The girls were apprehensive about what to do with their sudden freedom. They looked about, cowering.

"*¡Vayate!*" the thug beside them commanded.

The *señoritas* scurried down the pyramid's steps. The highway was quite visible from here, with its frequent buses running back and forth to Mexico City. Shortly they would be aboard one of those buses, safely returning to their anxious families.

Though this demand was trivial, Mehrukenah treated it as though I'd demanded that he chop off a limb.

"We will make no further concessions," he growled.

"If it means getting the sword, you'll make as many as I choose," I retorted. "Now I will return to my car. Bring Jenny and Renae to the fork where the road into the park divides. Bring only one vehicle."

"And then?"

"We'll discuss it at that time."

I turned around and began descending the pyramid's steps. They made no effort to stop me. Even *I'd* underestimated my powers to gain their cooperation. Their lust for the sword was consuming their minds. As my feet reached the Avenue of the Dead and started northward, I realized I was hyperventilating in an effort to keep the tears from flowing. I wouldn't let myself think about Garth. I had to stay focused. But the harder I tried, the more easily his face appeared, laughing, scolding, smiling in friendship. In spite of my efforts, tears burst from my eyes. *Why, Heavenly Father? Why couldn't it have been me?* How could I be expected to finish this mission without him? I needed his strength, his force of will, his conscience to guide me.

As I reached the platform steps which led up to the north parking lot, I dropped to my knees. Shaking, I gripped the bottom of my shirt in both fists and wiped my eyes. Then I inhaled a few hearty breaths and began climbing the final stone staircase.

I still faced the horrible prospect of mourning the loss of three loved ones before this day was over. I had to clear my head. One of my motives for telling Mehrukenah that we would discuss the details of what to do when we got there was because I still had to figure it out!

The Mazda was the last automobile in the north parking lot, except for some trucks belonging to groundskeepers. Still praying for inspiration, I drove down the road and exited the park. As I reached the designated intersection, the blue Suburban had already arrived. Just as I'd instructed, the vehicle was alone. I pulled onto the grassy shoulder about ten yards beyond them. Mehrukenah and Shurr climbed out of the Suburban and met me halfway. Mr. Clarke remained in the Suburban's backseat with Jenny and Renae.

"We're going to trade vehicles," I announced.

Mehrukenah flared. "Do you think I'm a fool?"

"Hear me out. The three of you will transfer the girls to my car. I will drive the Suburban. Then you will follow me to the place where I've hidden the sword. When we get there, our cars will park a hundred yards from each other. You will then toss my car keys onto the seat, and I will watch you do it."

"Then what will happen?"

"All of you will walk away from my vehicle and return to the Suburban."

"Unacceptable," stated Shurr. "The prisoners will take the keys and escape. Since you value their lives more than your own, you will not fulfill your end of the bargain."

"Then keep their hands bound," I suggested. "That should keep them from driving away, don't you agree?"

"What happens next?" asked Mehrukenah.

"Then I'll tell you where the sword is hidden, and we'll depart."

"Again, unacceptable," parroted Shurr. "How are we to know the sword is hidden where you've said?"

"You'll have to take my word for it."

Mehrukenah laughed. "No, this arrangement will not work. Not unless *you* retrieve the sword."

"I'll agree to that," I replied, "but I won't hand it to you directly. I'll display it from a distance and drop it on the ground. Then you will allow me to return to my vehicle and drive away."

Mehrukenah remained wary. I could see the wheels spinning in his mind, trying to find a trick, a flaw. Something occurred to him. I realized he was remembering that night when he was attacked by Muleki. He'd been confident that the Nephite had no way of following us, yet follow us he did.

"These terms are acceptable on one condition," said Mehrukenah. "That we first be allowed to search you and your car."

"Certainly," I said. "Do you hope to find the sword?"

"No. A spare key."

Mehrukenah indicated the ignition key still in my hand. It was on the same ring with every key I owned—the one to my apartment, the one to my P.E. locker, and the one to my post office box.

"In case you attempt something stupid, I need to know that yours is the only key," he stated.

I pretended to be surprised by his request, then shrugged. "Be my guest."

I lifted my arms, and they searched me thoroughly. Then they searched every inch of the car's interior, including under the floormats. The search took a good ten minutes, with Jenny and Renae watching all the proceedings. Their windows were open, so I was sure they had overheard most of the conversation.

Satisfied that no spare key existed, Mehrukenah coordinated the transfer of prisoners from one vehicle to the other. I was made to stand on the opposite side of the road while Mehrukenah and Shurr, each with a knife at one of the girl's throats, guided them, hands bound behind their backs, to the Mazda.

Jenny and Renae appeared grief-stricken and disheveled. They looked into my eyes for assurance. I smiled tightly, as if to say, "Don't worry. Everything's going to be all right."

The Gadiantons thrust the girls into the backseat. Mr. Clarke approached me and requested my keys, while at the same time handing me the ones to the Suburban. There were two or three keys on their key ring as well, but of course only one for the ignition.

"Is this *your* only ignition key?" I asked him.

"You'll have to wonder," replied Mr. Clarke and turned around.

His coy reply didn't fool me. The Suburban had no spare.

I climbed into the driver's seat, put their key into the ignition, and started the engine. Mr. Clarke did the same. Mehrukenah sat with Jenny and Renae in the backseat, holding his knife where it was plainly visible to me in case I was harboring any foolish notions. They waited for me to pull past them. Afterwards, they were quick to follow.

We drove several more miles, finally turning off the main highway and following a road with more potholes than pavement. Parallel to this road ran a high-flowing canal, about eight feet wide. There were a few scattered neighborhoods of small stucco homes nearby; otherwise the scenery remained quite rural. We crossed a railroad track and continued on another quarter mile to an empty park and picnic area on the south side of the road, across the canal. Once it may have been a thriving recreational retreat with a green and inviting lawn, but now the landscape was choked with weeds. The swing set was a rusted skeleton without swings or chains. The picnic tables were good for nothing but slivers. Farther south, a wire fence line separated the picnic area from the remains of two roofless and crumbling buildings. Beyond this was a dump site with half-buried garbage, planks of wood, and rusty pipes. On either side of this dumping zone were acres of the tall cactus plants from which the *tuna* fruit was harvested.

The park was like an island encircled by a two-tire dirt road. The island was accessed by two crossing points—cement bridges on the east and west ends. The east end of the park looked quite muddy, as if the canal was overflowing nearby. I stopped the Suburban just this side of the west-end bridge and waited for the Mazda to pull up beside me. Shurr's passenger-side window was open.

"Park it here," I instructed, "but first turn it around to face back toward the highway."

They appeared reluctant, knowing this positioning would give me an easy escape. Nevertheless, they did as I instructed. I drove the Suburban on across the west bridge and around the muddy circle until I'd reached the other end of the park, a good hundred yards from where I'd instructed them to park my vehicle. Then I opened the door and stepped outside.

I felt I'd chosen my location well. It was far enough off the main highway that their minions would have a hard time following us. There were so many places to hide something that it would have been foolish for the Gadiantons to hold the three of us at gunpoint and search for the sword themselves. Besides, they had no way of knowing if I was telling the truth or not. Maybe it wasn't here at all.

Mehrukenah, Shurr, and Mr. Clarke were all standing outside the Mazda now, scrutinizing me. Jenny and Renae were still in the backseat. The driver's-side door was open. Mr. Clarke was standing beside it.

I held their key ring over my head for them to see the keys dangling. Mr. Clarke did the same. I tossed their keys onto the Suburban's front seat. Mr. Clarke conspicuously did the same. The sound of me shutting the Suburban's door was echoed by their shutting of the door on the Mazda. We walked toward one another, finally meeting under the rusty swing set.

"I won't bring it out of hiding until I see all of you standing over by the Suburban," I told them.

Mehrukenah stepped up close and glared into my eyes.

"I warn you, Jimawkins, if you attempt to betray us, the next time I'll kill you and the others without hesitation—whether we have the sword or not."

The Gadiantons walked past me. I waited patiently until they had all reached the Suburban before I went into action. There was a shallow, dry ditch running along the park on the west end, parallel to the canal. From the Gadiantons' point of view, they would have seen me step into it, momentarily hidden by the high weeds, and emerge again holding aloft the guitar case that I'd planted there an hour or so earlier. They would have seen me open it, reach inside to grab something, and close it again. As I expected, they were not true to their word. The moment they saw the guitar case, they began stalking in my direction. Spies had undoubtedly reported to Mehrukenah that Garth had taken just such an odd case out of our trunk the same day we'd picked up Jenny from her apartment. Immediately, I tossed the guitar case into the canal and made a mad dash for our car, allowing the current to carry the package downstream, toward the Gadiantons. As the guitar case was thrown, and as it landed with a sizable splash, they should have heard a bulky object bouncing around inside. They also should have noticed that the guitar case floated low in the water, as if it contained something quite heavy. As I'd hoped, their pursuit faltered. Mehrukenah commanded Mr. Clarke to jump into the water after it.

Just as Mr. Clarke had seized the case and was trying to swim it back to the edge, I reached the Mazda and threw open the front door. There was no time to enjoy my reunion with Jenny and Renae, or even to untie them.

"We've gotta get outa here!" I cried. "When they open that case, all they're gonna find is the tire jack."

"Then where's the sword?" asked Renae.

"Where the tire jack used to be," I replied. "Under the carpet in the trunk."

"You mean it was here all along?" shrieked Jenny.

Renae added, "So that's what Mehrukenah meant when he said he felt the sword was very near."

Fortunately, he hadn't known *how* near. The Gadiantons had been very thorough about searching every inch of the car's interior, yet it hadn't occurred to them to search the trunk. I recalled that they had already searched it once back in San Luis Potosi. I picked up the key ring off the seat. After a quick assessment of the keys, I snorted and tossed the whole bunch of them aside.

"What's the matter?" asked Renae.

"Mehrukenah is too predictable," I declared. "The ignition key is missing from the ring."

I saw in the rearview mirror that the Gadiantons had found the tire jack. We heard another splash as it and the guitar case were angrily tossed back into the canal. Now the Gadiantons were marching toward us with their guns and daggers drawn, a slavering Mehrukenah leading the way. Jenny and Renae looked back in terror.

"They promised to kill us immediately if you betrayed them, Jim!" gasped Renae.

The girls were near hysteria, when suddenly they heard the car's engine turn over as I twisted the spare key in the ignition. Mehrukenah screamed out a terrible curse and began charging us. The other Gadiantons were thinking much more practically and began running back toward the Suburban. As I hit the gas pedal, my wheels sent a spray of black Mexican mud onto Mehrukenah's clothing. The Mazda peeled away down the road, back toward the main highway.

"But I saw them search you," Jenny declared. "I saw them look under the floor mat. Where was the key hidden?"

"In the guitar case," I revealed. "When we reach the main highway, I'll untie you."

"Never mind!" Renae insisted. "They'll be behind us any minute!"

"I don't think so," I said.

"What are you talking about? Why not?"

"Because warped minds think alike," I replied, and to prove it, I held up the Suburban's ignition key.

CHAPTER 24

"Garth isn't dead," Jenny declared. "No matter what they might have told you, I don't believe it."

"Explain to me everything that happened," I urged.

"After we visited that old Catholic church," Jenny began, "we wandered up to the plaza where we'd parked the car to look at the Christmas lights. That's where they attacked."

"They threatened Garth with death if he didn't tell them where you were," added Renae. "When Garth continued to resist, Mehrukenah told Shurr to take him somewhere quiet where no one would hear him scream. Shurr and some other men put him in one of the other cars and drove away."

"Where were they taking him?"

"I don't know," Jenny admitted. "But Shurr met us on the highway about two hours later. We watched them through the window. We couldn't hear what they were saying, but we could tell Mehrukenah was furious, as if Garth had escaped. A few minutes later they told us he was dead, but I didn't believe them."

"Jenny, maybe . . . maybe Mehrukenah was angry because Garth refused to give in all the way to the end."

"No!" Jenny insisted. "I know he's okay. Even when they told us he'd been killed, I couldn't cry for him, because I knew it wasn't true."

It occurred to me that if Garth had escaped, the first place he'd have gone would have been the Hotel Filher in San Luis Potosi to try and find me. We had to locate a phone.

I turned north on Highway 130 and found a tiny motel. We parked our car where it couldn't be seen from the highway and asked the motel's desk clerk to help us make a long-distance call to the Filher. Renae spoke with the Filher's manager, asking if Garth had returned—asking a half-dozen different ways to see if it might inspire a memory. Disheartened, she got off the phone and shook her head.

"I don't care!" Jenny cried. "He's alive! Call it intuition—call it anything you like!"

A psychologist might have called it denial. But despite our dread, Jenny's conviction gave us all a sliver of hope.

"We should go back to San Luis Potosi and look for him," I suggested.

Jenny eagerly agreed, but Renae became the voice of reason.

"Even if he *did* escape, he wouldn't have stayed in San Luis Potosi. He would have tried to follow us, Jim. Whether he's alive or not, he would have wanted you to continue on to Veracruz and complete the mission. You *know* he would."

Renae was right. But taking the shortest route to Veracruz—southward back through Mexico City—would have undoubtedly placed us right in the middle of a desperate ambush. At Renae's urging, we continued *northward* on Highway 130. Our destination was the city of Poza Rica, where Renae had once been an exchange student. She said we could stay with a family she knew there, maybe get some help, and rest up on the Sabbath. I almost objected to waiting a day, knowing the delay would give the Gadiantons time to position themselves at the Hill Vigia. But our going to Poza Rica was going to give them an eight or ten hour advantage over us anyway. Besides, Garth would have approved of our resting on the Sabbath.

It was dark by the time we reached a town called Tulancingo. Our anxiety over Garth kept anyone from feeling hunger, but to keep up our strength, I insisted we get something to eat. We found a place with a big sign reading *Hamburguesas*.

Before we'd even ordered, Renae announced that she was feeling ill. For the last couple of hours, I'd felt sickness coming on as well, though I hadn't told anyone. Somebody had to get us over the winding mountain roads that Renae said would dominate the rest of our journey into Poza Rica. Renae ate one bite of her hamburger and asked to be excused. I forced my own meal down with another bottle of apple soda. After dinner, we found Renae curled up in a blanket in the backseat of the car, her face ghostly white.

"You gonna be okay?" I asked.

"Sometimes it doesn't matter how hard you try," she confessed, "you still get a touch of the 'revenge.' Don't worry. Normally it only lasts twenty-four hours."

We continued into the mountains. The perils of driving this stretch of highway at night were many; nevertheless, I navigated without the help of the sword. Only an hour out of Tulancingo, my nausea was overwhelming. Tonight's meal ended up in a ditch along the side of the road.

"Jen," I moaned, "you're gonna have to take over."

"Here?!" she cried. "On these steep roads? I can't!"

"It's either that, or we spend the night here in the mountains."

"When my curse kicks in, we'll spend the night in the mountains anyway—at the bottom of a gorge!"

"Please, Jenny," I begged. "You have to try."

Only after I'd pleaded another minute would she give up her place in the passenger's seat. Swallowing her fears, my sister pulled back onto the roadway. Renae handed me a couple of pills left over from her first trip to Mexico, saying they'd keep us from having to stop at every other rest room.

The road became even narrower and more dangerous. The curves were so sharp and obscure, there was little way of telling if another vehicle was approaching. The asphalt was even more broken and decayed than the road into Chihuahua. But to make matters worse, one false move, instead of sending us hurling into the desert, would send us tumbling into a chasm hundreds of feet deep.

Every time a pair of oncoming headlights appeared, Jenny would squint and slow down. Once the headlights were a semi-truck, barreling down the slope at maximum speed. Jenny froze. She hit the brakes and brought the Mazda to a complete stop in the middle of the road. She covered her eyes and the truck whizzed by, missing us by an inch. Maybe it was a foot. My illness had put me in too much of a delirium to say for sure.

We sat still in the Mexican night for what seemed like several minutes, until a car came up from behind, honked its horn, and drove around us. At that moment I saw that familiar grit rise from Jenny's soul—the sternness of a sea captain. The Mazda lurched forward, soon even passing the car that had overtaken us.

Since leaving Teotihuacan, we'd seen three different kinds of terrain. Soon after entering the mountains, the dry plateau had become a coniferous forest. After our descent toward Poza Rica, we entered what appeared to be a tropical jungle, about as thick as any jungle can get—the hillsides flourishing with vast plantations of bananas, vanilla beans, and coffee.

Ever since I was a little boy, I'd dreamed of seeing a jungle. The only thing missing was that I was no longer a little boy, nestled in cheerful fantasies. Though the sword had remained in the trunk, where I thought I was free from its influence, there were moments that I swore it was whispering to me, insulting me, desperate to convince me that without it, I was nothing. As sick as I was, full of grief, and trying to solidify my convictions for truth and right, these were not the kind of whisperings I wanted to hear.

It was just past midnight when Jenny announced that we'd arrived in Poza Rica. The streets were busy with traffic and pedestrians. Nobody seemed to sleep in this country. It was the Christmas season, and every night was a time for *fiesta*.

Wearily, Renae sat up and instructed us to turn at the next intersection.

We entered a quiet, darkened neighborhood where the car high-centered twice on the uneven dirt road. A few blocks farther, Renae directed us into the driveway of a small but well-constructed home with a yard full of plants and fruit trees. There was an old, mud-splattered Chevy pickup in the driveway ahead of us.

Curious faces pressed against the screen on the front doorway. As we emerged from the car, I heard the children shout "Renae!" and lunge forward to embrace her.

Renae mustered her remaining strength to wrap them in her arms and cry, "*¡Rosalinda! ¡Nephi! ¡Como te has crecido!*"

This was the Corral family—Latter-day Saints extraordinaire, right down to the poster of the Mexico City Temple on the front room wall and the five boys named, from oldest to youngest, Mormon, Helaman, Ammon, Moroni, and Nephi. One of the girls was even named Sariah. The father, Guillermo Corral, was a member of the bishopric. He and his wife, Julia, had been baptized as newlyweds and sealed two years later in the Salt Lake City Temple. Though the home was phoneless, with only throw rugs, Guillermo was actually one of the richer members of the community—considered upper-middle class. He operated a distribution business, supplying rubbing alcohol, aspirin, and vitamins to many of the drugstores, or *farmacias*, in the state of Veracruz.

There was a ninety-year-old grandmother living with them—her eyes sparkling the way my Grandma Tucker's had in the years before she passed away. She took my hand in hers and said, "*Es su casa* (Consider this your home)."

Guillermo spoke decent English, thanks to Renae's tutelage. We told him about our plight, omitting some of the more incomprehensible details. Guillermo trusted Renae and anyone associated with her. Though we couldn't fully explain why we had to reach Santiago Tuxtla and the Hill Vigia, he didn't push, and asked what he might do to help.

"We need a place to stay," Renae told him. "And we'd like to go to your sacrament meeting—if we can make it. Jim and I are a little 'under the weather.'"

"We'll be gone early Monday morning," I promised.

Truly, these people were a Godsend. It wasn't long before the mother was concocting a recipe of her own to relieve our sickness. Although we told them we'd happily spread out our sleeping bag and blankets on the floor, the parents and two of the older children had already dragged in their own bedding, insisting that they would give us their rooms and sleep on the floor themselves. Everyone showered us with love and attention. The fifteen-year-old daughter noticed the bruise from Mehrukenah's blow under my ear and created a poultice for it. And I thought *my* family was accommodating!

That night, though I was lying in my sleeping bag on a comfortable mattress, sleep came only with patience and effort. The walls were thin, and I could hear Jenny sobbing in the next room. In daylight she could confidently declare that Garth was still alive, but it was dark now and her subconscious doubts were rising to the surface.

Through my bedroom window I watched a canopy of shadowy clouds float in off the Gulf of Mexico. When a hole appeared and the glimmer of a few Mexican stars broke though, I was finally able to fall asleep. I'd always felt that Garth and I could travel to the ends of the universe and back. As long as the universe was still up there, Garth had to be alive in it somewhere, looking up at those same stars.

By the next morning, Renae's health had returned. Though I was still in the last hours of recovery, I was at least well enough to attend church with the Corral family in their newly constructed stake center. Jenny and I sang "Now Let Us Rejoice" and "I Know That My Redeemer Lives" in English while everyone else sang it in Spanish.

The sacrament talks and Sunday School lesson were hard to follow since Renae just couldn't interpret the words fast enough, and in priesthood I had to be content just to sit there and smile. But it really didn't matter what they were saying. What mattered was that today I was among the Saints. I realized it made no difference where I was in the world; if there were Saints, I was home.

I hoped the Corral family didn't consider us rude, but after we'd eaten a hearty lunch with the children, the three of us were so exhausted from the trials of the previous days that we napped all afternoon. Jenny and Renae went right on napping into the evening.

I was unable to sleep much later than seven o'clock on account of some pressing and difficult matters on my mind. I approached Guillermo with a very serious request. The primary problem I faced in getting close enough to the Hill Vigia to fulfill my mission was Jenny's Mazda. By now, our enemies had trained themselves to spot it. According to the map, there was only one highway into Santiago Tuxtla. I felt certain I would never make it there if I drove the Mazda. So I asked Guillermo if I could borrow his mud-splattered Chevy.

He was hesitant at first. Guillermo depended upon his truck to operate his business. A car couldn't carry a dozen crates of rubbing alcohol. But the fact was, his truck was worth about five hundred dollars, whereas the Mazda might bring in a couple thousand. I told him if we returned his truck inoperable, he could sell the Mazda for a much worthier set of wheels. I was sure that Jenny would agree. With a smile, Guillermo accepted my terms. Hesitantly, I made one more request.

"I can't take the girls," I told him. "Where I'm going, I have to go alone. Jenny and Renae would never hear of that. They would strap on the seatbelts and refuse to get out of the truck."

"Especially Renae," Guillermo chuckled.

"They believe we're leaving in the morning. Instead, I will leave tonight—right now. Please take care of them until I return—and whatever you do, don't let them follow me."

Guillermo saw the solemnity in my eyes, and he knew how much pain it brought me to have to make such a decision.

"I will do this for you, Jim," he agreed.

I also persuaded their oldest boy, Mormon, to loan me his sunglasses and visor cap with the slogan *"¡Qué Sabroso!"* stamped across the front to advertise a bottle of soda pop.

After retrieving my duffel bag from the bedroom, I quietly made my way past the rooms where Jenny and Renae were sleeping. The door to Renae's room was slightly ajar. Peering in, I watched her for a moment. The crimson light of the lowering sun was creeping in from her window, illuminating her face and reflecting off the flowing locks of ebony black hair that curled around her pillow.

"I love you," I whispered, unheard.

As I drove away, I was haunted by the regret of never having spoken those words to her out loud. Would she ever hear them? I determined in my heart that if I ever saw her again, they would be the first words out of my mouth.

It was the last leg of my journey. The sword was firmly set in its scabbard on the passenger's side of the seat. I turned onto Highway 180 and ascended the tropical hillsides above the town, rife with sugar cane, banana, and coffee. Within an hour I was driving parallel with the angry, sapphire seas of the Gulf of Mexico, its waves crashing against the grassy beaches, trying to escape a storm swirling out on the horizon. There was lightning out there too, the fiery white projectiles becoming more bright and menacing as the sun faded behind the inland mountains.

A few hours later, as I crossed the bridge at Santa Ana, I heard a voice, as distinct as if I'd been entertaining a passenger beside me, but the voice had not been created by sound.

I know where you're taking me . . .

I looked at the sword, still as frozen and dead as the first time I'd seen it, yet somehow, tonight it was breathing. A burning began in my breast, spreading outward to my limbs, pulsating, trying to imitate God's confirmation of truth. I turned forward again and tightened my grip on the wheel.

. . . but I don't think you understand.

Muleki was right. I'd sensed an increase of power in this object through every mile of our journey. I was now close enough to the land of its creation to feel the heat of the smelter that had forged it upon my brow. Words continued streaming into my head, as if they were my own thoughts. Maybe they were.

This is not a land of death, Jim. It is a land of glory. Not the glory of cowards like yourself. The glory of heroes.

I couldn't believe this. A hunk of metal was calling me names! I laughed out loud. It didn't seem to appreciate my sense of humor.

You don't have to be a coward, Jim. I can make you anything you desire. Anything you're brave enough to dream.

Then I want to be left alone, I said in my mind. I want my thoughts to be my own, and I want to *know* that they're my own.

Do you think they're not? Do you think I can create such aspirations out of the blue? I cannot—not unless the thoughts were there to begin with. You've never been a man who bows down to medioc-

rity, Jim. There's a whole world out there. A world you've always dreamed could be yours. There's no greater pain than to have a passion for greatness with no certain means of obtaining it. Why be tortured by failure and shattered hopes? Why waste all of that time and energy? Why, Jim?

Because it's my time, and it's my energy—not yours. And it never will be.

Never? Never is a long time, Jim Hawkins.

* * *

This was oil country, and Veracruz was one of the largest ports for crude export in the world. I could see its lights glowing up into the night from twenty miles away, reminding me of the lights of Las Vegas from way off in the desert. I never saw its streets, only the lights. It was unnecessary to drive directly through Veracruz. The highway bypassed it on the west, and soon its glow faded well behind me.

Before long the highway was paralleling the ocean again. There was a ten-mile stretch where the grasses on either side of the road were especially tall. Dozens of white crabs could be seen dashing out of the grass and making their way across the roadway in an attempt to reach the ocean. Many had been smashed by the wheels of previous cars, their exoskeletons carpeting the asphalt. Even at this early hour, local anglers patrolled the roadsides with a ready bag.

I crossed many more bridges and followed the highway farther inland. All along the route I half-expected to see familiar cars off to the side of the road, watching for my arrival in the Mazda. Curiously, I never noticed any—although darkened vehicles hiding in the shrubbery might have been easily missed.

At last I passed a sign announcing my arrival in the village of Santiago Tuxtla. Even in the pitch black of night, with an overcast sky, the landscape was still slightly darker than the heavens. Rising above the village, not far to the southwest, loomed the silhouette of a mighty hill, nearly the size of a mountain. This was doubtless the fortress locals had christened Vigia, or "Lookout Hill." What I hoped beyond all hope was that it was also the place where a quarter-million Nephites had made their final stand—the hill which the ancient prophet Mormon had called Cumorah.

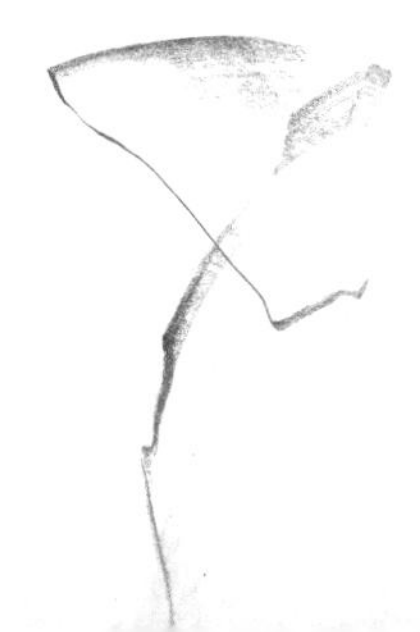

CHAPTER 25

It didn't take long to find Santiago Tuxtla's central square. I parked along its edge and turned off the headlights of Guillermo's pickup. It was four a.m. now, still hours before sunrise. I realized it would be insane to try and climb that jungled hill in the dark. The odds of losing my way in the light were bad enough. My body clock was all screwed up. Despite yesterday's rest, I was struggling desperately to keep my eyelids up. I slapped myself. I couldn't allow myself to fall asleep—not here, out in the open and vulnerable. Who knew what faces might be sneering down through my window when I awoke? Looking at the distant profile of Vigia, I could tell it would require an arduous two- to three-hour climb. In my present state of weariness, the very thought filled my head with dismal images. I had to get some sleep, if only for a couple of hours.

Neon lights across the square were flashing "Hotel Castellano." It was by far the tallest structure in the community—an eight-story circular edifice, not unlike the Leaning Tower of Pisa, without the "leaning" part. I wondered how such a large hotel in this small of a town could ever make any money.

I strapped the sword to my waist and cautiously exited Guillermo Corral's rusty Chevy. The village square was graveyard calm, empty except for the myriad of tropical plants. The humidity was so thick I thought I might have to cut my way through it with the sword. There was a gigantic boulder in the middle of the square, about seven or eight feet tall and wide. Someone had carved it to look like a massive head.

Only a few lights illuminated the neighborhood, the brightest being the ones shining from the hotel lobby. Inside, I found a boyish desk clerk with his nose buried in paperwork. My voice startled him when I requested a room. It wasn't exactly a common hour for receiving new patrons. Though he spoke only a little English, we were able to agree that I would stay until Tuesday morning. After I forked over one hundred and sixty thousand pesos, he handed me a key to room 307. In my wallet there was only a little over one hundred thousand pesos remaining, or about thirty-five dollars—not even enough for the gas it would take to get back to the U.S. border. Renae had told me that the residue of our American money had been stolen by Mehrukenah's men. The rest of our finances had been with Garth. Even if he was still alive, would they have left his bankroll intact? It seemed doubtful.

I signed my name to the register. I was too sleepy to come up with a creative pseudonym. I simply spelled out "George Bush" and gave myself an address in Washington, D.C.

Even though my floor was only two flights up, I chose the laziest means of ascension—the elevator. As I approached the elevator doors, I passed under the center circle of the hotel, hollow all the way to the ceiling—an architectural view even more dramatic than the one in the Hotel Filher, but without the weeping vines or colonial elegance.

All the rooms on the third floor, as on all the floors, were situated at the outermost ring of the circle. The elevator was built into a side hallway, or rather a gap in the outermost ring. The hallway led around to each room's door, meeting back where it started, and was contained by a solid plaster handrail. Twenty feet and two flights below, I could see the cushy furniture of the hotel lobby. My room was just around the corner and two doors to the right.

I almost wished I'd left my duffel bag in the truck, instead of adding to the tremendous burden of carrying the sword. It had become so inexplicably heavy. I was certain it was only an illusion, but illusion or not, when I unbuckled it from my waist and let it drop to the floor, I felt like I'd unloaded a granite-filled backpack.

I nestled myself onto the soft mattress of the double bed without removing my shoes or clothes. My intention was only to doze until it was barely light outside. Unfortunately, when I finally awakened, it was four hours later.

The sun was bright outside my window—too bright. I narrowly avoided cursing. I'd hoped to begin my climb in the dimness of sunrise, when pedestrians were scarce and I could spot my enemies more readily. It was almost nine now; the narrow streets of Santiago Tuxtla would already be bustling with natives.

I slapped water on my face and washed away the dog tears around my eyes. There were two bottles of mineral water on the nightstand between the beds. I guzzled them both, and wiped my mouth with the back of my hand. After restrapping the cumbersome scabbard and sword about my waist, I cautiously opened the door and poked my head out into the hall.

The coast was clear, except for a maid's supply cart outside one of the open rooms across the circle. It was somewhat comforting to know that even if I'd failed to wake up when I did, the maid's knock would have alerted me in a few minutes anyway. I hailed the elevator and pressed the button to the lobby. The elevator opened facing the hotel's front entrance.

I paused as I stepped into the street. The first daylight view I had of *El Cerro Vigia* held me breathless. Behind it, far to the west, were the remains of last night's overcast sky, giving the jungled hill, its base terraced with bright green pastures and crop-filled fields, a darkened backdrop that made it all the more menacing. A horseshoe of clouds hung around Vigia's summit, illustrating my destination like a circle on a map.

I hesitated no longer. The base of the hill was just beyond the borders of the village. As I climbed back into Guillermo's truck, I noticed that I was being watched. Not by Gadiantons—at least I didn't *think* they were Gadiantons—but by the police. A patrol car was parked at the north end of the plaza, its officers enjoying breakfast at one of the food stands. I wished I knew what they were thinking. Maybe they'd seen the unconcealed sword. Or maybe they just thought it strange that a gringo should be climbing into a truck with Mexican license plates. What proof did I have that I hadn't stolen it? Boy, all I needed was more trouble from the cops. Fortunately, as I started the engine and rolled past them around the square, they stayed in their places and continued chewing their food.

I drove through the village's muddy, cobbled streets, dodging more burros than cars. It didn't take long to find the street that brought me closest to the hill. All roads seemed to converge into it, but before long, the pathway became so narrow and ill-defined that traversing it with a vehicle was quite impossible.

After parking on a grassy patch along the edge of a grove of orange trees, I donned the cap and sunglasses that Guillermo's son had given me in Poza Rica. It was a miserably meager disguise. But even if I'd been wearing "Freddy Kruger" makeup, the sword would have made me identifiable in a cast of thousands. As a final solution, I reached into the pickup bed and grabbed a plastic tarp which Guillermo must have used on rainy days to cover his stock. I wrapped the sword inside it and bundled it all together with an accompanying strip of cord. Over my shoulder, it looked like a bedroll of sorts. The very end of the sword's hilt stuck out of the bundle, making it easy enough to draw, should the situation require it. I knew this getup would only deflect attention for a few seconds, but maybe that few seconds would be all I needed.

After abandoning the pickup, I continued up the narrow and muddy road. It led me down a final declivity, bypassing a last row of shabby homes, gawking housewives, children, and farm animals. A maroon-spotted pig, at least twice my weight, snorted at me in disapproval and kicked its heels. It seemed to know I didn't belong here. Fortunately, a thick rope kept it from getting too near.

At the bottom of the hollow there was a makeshift bridge of wooden planks. It crossed a stream of the clearest water I'd yet seen in Mexico, gushing from a fountain of fresh spring water somewhere amidst Vigia's slopes. Lizards darted from stone to stone. One was a good fifteen inches long, counting the tail, with a fin on its head like a dinosaur. It escaped across the water on two legs that were spinning so rapidly the creature didn't sink.

The path became cobbled, though still very muddy, despite the fact that it was Mexico's dry season. The way got steeper; I'd officially begun my ascent of the hill. Several Mexican villagers passed me coming down. They smiled and nodded, finding my presence curious but not something to stop the presses. They'd seen American tourists before, many of whom I'm sure were Latter-day Saints.

I was dripping so much sweat you'd have thought I'd just stepped out of the shower. Oddly, the villagers looked perfectly dry and comfortable, even with heavy loads of stick bundles and coconuts strapped to their backs. They were usually barefoot, with mud caked all the way up to their knees. The mud was climbing just as high up my jeans.

The jungle grew denser. The number of huts off to the side of the trail seemed to be tapering. It wasn't long before I found myself panting and turning back to check my altitude. Either the village of Santiago Tuxtla was sinking, or I'd made a considerable amount of progress. I could see the hotel where I'd slept and the highway leading back toward Veracruz. The landscape was enchanting, like something out of a Terry Brooks novel. Everything was green and burgeoning with life and sustenance. Still, I couldn't allow myself to get caught up in the scenery. I had to maintain my focus on the task at hand. The weight of the sword seemed to have doubled just since I'd started the climb. And there was so much farther to go.

I was surprised by the approach of a man with a machete. He was older, with a heavy touch of gray in his black hair. Though he didn't seem to be attacking, he was yelling at me frantically, half in Spanish and half in English.

"*¡No se adelante! ¡Mala gente los espera en El Cerro Vigia!* Bad people on mountain! *¡Les esperamos y ya llegaron!* They are here! You stop and go back!"

"I don't understand. *Who* is on the mountain?"

"The Gadiantons," announced a familiar voice behind me.

I turned abruptly, just in time to see Garth Plimpton emerging from the trees.

* * *

This was likely the closest I'd ever come to understanding the joy felt by onlookers who saw Lazarus rise from the tomb. My soul was spinning somersaults as we grasped each other's shoulders. Garth's first concerns were for Jenny and Renae.

"They're fine!" I reported. "Mehrukenah tried to use them as bait for the sword, but I outwitted him. They're staying with an LDS family in Poza Rica, about six hours north."

Garth looked relieved. "I've been hiding here since Saturday night, watching for them and for you. I knew you'd come this way. It's the only trail on this side of the hill. Antonio here has been helping me. He's an Indian. That's his house over there. I trust him."

"Garth, how did you get here?"

"By bus," he explained. "Mexico has buses to every corner of this country. Actually, Santiago Tuxtla is a major stop from Veracruz. It's on the main highway to the resort area of Lake Catemaco."

"Then . . . Mehrukenah and the rest are here?" I asked.

Garth nodded gravely. "They arrived yesterday afternoon. About twenty of them climbed this trail. But Mehrukenah and Shurr didn't leave a single man behind to watch for us. I get the feeling that they want to keep everyone in fairly close proximity, as if they fear that one of their men will get hold of the sword first and steal it for themselves. They're up there waiting for us now. We've got to go another way. Antonio gave me directions to a road that he says leads to the very top by a completely different route. He helped build it many years ago to get equipment up there for an electrical relay station. It's a long jungle road, crossing a score of other hills before it reaches the base of Vigia. There might be a few places washed out by last season's rain, but according to him, it's the only other way."

"You go now," said Antonio. "Get back before dark."

Garth took off his shoe and reached in to grab some ten-thousand peso bills. Stuffing the money under his foot hadn't been such a silly idea after all. He handed the bills to Antonio, saying, "*Muchas gracias por todo su ayuda.*"

Antonio took the money gratefully. I felt sure it was more than he normally made in a week.

Before we left, Antonio pointed back up the hill and asked, "Those men, they thieves or witches?"

Garth considered his question. "A little of both, I reckon."

"Thieves, we have no use for," Antonio said. "I get neighbors, we fight. But witches . . ." His tone grew somber. "We no mess with witches."

As we walked back down the hill, Garth told me how he'd escaped from Shurr and the two other thugs who had been brought along to witness his execution.

"I was in the backseat with Shurr as we drove out into the country—looking for some private and secluded place to conduct their 'interrogation.' The knots on my hands gave a little. I'd slipped my left wrist free just as the car slowed down to avoid barreling through a large fiesta crowd outside a country church. A fat man—I'd swear he was drunk—started banging on the car's hood and then on Shurr's window. While Shurr was distracted, I threw open the door and dashed into the crowd. I'm sure they pursued me, but I ran for an hour across the countryside without looking back."

"Why didn't you go back to the hotel?" I asked.

"I did," Garth insisted. "But by then it was nine o'clock. You'd already left."

"You should have left a message. Mehrukenah told Jenny and Renae that you were dead!"

"Can we call them?"

I shook my head. "The people they're staying with don't have a phone."

Garth sighed. "I'm sorry. All I could think about was finding a bus to Veracruz and then to here. I knew my only hope of ever meeting up with you again was to arrive first."

"Well, then, let's get this sword to the top and finish the mission," I declared. "How long is the drive up this road?"

"Antonio said a couple of hours—about the same length of time it would take to climb."

"And you don't think anyone will oppose us?"

"I hope not," said Garth. "Antonio says that not many outsiders know about the road. But the reality is, either route takes us to the same summit. If they're waiting for us at the very top, I'm fresh out of ideas."

We reached the stream and bridge. A minute later we were climbing back into Guillermo's Chevy. My energy level had plummeted. I was desperately hungry. We decided to return briefly to the hotel to find something to eat. As we parked again alongside the city square, I asked Garth if he was still convinced that we'd found the right hill. He pointed out the ancient stone head in the middle of the plaza.

"Antonio says the villagers found that head on Vigia many years ago. It was up there three thousand years, carved by a people that archeologists call *Olmecs.* The Olmecs are considered by many to be among the oldest civilizations in the New World. Some LDS scholars believe the rise and fall of the Olmecs corresponds so closely to the rise and fall of the Jaredites that, for all practical purposes, Olmecs *were* Jaredites."

We walked back toward the hotel. As Garth spoke, I kept my eye on the policemen, still visiting with local merchants along the south street of the plaza. Either they hadn't seen us return, or they'd lost interest.

"What's even more fascinating," Garth continued, "is that according to Antonio, the villagers here are taught that the Olmecs fought a great battle on that hill."

As we entered the hotel lobby, I told Garth my room number. Then I pointed toward the restaurant and asked him to order us some lunch while I went upstairs to change into some pants and sneakers that weren't caked in mud. As I carried the tarp-bundled sword into the elevator, the mud on my shoes left some ugly tracks. I felt bad for the poor maid who'd just mopped it.

After I'd closed the door of my room behind me, I proceeded to change into another pair of jeans. I'd also brought an extra pair of "high tops"—not quite as comfortable as the first, but at least they were clean. As I was tying the last shoelace, there was a knock on the door.

I hesitated, then asked, "Is that you, Garth?"

"Maid service," said a heavily accented female voice.

I looked around the room. The wrinkled covers on my bed had been pulled taut. There was a new towel hanging above the sink, and two new bottles of mineral water on the nightstand.

"You've already cleaned in here!" I called out.

There was no reply. I waited another moment. Apparently she'd recognized her mistake and decided to move on. I felt very nervous all of a sudden. Would a maid who cleaned this building every day have made such a mistake? It occurred to me that she might have seen the mud tracks leading up to my door. It would have been easy enough to find the culprit—just follow the trail. Then it occurred to me—anyone who'd seen me enter the hotel could have located me just as easily.

I lifted the sword and bundle back over my shoulder and carefully approached the door, trying to keep the floor from creaking. Before opening it, I listened.

I called out again, "Hello? Are you still there?"

Again, there was no reply.

I swallowed. Had it been a mistake to come back here? Had Garth been mistaken about all of Mehrukenah's men climbing the mountain? Why couldn't I acquire an instinct for these things? I felt angry inside, as if the Lord should have been doing more to keep me out of these situations.

Slowly, I opened the door, ready to slam it shut again if someone tried to force their way in. Peeking out into the hallway, not a patron or maid was in sight. I had to conclude she'd disappeared into the elevator or stairwell. I moved slowly into the hallway and made my way around the circle. Halfway to the elevator, I had the peculiar feeling that I was being watched. I glanced over the handrail and down at the lobby two floors below, certain that I would see someone looking up.

My guess was exactly wrong. Behind me, the door to room 306 flew open with a crash. A female voice shrieked. Standing in the doorway was Todd Finlay, aiming a handgun at my belly. His other arm held the maid around the throat. Having no further need of her, Todd pushed the girl back into Room 306 and slammed the door, growling, "Come out and I'll kill you!"

He turned his maniacal grin back on me.

"I wish you had listened. I always liked you, Jim. I don't know why you turned against me."

"Todd," I pleaded, "can't you see what the sword has done to you?"

"You're wasting my time! The sword and I have a mission—a *great* mission. Hand it over."

I let the tarp bundle slide off my shoulder and drop to the ground. I couldn't believe I had lost. It seemed so tragic to have come so far. We were so close; our goal was only a stone's throw away. I looked down at the sword's shining hilt. It was right beside my hand. It would slide out of the bundle so easily.

I can protect you, if you let me.

A split second later I found myself hoisting the sword out from between the layers of tarp. I held it aloft, prepared to follow an impulse to strike.

I heard the elevator arrive.

But the sound was overshadowed by the echo of Todd's gun. *He'd pulled the trigger!* For a moment my mind blacked out. No—I was conscious, but I no longer had control. The blade of the sword adjusted, but I don't believe it was my muscle that moved it. Yet who else's muscle could it have been?

The explosion from the chamber of Todd's pistol was nearly simultaneous with the chink of metal-on-metal, like a rod against a tuning fork. But the note ended bluntly, drowned out by Todd Finlay's scream as a spark created by the bullet's ricochet flashed on the muzzle of his pistol. He released the weapon as if it had shocked him, letting it fall to the floor.

Peripherally, I saw Garth emerge from the elevator, dropping our sandwiches. But I had no time to consider him. My next action seemed so obvious, so clear. Todd Finlay had to die.

But *I* couldn't do the killing! It wasn't in my nature! Yet if that were true, why were my arms hefting the sword overhead? Why was I stepping toward him? Surely my actions were involuntary, and yet they weren't involuntary at all. I was fully aware of what I was doing—it just didn't matter. The hatred was so overwhelming—so all-consuming. Something horrid had sprung to life within me, something I never knew existed—*never wanted to know!* And yet at this moment, I actually *liked* it.

"Nooooo!" Garth screamed.

Todd was cowering on the floor, writhing like a mealworm. Destroying him was good. Nothing could be so righteous. The blade was falling. But before it could strike, Garth's shoulder hit my chest like a freight train.

The impact forced every ounce of oxygen from my lungs. My waist hit the railing—and I was still tripping backward! Garth had sent us both plummeting over the handrail! We were doomed to fall twenty feet to the stone tile floor of the hotel lobby! Had Garth gone nuts? My best friend had just succeeded in killing us *both!* We flipped once in mid-air—the ceiling, the second-floor handrail, the lobby—all of them were rotating in my vision. Garth became positioned beneath me for impact—and impact we did, but not on the stony floor. Garth's back collided with one of the lobby couches, but it was not a bull's-eye. The back of the couch split from the bench. I heard the crack of Garth's upper leg against an armrest. The sword bounced from my grip as we hit, leaving a gouge mark in the tiles and sliding over near the front desk.

I bounced off Garth and onto the floor, rolling onto my back, shocked and disoriented, my elbow and ribs throbbing with pain. My eyesight was blurry; the desk clerk's voice was echoing. The moment my vision normalized, and I could see that Garth was alive and moving, I yelled, *"Are you crazy?!"*

"You would have killed him, Jim," he mumbled, wincing at the pain in his leg. "You would have become one of them."

I hobbled to my feet, walking in a circle, trying to reorient my mind. Where was the all-consuming hatred? Had I really been a fraction of a second away from slaughtering a defenseless man? It seemed so long ago—so incomprehensible now! I felt nothing anymore, nothing but the instinctive fear that prey feels for a predator still lurking.

My head quickly turned as I heard the elevator doors open. Todd was emerging, the pistol back in his grip.

"¡Alto!" a stern voice commanded.

The police officers from the square were standing in the entranceway of the hotel, their weapons aimed at Todd, cocked and ready to fire.

"¡Pistola al suelo imediatamente—o te mato!"

I could tell it was a difficult decision for Todd to drop his weapon; nevertheless, his survival instincts prevailed. He set down the gun and raised his hands in the air.

It was Todd Finlay who would live out my nightmare of incarceration in a Mexican prison.

CHAPTER 26

A moment later, the Mexican police had Todd in handcuffs. As they began to escort him to their patrol car across the square, Todd turned and looked at me. His expression was no longer a threat of vengeance. Instead, I saw bitter sadness—not remorse, but regret—and a lostness. He shook his head as if to say, "Why couldn't you have just given it back to me?"

One of the officers called back to us, *"¡Quedense!"* and gestured with his hand for us to stay put.

Many of the hotel and restaurant staff had gathered around; villagers on the sidewalk were peering in. The desk clerk was strangely drawn to the fallen sword. He picked it up to admire its workmanship. I stepped over and snatched it from his hands. My sternness startled him, and he looked deeply embarrassed and apologetic. I turned back to Garth, still lying on the displaced cushions of the broken couch.

I put my arm around his neck. "Can you stand?"

He made a feeble attempt and replied, "I'm afraid not. Don't try to move me. And don't wait here, Jim."

"But the policeman told us—"

"I'll handle the police," Garth insisted. "I'll tell them Todd attacked *me*, not you. If they find out the sword inspired all this, I fear they'll take it away. If they do, it's almost certain we'll never see it again. Everything we've sacrificed will have been wasted. Find Antonio, Jim. Persuade him to take you to the summit. Give him anything he wants."

"But I can't leave you—"

"I'll be okay. Find me later—after you've destroyed it. And Jim—" His eyes became desperately pleading. "Promise me you won't . . . promise me that . . ."

I knew what he was trying to say. He'd seen me succumb to the sword again. He was a witness to the moment that I nearly lost my soul. Was it useless for him to hope I could resist it now?

"I'll make it," I promised. "We're so close. I don't have much farther to go."

I took the sword, now without a scabbard, and fled out the back door of the Hotel Castellano, around the leaf-strewn surface of the swimming pool, and through the gate of the rear parking lot. As I crept around to approach my pickup, I could still see the patrol car across the square, Todd Finlay in the back. One officer had remained with the prisoner. The other had made good on his promise to go back and question us. I kept the trees and shrubbery of the plaza square between myself and the policemen's car until I had climbed back into Guillermo's Chevy and closed the door. I made a discreet escape, attracting no further attention. Since Garth hadn't had time to give me directions to where the road began which led to the top of Vigia, I followed his advice to seek out Antonio. After parking again beside the orange grove at the end of the road, I hastened down the path, crossed the stream, and climbed into Vigia's foothills. My last pair of shoes became caked in mud.

I found Antonio just off the trail, working in the forest. His legs wrapped around the base of a palm tree, he was completing his descent after having severed five or six coconuts from under its leafy hood with his machete. Upon seeing me, his expression was a mixture of pleasure and concern.

"Where is Garth?" he asked, the accent making his speech almost incomprehensible.

"He has broken his leg," I said, using my hand to illustrate by swiping it against my calf.

"Broke?" he repeated.

"Yes, broke. I need your help, Antonio. I need to reach the top of the hill."

Antonio furrowed his brow. He turned to look up toward the summit. It was now hidden entirely inside a bank of clouds, like fog around an evil castle.

The Indian turned back to me. "Garth say men were thieves and witches."

I couldn't lie to Antonio. What Garth had told him was true enough.

"I'll pay you fifty thousand pesos," I offered.

Antonio's brow perked up, but not enough.

"All right, I'll give you everything in my wallet." I opened it for him. "One hundred thousand pesos."

His superstitions seemed to melt at the prospect of money. Nevertheless, it still wasn't quite enough.

"Everything in wallet . . . and *wallet.*"

My wallet had been a present from my Uncle Spencer shortly after I returned home from my mission. It was handcrafted with a picture of the Salt Lake Temple and the Angel Moroni pressed into the leather. Still, I agreed to the old man's terms, taking out my license, BYU ID, and temple recommend. I also began removing the pictures of four or five previous girlfriends, but he stopped me.

"Leave girls," he said.

This guy was a tough negotiator. I wished Renae were here to witness this. It was solid evidence of my overwhelming love. I gave him the wallet—girls and all—but half the money I stuffed into my pocket.

"I'll give you the rest when we get there."

Antonio retrieved his straw hat from off the ground. "We go quickly. Get back before dark."

Antonio also brought his machete. When we got back to the pickup, I asked him to place it in the bed. I'd gone through too much to allow myself to fully trust a man I'd only met this morning.

Antonio directed us down a street which proved to be a shorter route to the highway. Then we turned left, back in the direction of Veracruz. About five miles later, Antonio pointed out a one-lane cobbled road ascending into the jungle on the left side of the highway. It seemed so indistinguishable from the other field roads and driveways, I was almost certain Garth and I would have backtracked half a dozen times before we'd found it.

The sound beneath our wheels changed from the smooth glide of pavement to the disquieting rumble of loose stone. Steadily, the road ascended into the hills. In the distance we could see Vigia, the summit still veiled in clouds. It seemed so far away. It was so hard to believe that this, or any road, could reach it. The jungle grew thicker, the earth breathing only when an outcropping of volcanic rock forced the foliage to separate, or when a field had been cleared for coffee or corn. Even here, people lived. Deep in the jungle I could see humble native huts—dwellings whose occupants for the most part had never seen the world beyond the view of these slopes. As we passed several men riding burros or carrying bundles, Antonio would smile and call out to them, and they would wave and call back.

"Do you know *all* these people?" I asked.

"*Sí.* Many," he replied.

A quarter mile later, we passed a man herding a dozen cattle across the road with a whip.

"Bad year for cattle," Antonio commented.

"Oh, yeah? Why's that?"

"Thieves. Steal cattle and eat. Man I know lose eighty cattle."

"Can't you catch the thieves?"

Antonio shook his head. "We try. Only steal at night. That why we must get back before dark. They steal truck—steal all we own. Maybe kill us."

I turned to him. "Are you talking about the men you and Garth saw yesterday, or other men?"

"Other men," he confirmed.

This seemed to be a bad neighborhood altogether—like an inner city street in New York. It was interesting that in Mexico people seemed much more fearful of the country than the city. Cities were places of refuge. Criminals were thought to mostly reside in the mountains. The attitude seemed exactly opposite from that in America.

Antonio also revealed that witchcraft was very common in these hills. Lake Catemaco, which was only twenty miles away, was considered the Mexican equivalent of Salem, Massachusetts. He said *El Cerro Vigia* was a kind of mecca for witches—*American* witches. Every second week in March, foreigners would gather near Antonio's home and light candles, following the trail to the top for ceremonies he'd never witnessed.

To me this only made sense. If it truly was Ramah/Cumorah, and two civilizations had been wiped out on its slopes, tradition would not make it a sacred place, but a place of evil.

But in spite of that, Antonio was convinced the cattle thieves were not witches, only scoundrels, and he hoped they would soon be caught. What he had in mind for them sounded a little like Judge Roy Bean-style frontier justice.

"Where did you learn English?" I asked, trying to lighten the conversation.

"Naycha-list from United States," he said.

"You mean a naturalist? A scientist?"

"*Sí.* He study animals, bugs, plants. I work his assistant for two years. This many years ago."

"How many children do you have?"

Antonio took a moment to recall the number in English. "Twenty-six."

My eyes bugged out. "You have *twenty-six kids?* How many times have you been married?"

"Three."

"Did you outlive them all?"

"No."

"You divorced the first two?"

"No."

"You have *three wives?* And they're all *still alive?*"

He laughed, amused by my surprise. "*Sí.* Yes."

"Do they all get along?"

"No," he smiled. "They no like each other—jealous. They live separate houses."

He told me he got his second wife by paying the government a fee. The third one was not really an "official" wife, though she'd borne most of his children. Though Antonio would have welcomed it, I decided not to dig further into his family life. All I knew was, if the Lord ever restored polygamy, it would be a principle eagerly supported by a certain Indian named Antonio—though clearly not so much by his wives.

The truck continued to climb, sometimes spinning its wheels to escape the mud or traverse a steep corner. We saw fewer and fewer houses, though evidences of civilization were never entirely absent. Antonio got out of the car to open and close several gates. There always seemed to be crops growing in a field somewhere nearby, no matter how steep or inaccessible the terrain.

"Are there jaguars around here?" I wondered.

"No," Antonio confirmed. "Once many. Now only farther south. But in river near my home many crocodiles."

The jungle leaves on either edge of the road were larger than umbrellas; Antonio revealed that many times umbrellas were exactly what they were used for. We soon entered the cloud bank which hid Vigia's summit. Visibility was reduced to about a hundred yards. I felt certain the top of the hill, and the power relay station Garth had mentioned, would come into view any moment. It seemed to me if the Gadiantons were still on the hill, they wouldn't go near the very summit, where an on-duty operator might think their presence was suspicious. I felt sure they'd wait for me somewhere below, along the trail.

I stopped for another gate. As usual, Antonio got out to open it, but this time he seemed to sense something different in the air. He paused before unlatching the wire loop from around the fence post and listened.

My window was open. I called out, "Is something the matter?"

"No," he responded. Yet he remained quite cautious as he pulled back the gate and waited for me to drive through. After he climbed back into the truck, I asked him again if something was wrong, but he reassured me by saying, "I imagine things sometimes. Happens when old like me."

A short distance later, as the road ran parallel to the fence line, Antonio pointed out another gateway off to the side, only this one was meant for pedestrians. There was a muddy path coming up from the steep slope below and leading through it.

"That where trail lead down to my home," said Antonio.

My heart started pounding. It took a moment for me to put together why I found Antonio's statement so disturbing. Then I realized—he was saying that from here on out, the road and the trail were *connected!*

"I thought the road and the trail were completely separate routes all the way to the top."

"No," Antonio confirmed. "From here they are one."

I shuddered. If my suspicions about Mehrukenah placing his men somewhere along the trail below the summit were correct, this meant we were driving along the very section of trail where such a positioning would take place. I slammed on the brakes.

"Is there another way to the top?" I demanded.

Antonio shook his head. "I know of no other way. The jungle here very steep."

"Can you drive?" I asked.

"*Sí.* Of course."

"Then let's switch places," I said. "I'm going to lie low on the floorspace the rest of the way."

Antonio cocked an eyebrow, then shrugged. "Okay. But first drive through gate."

About ten yards ahead, another gate blocked the road.

"Tell you what," I said, "you open the gate and then come back and drive through. From here on out, I want to remain unseen. Onlookers must think you're up here alone. Understand?"

Antonio nodded, still confused and somewhat alarmed by my actions. I guess the thought that we might be out-and-out attacked in broad daylight had not occurred to him.

After he'd stepped out of the pickup, I scooted over to his side of the truck and slipped uncomfortably into the floorspace, with my knees in my chest and my neck bent out from under the glove box. On the seat and under my left hand, I continued to hold the sword.

When Antonio returned and opened the driver's side door, the news was not good. "There is chain and lock on gate," he said.

"Is that normal?" I wondered.

"No. Not normal," claimed Antonio. "Never lock on gate. Something very wrong."

"Turn back," I insisted. "Get us out of here. We have to find another way to the summit."

"Maybe trail other side of hill," thought Antonio. "Don't know for sure. Never had reason to go up that way."

"Please turn the truck around—*quickly!*"

Turning was not an easy task. As Antonio pulled forward, the hood of the pickup pushed back the foliage. He then turned the wheels sharply, backed up, broke a few more branches, turned the wheels again, pulled forward. After three or four more maneuvers, the truck was facing downhill.

I was biting my nails—something I hadn't done in years. If we could just get beyond the next gate, I would feel so much better. Suddenly Antonio accelerated the speed—but why?

He'd seen something in the jungle. I lifted my head just enough to look. They were *everywhere,* shadows weaving through the foggy forest and vines, following along with the truck. Remaining on the floor was useless—an idea instigated too late. I'd already been seen. I climbed back up on the seat and prepared to jump out and throw open the next gate. It was just now coming into view.

Antonio stopped the truck. I leaped out and rushed up to the fence. As I began lifting the wire hook, I saw the chain. In the last few minutes, this gate had been padlocked as well. We were trapped.

I jumped back into the truck. "Antonio, we have to smash through!"

He nodded and backed up about fifteen yards. Behind us, men were emerging from the woods and rushing toward us. Some I recognized from earlier encounters, some I'd never seen before. Antonio made a Catholic cross across his chest, then punched the gas pedal.

We rammed the fence. The two side posts snapped at the base. The gate's barbed wire stretched across the hood. The barrier was a shambles—but it was not broken. Antonio fought desperately with the steering and lost control. The right tires slipped off the road and the vehicle came to a stop, stones grinding underneath the frame. The left tires continued to spin and rip into the gravel, but the effort caused the tail of the truck to slide off the road as well. We were hopelessly stuck. The Gadianton minions were closing in—and cheering.

"We go on foot, through jungle!" cried Antonio. "You follow!"

Antonio pushed open the driver's side door and leaped out. I tried to open my side, but the door was obstructed by barbed wire. Nevertheless, I pried it open enough to slip out, dragging the sword behind me. Antonio didn't wait. He vaulted over the fence, losing his straw hat, and disappeared into the jungle. I'd escaped the car, but it was another matter to escape the nest of barbed wire and fence posts that our smash-up had created. I tried to step through, but my pant leg got caught—the barbs were biting my flesh! The enemy was arriving. Among them I recognized Shurr. There were also a number of local men with big machetes. Perhaps these were some of the thieves Antonio had mentioned—now Gadianton proselytes. In a panic, I tried to tear myself free, but my efforts only worsened the tangle, and the barbs began biting my arm. I fell, dropping the sword. The fence had become a net, and I was the fish. I could no longer move—the barbs would only dig in deeper.

The minions had gathered around me. They were laughing hysterically at my predicament. Shurr was cackling as well. His hand reached through the coils and found the hilt of the sword. Carefully, he lifted it out and brought it close to his breast. With his other hand, he stroked the silver blade and sighed long and deep.

Then he held it aloft to the gawking crowd and announced, "Coriantumr's sword is ours again!"

They cheered, and I fainted—from the pain, and from the crushing blow of failure.

CHAPTER 27

I know I wasn't unconscious long, because I felt the barbs further tear my clothes and scratch my skin as they dragged me out of the nest. A noose of the wire had been coiled about my neck, fortunately not where a barb dug into the skin unless I moved about. The other end of the wire was tossed over a tree limb and secured to a branch around the other side. They propped me against the trunk, as high up the bark as they could without suspending my feet. My hands were left free to try and relieve the pressure on my neck, but it was impossible to twist loose.

I remained in this unbearably awkward position for well over an hour while a runner went to fetch Mehrukenah, who'd been lying in wait with Mr. Clarke and several other thugs at a point closer to the summit. When they arrived and looked upon my miserable state—coughing and bleeding, my fingers all that were saving me from choking to death—a grin formed on Mehrukenah's mug from ear to ear.

"Welcome to the Hill Ramah and the Land of Desolation, Jimawkins," he said. "We were beginning to think you'd never come."

I didn't reply.

He continued. "Actually, this is my first visit as well, in your time *or* mine. I'm sure it's much more accessible now, what with all the roads and people." He stepped up close. "Have you nothing to say? No clever comments?"

I remained silent, though I couldn't fully hide my feelings. They were expressed loudly by the fear in my eyes. Mehrukenah grinned again, sufficiently gratified.

He turned to Shurr. "Give me the sword."

Shurr was balancing himself on the hilt, with the point in the dirt. He gave Mehrukenah a queer look. "You know I can't," he refused. "Gadianton's wish was that once it touched my hands, it would not touch another's. It was for this purpose that my brother sent me."

"Your brother is too distrusting," scoffed Mehrukenah. "I request only the honor of using it to spill the first blood. Then I'll give it back, and you may keep it in your possession until the very moment it's presented to Gadianton."

Shurr hesitated, but only for a moment. Mehrukenah's request seemed harmless enough. He presented the wizened old man with Coriantumr's sword. Mehrukenah took it in his grasp and held it in awe. He tested its weight and swiped it against the air. Then he thrust it to the sky.

"Such glory!" he cried.

No doubt the sword was soothing him with the same promises it had given me. I was strangely jealous—resentful that the sword could be so fickle, telling the same lies to anyone it touched. That must have been how it had survived all these centuries since Akish. The sword played no favorites and therefore, among those who wielded it, the sword had no foes.

Mehrukenah glowered at me and shook his head. "How can a man so young be so misguided, Jimawkins? Couldn't you feel its power? Why would you want to destroy something so perfect?"

"Because it's *not* perfect," I replied. "It's the epitome of *imperfect.* If only you understood the destiny of the being you worship, Mehrukenah, the destiny of the founder of Gadianton's oaths and combinations—the founder of the power in that sword."

"You baffle me," said Mehrukenah. "I'm baffled by *all* Christians. You beg for blessings, sometimes receiving, most of the time not. I can only conclude that your god is very weak. Whereas the power which binds our band—the power by which we live and breathe—is the very power of the earth, ultimate and eternal. Our formulas are as pure as spring water, and with them one can soar as the eagles."

"But each time you follow those formulas," I said, "the eagle soars with one less feather. One day soon, Mehrukenah, you're going to plunge to the earth and be crushed."

He stepped up close. "*You're* the one whose god appears to have left him shy of feathers. No, wait. There's one feather remaining." Slowly, he moved the sword's tip forward and touched it against my throat. "This is the quetzal feather I'll pluck for myself now."

He retracted the sword, placing the cold silver blade against his brow. Then he closed his eyes and turned away, as if in concentration or prayer. The crowd around us watched in silence. Even Shurr lowered his chin and shut his eyes to reverence the moment of my execution.

I refused to close my eyes. Somehow I felt if I kept them open, I couldn't die. My soul was calling out to my Heavenly Father—but He didn't seem to be answering. Why wasn't He answering? Perhaps He no longer believed in me. Had the sword corrupted me beyond redemption? What would be the state of my soul in the life to come? A horrible dread churned inside me. How I wished I'd never touched it—never listened to its voice!

From here, everything seemed to move in slow motion. Mehrukenah began to scream. He brought the full weight of the sword to bear behind his shoulder and began twisting forward with a mighty swing. But his eyes and the sword swung right past me. Was he spinning around a second time for more momentum? But instead, his eyes fixed on Shurr, still standing in silence. With all his might, Mehrukenah drove the blade into Shurr's belly. The brother of Gadianton opened his eyes and stared at his comrade's face in horror. Mehrukenah kept the blade inserted until Shurr dropped to his knees. Then Mehrukenah put his foot against Shurr's chest and yanked it free. The eyes of Gadianton's brother rolled up into his head, and his lifeless body fell forward onto the dirt. All around Mehrukenah, the gathering applauded. Mr. Clarke looked especially pleased. Apparently this conspiracy had been planned long before. Mehrukenah's motives were perfectly clear. Why return to 50 B.C. now that he'd acquired a solid circle of followers here? Converts of this age and time would have had no desire to return to the primitive world of Gadianton—not when there was so much more to be gained in the twenty-first century. Mehrukenah knew the potential of that sword better than any man alive. With it he could inspire a following greater than Todd Finlay had ever dreamed of.

The sword was still dripping with the blood of its previous victim when Mehrukenah faced me again.

"Now, where were we? Ah, yes." He turned around and made an announcement to the crowd. "Now witness the moment of death for the oldest enemy I have left in this life!" He turned back to me one last time. "I'm sorry you'll never live to see the greatness of the kingdom I'll build in your day, Jimawkins."

He hoisted the sword overhead once again, this time skipping all elements of ceremony, except for the scream. But the scream began in one pitch and ended in another as an arrow struck him in the shoulder. He staggered back and dropped the sword before he could finish his swing.

The gathering scrambled in confusion. The jungle was swarming with villagers, armed with machetes, clubs, and—as was apparent from Mehrukenah's wound—at least one crossbow. They sprang out of the dense jungle foliage from all directions, causing Mehrukenah and his men to scatter. The villagers swung their weapons viciously. Though some of Mehrukenah's men had revolvers, few had time to bring them to bear. The villagers were thrice the enemy's number—maybe more. They pursued their prey in whatever direction they fled. I couldn't see all the action—the wire still kept me from turning my head—but I did see Mr. Clarke trying to escape down the road. The revolver in his hand had been fired twice at his attackers, but several more villagers sprang from the trees, and before he could empty another chamber, Mr. Clarke fell under a machete's blade.

From behind me, another machete swiped at the tree trunk above my head. After several more swipes, the wire snapped. I would have collapsed, except that someone caught me. When I looked up to see my benefactor, it was the beaming face of Antonio. He helped me to untwist the wire from around my neck, then he retrieved the crossbow he'd laid down behind the tree.

"I could have bring more, but I no think there was time."

"Your timing was perfect, Antonio. You saved my life."

"I think I save many cattle, too. Me think we have no more trouble with thieves, eh?"

"No," I replied. "I don't think you will."

Antonio left me there and ran off to assist his fellow villagers. I picked the sword up from the ground where Mehrukenah had dropped it and got out of the area as quickly as possible, fearing the villagers might consider me a straggler and attack me as well.

As I climbed up the road, I must have looked like I'd been through the Battle of Waterloo. My clothes were in shreds, blood-stained from the cuts the barbs had inflicted on my skin. My neck was raw from the wire noose, and my mouth felt bone-dry all the way down my throat. Add to all this a terrible nausea, as if my insides were being twisted around in a hurricane. At one point I dropped the sword and fell on my hands, ready to throw up, but with nothing inside my stomach, I only heaved and retched in pain.

When I lifted the sword again, I swore it weighed no less than a ton. I nearly decided to drop it, but strangely it rose into my arms as easily as it ever had. The sword had overplayed its weight game. The illusion unwittingly provided me with strength. If I could lift a ton, I could certainly lift myself the rest of the way up this hill.

It was late afternoon. The fog was still very thick. I couldn't see any patterns of landscape in any direction, and I had no idea how much farther it was to the summit. Maybe I should have waited for Antonio's help, but I knew by the time he was finished rounding up the villains, it would have already been dark. Somehow I knew I couldn't have succeeded in the dark. Nor could I have waited until tomorrow. So I set off on my own.

Soon after traversing that final gate, the tower of the relay station began to emerge from the mist. There was only one more switchback, and I would be there.

What will it accomplish, Jim, if you destroy me? It will not change the course of the world. It will not put an end to the blood and horror.

Maybe not, I thought, but it may temper it some, and it may save a few souls.

It will save nothing! In fact, it may accelerate the damage. Haven't you learned anything since we became friends? I've saved your life at least twice. Together we can save many lives, and do much good.

No. Any good which you could ever inspire would be more than offset as soon as you gained possession of my soul.

I am always subject to the will of him who bears me.

That's a lie.

But I love you, Jim. I love you more than anyone who has ever borne my weight. If you hurt me, it would be as if you'd murdered your own child—your own flesh and blood.

Sorry. If you loved me, you would have stayed Mehrukenah's hand. You wanted to see me destroyed even more than he did.

How can you say that? You're still alive, aren't you? Maybe you should think about that.

I'm alive because of Antonio—and God. No one else receives any credit.

You're being very ungrateful. If only you knew how much I would miss you. If you knew, you would not hurt me. You would trust me just a little longer, so I could prove my worth to you. What if I healed your wounds?

It would only be an illusion, just like the illusion of your heaviness. The sickness would still be there; you'd only cover it up.

You're wrong. Do you really think so little of my powers?

Yes. It's all an illusion—like any promise of Satan.

You have so much to learn. If only I could have time to teach you.

There was no fog obscuring my view of the summit now. I could see it. The road led right around to the top. Two buildings made up the power relay station, along with the giant tower. The first building was directly in front of me now. It was surrounded by a chain-link fence; apparently it was used only for equipment storage. I could hear the hum of an electrical generator farther up the road. I followed that sound and found myself climbing the final bend to the top of the hill.

The jungle foliage remained quite dense on either side of the road. Just as the uppermost two-story building came into view, something flashed out of the corner of my eye—something lunging at me from the darkness of the foliage. It was Mehrukenah, charging like a phantom through the air.

Raise me, and I will save you. If you don't, you will die.

The broken shaft of the arrow was still embedded in Mehrukenah's right shoulder. I did not raise the sword. I rejected its promise and let Mehrukenah barrel into my chest. As I fell against a rocky outcropping of soil at the side of the road, the sword dropped from my grip.

Mehrukenah wasted no time retrieving it with his right hand. Instantly his bleeding appendage received strength. He hoisted the weapon overhead. As the blade was coming down right between my eyes, I rolled. The sword split the stones which had been underneath me. Scrambling, I hoisted myself upward, my fingers clutching a bush's brittle branches for leverage. Yelling furiously, Mehrukenah continued swinging at me. I plunged deeper into the foliage on the hillside between the upper and lower buildings. The undergrowth made it impossible to see where I should place my feet, yet I continued running. I set my sights on the tower, hoping someone up there might hear us and rush out to help. But the roar of the nearby generator muffled Mehrukenah's screams.

He kept pursuing, looking for another moment to strike. I thought I had a free run all the way across the hillside, but suddenly I was face down on the ground. I'd tripped on something in the undergrowth! I looked down at my legs and saw that I'd further unearthed a section of insulated cable extending from the generator to the upper station. Mehrukenah stood over me, panting. He smiled, showing me the gaps in his teeth one final time.

"Good-bye, my quetzal feather!"

As he raised the sword high overhead, I grabbed the power cable with my left hand and rolled onto my back. The cable unearthed another few feet. I thrust it upward just as

Mehrukenah's blade was coming down. The sword sliced down upon it, cutting into the insulation, penetrating to the copper core.

I released the cable and rolled out from under the sword. There was a surge of noise from the generator as it adjusted for a sudden power loss. I looked back at Mehrukenah. His eyes were wide. His hands, still gripping the metal hilt, were shaking. The volts of electricity vibrated through his body for at least a quarter minute. Finally, the old wizened wraith fell forward into the undergrowth, convulsing once, and then lying still, his contorted expression frozen with the agony of his final moment.

The sword was lying on the ground, still wedged in the cable. The earth around me became fuzzy with an electric charge. Using a dead branch, I knocked the cable free. The power surge from the generator ceased, and the fuzziness in the ground dissipated.

The sword was hot now, as well as heavy, but the heat was no illusion. I picked it up, using the bottom of my shirt as padding. The smell immediately around Mehrukenah made my skin crawl. Hastily, with my free hand covering my mouth and nose to keep out the stench, I scrambled across the hillside and again found the road. As I peered back through the dense foliage, I spotted the two on-duty operators coming around the other side of the hill, making their way down a trail leading to the generator in hopes of discovering what had caused the unusual loss and surge of power. I remained out of sight and followed the road around its final loop.

Do you believe me now? If I didn't love you, why would I kill Mehrukenah for you? Now it's three *times that I've saved your life, Jim Hawkins.*

No, no. Again, this was the Lord's work, and a simple phenomenon called electricity. Again, you had nothing to do with it.

You're the liar, Jim, not giving credit where credit is due.

I'd reached the rocky precipice directly in front of the two-story upper building of the relay station. The door was ajar, left open by the operators who'd run around back. In thanks to my Father in Heaven, I dropped heavily to my knees. This was it! This was the destination I'd risked my life and the lives of those I loved most in this world to reach: the top of Cumorah—the final battleground of the Nephites and Lamanites, the summit of Ramah where Coriantumr, with the very sword I now held in my hand, had guided the Jaredite armies to their suicidal climax.

Yet one mystery still remained unsolved. I opened my eyes and reassessed the ground upon which I knelt. Something was chillingly wrong. All my opposition had been crushed. Mehrukenah himself was lying dead a short ways down the hill. Garth's leg had been broken. My own body was racked with wounds and sickness—and all for *what?* This building and the tower it supported had been erected *precisely upon the highest summit point of Vigia!*

Ether's coffer was gone! We were thirty years too late! Whoever had excavated the foundation of this station had destroyed the stone box in the jaws of their Caterpillar, crushed it into a pile of rubble and dust unrecognizable as ever having been fashioned by ancient hands. The only means of destroying Coriantumr's sword had itself been destroyed by the progress of man.

The sword was laughing hysterically.

I'm not laughing at *you, Jim. I'm laughing* with *you. It's clear now that you can't get rid of me, and obviously you can't pass me along to anyone else. Therefore, your destiny is clear now, Jim. That destiny is with me! Now and for the rest of your life! Don't be disappointed. We have many great things yet to do together—righteous things. Oh, I promise it. Righteous things.*

It was taunting me. It must have known it. And yet it was right. I could never part with it now. Its curse was mine to bear—and I knew it *was* a curse—a punishment laid upon me for ever having let myself be enticed away from my God, even for a moment.

My life as I knew it was over. I would never graduate from college. I would never marry Renae. I would never raise a single child. I had to steer clear of anything that might put another's salvation at risk. Only one course was before me: to be the Keeper of the Sword—to live with it, defend it from theft, listen daily to its haunting temptations, but never, *never* to give in, not even in the face of my own death or the death of someone I loved. Now more than ever, I had to depend upon God for all my answers, all my decisions. I couldn't be irresolute about a single conviction. If ever I listened to the sword—or even to myself while under its influence—I was doomed.

And yet in spite of all this understanding, every fiber of reasoning within my soul told me it was impossible. I was not a perfect human being; I was so far from perfection it made my head swim. Sooner or later, the sword would secure its grip around my throat—just as it had every other soul who'd ever wielded it.

Garth was right. There were only two forces at work in this world. Lucifer had dragged down a third of all the hosts of heaven. His goal for the other two thirds was not necessarily to make every last one a son of perdition. If a soul was aiming for the terrestrial kingdom, and he could drag them down to the telestial, his purposes would have been successful. If a soul was aiming for the highest plane of celestial glory and he could drag them down to the level of a ministering angel, his vengeance had been met. To whatever rank of misery Satan could sentence mankind, that would be the rank he would shoot for.

I dropped to my knees in anguish, certain that the state of my soul was the most miserable of all. If any man ever needed God's mercy, I felt it was me. But then a thought entered my mind, as bright as sunlight so blinding it can't be escaped by closing the eyes: God had already extended that mercy in the boundless Atonement of His Only Begotten Son.

I felt an urge to raise my head, as if an unseen but sacred hand was lifting my chin. I turned my gaze toward a grassy offshoot of the hill, southwest of where I knelt. It was a thin promontory off the main summit, protruding out about two hundred yards to a tiny cluster of trees. From where I knelt, it appeared to be perhaps a few feet higher than the spot of ground where the relay station had been erected.

Rising to my feet, the sword still firm in my grasp, I took several steps toward it. Then I stopped again. Somebody was waiting for me there. As I squinted, I could see a man standing in the midst of that tiny cluster of trees. He was waving me toward him.

I passed by one of the steel supports to the tower and climbed over one final crossing of barbed wire. For the next hundred and fifty yards I forged through grasses as high as my elbows. As I neared the man who urged me onward, his identity was revealed to me. It was Ether, the great prophet of the Jaredites and the compiler of their records—the man who'd witnessed the final Jaredite struggle from his vantage point in the cavity of a rock. The only difference I noted from the way I'd envisioned him in my dreams was his lack of ancient clothing. Instead, his garments, as well as his hair, seemed to flow like a river of brilliant white.

The clouds were no longer shrouding my view to the western plains, now glowing red with the setting sun. Nor were they shrouding the waterways and swamps of the Papaloapan lagoon system in the distance. Nor were the clouds shrouding the hilly slopes of the western face of *El Cerro Vigia*. From here, it would have been an easy matter for Mormon to look down and view the fallen Gidgiddonah and his ten thousand, the fallen Lamah and his ten thousand, the fallen Gilgal and his ten thousand, until he'd accounted for all two hundred and twenty thousand Nephite soldiers who died on that first day of battle, excepting the twenty-four weary and wounded stragglers who spent that final night with him and his son, Moroni—perhaps on this very promontory, huddled from the wind within a cluster of trees, perhaps the seedling ancestors of the cluster I was now approaching. I drew close enough to see Ether's face and the beauty of his aquiline and eternal features, and to see his smile and the radiating compassion in his eyes—so deep, so indescribable. And then the ancient prophet faded away. All that remained was the cluster of trees, and in the center of it all, an old stump, scarred black by a single fulminating stroke of lightning.

You're a coward, Jim Hawkins! A pitifully misguided coward, turning on the spit of your own stupidity and blindness. Look at your life! The mediocrity, the failure, the loneliness, the misery, the weakness, the poverty! Don't you know I can change all that? Don't you believe it?!

Yes, I believe every word, and that's why I'm going to finish what Ether had wanted to do more than two thousand years ago.

With my free hand, I grabbed the blackened stump. It was hollow and deteriorated. Using my weight, and expending only a little exertion, I pushed the stump completely over on its side. As it fell, a layer of soil folded up at its base. Underneath it was a rectangular stone, thick and unevenly cut. I knelt to brush away the soil and roots. Then I utilized the sword in accomplishing the only worthwhile task of its existence, as a lever to pry open the lid of the coffer and push the stone aside.

As I peered into the box, there was only a reddish dirt, and what appeared to be slivers of metal, copper and silver—the remains of weapons long since eaten away by rust and time. I held the sword in both my hands, directly over its grave.

I curse you, Jim!! The rest of your days I curse you!! Look to death as your only escape, your only relief!! This is a promise I will *fulfill!!!*

I dropped the sword. It fell into the coffer, causing the soil there to fluff as it landed. I stood a moment longer in the wind, gazing down at Akish's creation. Suddenly it deteriorated before my eyes; the silver-plating on the copper flaked away and the jeweled hilt turned to dust. Then the blade itself shattered and cracked until everything which had once been Coriantumr's sword blended perfectly with the rest of the reddish dirt and slivers of metal around it.

A welcome, peaceful silence settled around me.

There were no more voices.

CHAPTER 28

Antonio found me early the next morning, sleeping tranquilly on that grassy summit within the cluster of trees. With his help, and the help of a few of his neighbors, we pulled Guillermo's rusty old Chevy from the ditch. I tried to give Antonio the rest of the money I'd saved for him in my pocket, but he refused to take it.

"You keep. You help us stop thieves on Vigia. I should pay *you.*"

To emphasize his point, he gave me back my wallet. After looking inside it, I smiled. He'd decided to keep the pictures of my old girlfriends.

I drove back down the narrow, winding road leading into the village of Santiago Tuxtla and found Garth Plimpton in a local clinic, a heavy plaster cast molded around his right leg. He was mulling over a selection of Mexican chocolates. I chuckled inside, remembering Garth's opinion that chocolate was often the best medicine for any ailment. When our eyes met, his face ignited into the warm, compassionate smile that was his trademark. He knew I'd accomplished the mission. We said nothing for several moments, and then Garth, upon noting my tattered condition, offered me a chocolate. "It looks like you might need one of these more than I do, my friend."

That night, we drove to Poza Rica. I couldn't help but feel a little apprehensive as we turned onto the dirt avenue leading to the home of Guillermo Corral. Renae and Jenny were not the type of women who liked to be left stranded, so I prepared myself for the tongue-lashing of my life.

As I approached the house, Renae was waiting at the end of the driveway, as if something had whispered to her that we'd soon be arriving. I did get a scolding, but it wasn't so bad. And after a moment, she tearfully drew me in for a heartfelt embrace. True to my promise, I told her I loved her and we enjoyed our first kiss. I was only vaguely aware of the Corral children giggling in the doorway.

Once I might have thought this moment should be circumscribed by sunsets or waterfalls. Though there may have been no pyrotechnics, there was a unity of heart, and I discovered that such unity carries a spectacle of its own, far more beautiful than any kind of fireworks.

Thanks to my parents, a two-hundred-dollar money order was waiting for us at the Western Union in Brownsville, Texas, to get us the rest of the way home. As we were crossing the border at Matamoros, Garth handed over all his leftover pesos, about thirty dollars' worth, to a boy with no legs, ambling around in the middle of the traffic on his hands. As an afterthought, Garth also gave the boy his Spanish Book of Mormon—the same one he'd held in such esteem since his mission to Guatemala. The boy stuck it in a vendor's pouch on his waist and offered a nod of gratitude. After parking in a border stall while the immigration officials searched our car, we looked back across the Rio Grande and saw this boy crawl into the shade of a giant tree, take the Book of Mormon out of his pouch, and begin reading its pages. Somehow, I still consider this the most glorious image I took back with me to Utah.

A week or so later, I did a little missionary work myself and sent the elders to Antonio's hut in Santiago Tuxtla. But alas, the old Indian was just too set in his ways. The elders did write me a letter, though, and told me their visits had inspired Antonio to hang a picture of the Mexico City Temple on his wall. I hoped that seeing this image every day would at least bring his family—all thirty of them—a little closer to their Father in Heaven.

It was the happiest Christmas I'd ever remembered. Though numbers around the tree were small, since my brothers were spending the holiday with their wives' families, the strings of bright and blinking lights nevertheless reflected on the faces of my mother and father, my beloved sister, Jennifer, my old comrade, Garth Plimpton, and my favorite Nephite, Muleki. Finally, the Christmas lights glowed on the tender features of my fiancée, Renae Fenimore, who had accepted my proposal on Christmas Eve.

In fulfillment of my desire that the girl I married remove the ring with the shiny blue stone from my finger, Renae set out to accomplish the feat. Requiring almost a full tub of margarine, it wasn't quite like Arthur removing the sword from the stone, but she got it off. Her motivation might have been fueled by my claims that it had been given to me by another girl.

The next week, Jenny, Renae, and I spent much of our time studying for finals. Our professors had agreed to let us take them the first week of January, before winter semester officially began.

Somehow I'd gotten it in my head that since Muleki's doctor said he should take it easy for a few weeks, the Nephite would stick around until at least the first of February. It was quite a shock for us on New Year's Day when he announced, just hours before our scheduled departure for Utah, that he wanted to be driven to the foot of Cedar Mountain.

I sternly objected. "But the doctor said your wound wouldn't be fully healed until—"

"It's okay, Jim," he interrupted. "I feel strong, and my work here is finished, thanks to you and the others."

"What about the Gadiantons?" I warned. "You said they might be guarding the way."

"Don't worry. I know a few tunnels they don't. Besides, I don't believe it's my time to meet God. There's still much to do in Zarahemla in preparation for the Savior's coming. I feel I have a future role in that, if only to protect the lives of my cousin's children, Lehi and Nephi. You've been a great friend, Jim, but it's time for me to return to my people."

I thought of chiding him further, accusing him of being as stubborn as his father, but I feared he would only take it as a compliment.

It was a cold day, the temperature near zero even with the sun high in a cloudless sky, when the five of us drove Jenny's faithful Mazda down the West Cody Strip to the snowy foot of Cedar Mountain. After scanning its slopes, I realized it would not be a difficult hike. Much easier, in fact, than the hike to the top of Vigia. The road, though buried under six inches of white, was still well defined and would take the Nephite right to the mouth of Frost Cave.

We all got out of the car to watch Muleki depart—even Garth, who was still on crutches. He winced when he accidentally stuck his bare toes, protruding from his cast, into the snow.

More tears were shed. One froze on Muleki's cheek as well. I embraced my ancient friend and made the mistake of calling him a Nephite one last time.

"Jershonite," he corrected.

Muleki finished his good-byes and turned away, climbing a few paces up the mountain before Jenny, shedding too many tears to freeze, cried out his name. Muleki turned back, and Jenny rushed forward to give him one final hug. He kissed her cheek and brushed her face tenderly where he had kissed.

"I'll think of you often," he told her, "and the wonderful family you'll raise in the latter days."

Garth fidgeted, a bit uncomfortable with Jenny's intensity of emotion. I think he'd hoped that she'd gotten over Muleki.

"Fortitude," I whispered to him.

Garth turned to me and smiled. "Right."

Jenny returned to stand with the rest of us, and the Captain of the Guard in the Palace of Helaman, Chief Judge of Zarahemla, raised his hand and cried, "Farewell, my friends! Whether we meet again in this life or the next, I know the reunion will be glorious!"

He choked a bit on that last word.

Wearing my old blue and white parka, faded Levi jeans, and a pair of high-top tennis shoes—clothing that I'm sure would be quite the conversation pieces in Zarahemla—Teancum's youngest son left his footsteps in the snow as he ascended the roadway which led to the top of Cedar Mountain. We watched him until he turned around to wave for the last time, then the Jershonite disappeared behind a switchback and a row of serried pine.

Garth didn't fare as badly as he might have thought. When we dropped him off at his home in Rock Springs, Jenny raised up on her toes and gave him the kind of kiss that leaves men stuttering. In fact, I doubt he was able to communicate in complete sentences again until long after we'd driven away.

In spite of the display, Jenny remained elusive to Garth's affections for another semester. But fortunately, my old comrade had taken my advice to heart. After he'd returned to Harvard, he got a part-time job, no doubt to support his long-distance phone calls to Heritage Halls.

In the succeeding months, he proposed to Jenny no less than three times—once when he came to BYU during Harvard's spring break, once just after school let out and he came to see her in Cody, and once in early June when she went to Rock Springs to see him. Each time the poor guy was tragically rejected by a woman who seemed eternally unready for that kind of commitment.

It wasn't until my wedding on June 16th, when I was sealed to Renae for time and all eternity in the Tower Room at the top of the spiral staircase in the Manti Temple, with Garth as my best man and Jenny as the maid of honor at our reception, that the heart of my little sister finally melted. Two days later she accepted Garth's fourth proposal. I'd swear we could hear his whoop of triumph all the way to the Hotel Filher in San Luis Potosi, Mexico, where Renae and I spent our honeymoon.

As the years passed, I used to feel sorrow that my destruction of Coriantumr's sword did not end poverty or pain in the world. It did not end bloodshed and crime, nor did it end misery and loneliness. I found some satisfaction in believing it may have slowed those things down some; maybe it prevented a few wars from being fought before their time, maybe it gave a few more people a chance to discover Christ and repent from their sins. But in the end, I came to realize that the primary soul which may have been saved that December was my own.

I had a resurgence of hope that when the battle lines of the last days became more distinctly drawn, and those with lukewarm convictions found it increasingly more difficult to remain Latter-day Saints, perhaps I would recognize the signs prophets had said might, if it were possible, fool the very elect. And perhaps I would be one of the survivors.

The memories of my adventures among the Nephites were not taken from me this time. I kept them sacred and did not abuse them, as I'm sure was the Prophet Helaman's fear all those years ago. When I was thirteen, his fears were certainly justified. It seemed I'd finally achieved enough spiritual maturity to have the blessing of recalling them out loud from time to time, usually when Garth and Jenny got together with us for holidays and special occasions.

Often, Garth and I would contemplate returning to that cavern at the top of Cedar Mountain to see if there was still an ancient world at the end of the tunnels waiting to greet us.

And who knows? Maybe one day something will force us to follow through with our contemplations.

The thought seems reasonable enough. In fact, it almost seems inevitable. Because one thing a man fears more than growing old, is growing too old for adventure.

PHOTO BY "PICTURE THIS...by Sara Staker"

About the Author

For over a decade, Chris Heimerdinger has brought adventure and fantasy to LDS readers. His first novel, *Tennis Shoes Among the Nephites,* published in 1989, continues to thrill readers young and old, and inspire a greater appreciation for the Book of Mormon.

The idea for *Gadiantons and the Silver Sword* was formulated shortly after the publication of *Tennis Shoes Among the Nephites,* though the concept did not become a reality until the summer of 1990 when Chris embarked on an epic drive with two Spanish-speaking companions from Salt Lake City to Santiago Tuxtla, Mexico, following the exact trail as his characters did in the story. Many incidents in the book were inspired by actual events and persons met during that journey, i.e. the incident with the police in Mexico City, the detour to Poza Rica, and the old Indian named Antonio.

Readers will also enjoy Chris' other books published in the *Tennis Shoes Adventure Series,* which include: *Tennis Shoes Among the Nephites; The Feathered Serpent, Parts One and Two; The Sacred Quest* (formerly *Tennis Shoes and the Seven Churches); The Lost Scrolls;* and *The Golden Crown.* His other books published by Covenant include *Daniel and Nephi; Eddie Fantastic;* and *A Return to Christmas* (currently published by Random House/Ballantine for a national readership).

Chris resides in Riverton, Utah, with his wife, Beth, and their three children, Steven Teancum, Christopher Ammon, and Alyssa Sariah. Check out Chris' web site and become a registered guest at **www.cheimerdinger.com.**

PROLOGUE

I'm entranced by the clouds. I especially love to watch them after a storm, when the billowing mass begins to break up, coil in on itself, and release the spiked rays of the sun.

As a little child, clouds would frighten me. Mostly because I had an older brother who attached macabre images to the evolving shapes over Rattlesnake Mountain. "Look, Jim, that one's an elk. It's been shot. See its tongue hanging out? There's a gargoyle. It's missing an eye and half its arm. That one's the bogey man's ghost. If it rains on us, the rain will make our skin dissolve." Once he frightened me so badly that I scurried home in a panic as soon as the first droplet hit my arm, losing one shoe in the street. Fortunately, Judd grew out of that stage, and today serves in a bishopric in Billings, Montana. Still, I can't really resent him for frightening me. I later did much the same thing to my little sister, Jennifer.

Few things take my breath away more than clouds. Not a canyon or a mountain, or even an ocean can fill human vision with such immensity and power. I've seen distant billows so magnificent it looked like the neighboring county had erupted in a massive volcano or exploded under a nuclear bomb. To me nothing in nature is more majestic. And it seems only appropriate, considering who the clouds will one day bring.

So I watch them, anxiously, breathlessly, the wind causing my eyes to tear when I forget to blink, afraid that I might miss a frac-

tion of a second of this glorious event. I know now what I await. I know it with such conviction that I sometimes find it difficult to carry on with the day's tasks. I focus, I concentrate, and still my mind drifts back to the clouds. But I know that only if I carry on, can I possibly abbreviate the wait. A short time ago I viewed this event as something that will inevitably occur, not as an event that I have the power to bring about; an event that all of us must bring about together.

So I carry on, and fervently. Because I will be there. Nothing fills me with greater anticipation. When those clouds finally part, if I am absent, I might as well shrivel into nothing. The thought that I might miss it makes me shudder.

A short time ago, these were unfamiliar emotions. It's not as if I had never known them. But sometimes our intimacy with the Spirit of God cools so gradually we don't know its gone. In college I had a Gospel Doctrine teacher who trumpeted the theme, "If you don't feel as close to God today as you did yesterday, who moved?"

So be it. I had moved. But I don't remember when exactly. All I remember is the pain. My heart was saturated with it. My bearings were lost. The future promised only blackness, thick and indispersable. Not even the simple things: a favorite food, a joyful song, or the laughter of my three children could dispel it. Especially not the word of God. For I thought I'd been abandoned by Him. Punished for some unknown and unknowable sin.

Three years ago my world was shattered so decisively I considered shutting the bedroom blinds and languishing in the dark until death took me home. I was prepared to quit my job, forget my family, and conclude my life as I had known it. Three years ago, on a stark October day, our family's vigil of futility came to an end.

Three years ago, she died.